What readers are saying about *Time Trap, Time Return and Time Lock*

"*Time Trap* is amazingly original and unexpected...I loved every second of reading it!" ~Alexandra Fedor, 15, has also read *The Book Thief, The Hunger Games*, and *Anna Karenina*

"Time Trap is a deliciously entrapping read you won't want to put down and leaves you thirsting for more when you finish." ~~ Angela Catucci, college student

"I really liked *Time Trap* and loved how Micah Caida created an entire world in the first pages...really want to know what happens next." ~~Duncan Calem, 14, Georgetown, TX who reads the Inheritance Series, Dark Life and Percy Jackson

"*Time Return* will grip you and keep you reading until the very end. The action is undoubtedly exciting, as well as the suspense. You won't want to put it down!" ~ Brooke McClure, teen

"*Time Return* is even better with the first one! The story heroes, Rayen, Tony, and Gabby, keep their promises and return to the future. But chaotic challenges ahead will test their loyalty and strength in the second book to the *Red Moon* trilogy. Absolute must read!" ~Alexandra Fedor, 17, has also read the *Divergent* trilogy, *The Sea of Tranquility*, and *Thus Spoke Zarathustra*

"*Time Return* drew me in from the first page, it took hold of my attention and never let go until the last sentence." ~Alex Bernier, teen, has also read also read all of *Rick Riordan's* books, the *Hunger Games*, the *Chronicles of Nick*, and the *Rangers Apprentice* series.

"I was intrigued from the first chapter. And I love the story because it surprised me (and my favorite books surprise me) and the characters are written with so much feeling. I just really like this book." ~Hannah G, 11, also reads Rick Riordan books

“As the thrilling conclusion to the *Red Moon* series, *Time Lock* does not disappoint and will leave you in awe…perfection on paper.” Angela Catucci, college student

“The issues addressed are timeless, and the characters are so realistic that I couldn’t help but be drawn into their story. Thanks to Micah Caida for a great read for every age, this is a gem of a series.” ~~ Emily Gifford, 17, read the Phantom of the Opera, A Princess of Mars and the Dresden Files

“Time Lock, and the Red Moon Trilogy, is a fast-paced, exciting fantasy that is so well written that it meets my expectations as an adult reader too! Loved it!” ~~ Sharon Griffiths, adult

“Time Lock is an awesome read. The story grabbed my attention from the first chapter and wouldn’t let go. The story is exciting and intense…” ~~ Hannah G, 12

“If I had found books like this (Time Trap) when I was a teen, I would have started reading much earlier, instead of waiting until my twenties!” ~~ Kay Barnes, adult

TIME LOCK

USA TODAY BESTSELLER

MICAH CAIDA

Cover Design and Interior format by The Killion Group
http://thekilliongroupinc.com

DEDICATION

To our readers – thank you for believing in this trilogy and supporting it from day one.

CHAPTER 1

I was down to hours to save Callan's life. He'd never see eighteen. At this rate, I might not either.

Callan was trapped in a place far into the future known as the Sphere, an artificial planet, and I was trapped in a small, cramped room somewhere out in the desert an hour away from a place called Albuquerque. The time-travel portal for returning to the Sphere was in an Albuquerque boarding school along with two friends I needed to help me open that portal.

Minutes raced past.

My heartbeat picked up speed.

"Come on," I begged my power that had yet to show up. I'd used it to kill a huge croggle monster in the Sphere, but I couldn't even open a lock right now. *Why?*

Then I remembered something that I'd figured out in the Sphere. Someone had been in danger each time I'd drawn on my power.

I could pretend, right? Clenching my fingers tighter around the doorknob, I dredged up an awful image of Callan's enemy—the TecKnati—swinging a sword and lopping off his beautiful hands. Nausea crowded my throat and I flinched at the gruesome image.

A spark of energy warmed my chest, swirling, then the heat spread to my arms and hands.

The knob heated beneath my fingers. A vision of metal parts blurred in my mind. They tumbled and clicked, banging into each other, faster and faster until I couldn't tell what they were doing.

Parts jangled together in a loud crash.

I snatched my hand away and jumped back, expecting

Takoda to burst inside any minute with another stun gun in hand. That's how I'd been stopped from running last night. Takoda was a Navajo who'd found me at the Byzantine Institute where I'd been dropped off a few days ago. I'd ended up there only hours after coming awake in the desert and being chased by a sentient beast.

None of that had made sense to me then.

What I'd learned *since then* was terrifying.

Silence outside my room taunted me.

No Takoda.

What if he had someone guarding this building?

Takoda had said he'd be back in the morning, which might be hours away if midnight was as close as I estimated. But it could already be past. My guess could be way off. Blood pounded in my ears, thudding with each heavy beat.

This was not the time for fear.

I had no idea how long it would take me to walk back to the school. To *run* back. Everything hinged on my returning before four in the morning.

I had to hurry and hope that Tony and Gabby were still there. My two new friends at the Institute had been with me when I accidentally opened a time-travel portal the first time. We'd already used it twice for traveling to the Sphere. Opening the portal again required all three of us present.

Callan and the other MystiK children who'd been captured and stuck there waited for us to come back.

Returning too late meant Callan would first suffer torture at the hands of the TecKnati, then he'd die a horrible death.

MystiKs and TecKnati were from 166 years in the future. The minute the red moon set in the Sphere and Callan turned eighteen, black wraiths would swarm him. He'd vanish into the ether. But the other MystiKs in the Sphere didn't know that.

I was the only one besides Callan who was aware of his horrible fate—the same fate of any MystiK turning eighteen in the Sphere.

I couldn't stop the moon from setting, but I might be able to do something to prevent his death.

I will not lose you, I vowed silently, repeating the words he'd said when he'd fought to protect me from a deadly plant on my last visit to the Sphere.

But nothing would happen if I didn't get out of this room.

Caution and the memory of being shocked by the stun gun had me waiting to see if anyone had heard the internal lock parts clanging, but I couldn't stay here any longer.

I listened one last time at the door.

No footsteps coming this way. Takoda had driven through miles of desert on the way here last night. He said only a few locals lived in this small town, but he hadn't told me if he was one of them.

How fast could I retrace my route to the school on foot?

I tested the doorknob again and ... it opened. My power had worked. This time.

Outside, the air was dry and cool where it had been hot as an oven during the day. Light from a giant, not-quite-full moon washed over the stacked pueblo rooms built high into the night sky. Takoda had used the term pueblo, but it was unfamiliar to me. To be honest, with few memories returning yet, the majority of everything I encountered was unfamiliar to me.

Takoda had talked continually on the drive last night, trying to act friendly and asking if I knew about Acoma Pueblo.

No I didn't and we weren't friends. My friends had never electro-shocked me with a weapon.

He'd explained what a stun gun was, then apologized.

Apology not accepted.

I kept picking my way through the town, looking all around. The place was built on a high plateau. In the distance, mountaintops dusted by moonlight rose against the dark skies. I had to get down from this sandstone mesa to the desert floor.

Had this place still been standing in the future when my people—C'raydonians—lived in the Sandia Mountains closer to Albuquerque? V'ru would know. I'd gained the only information I had on C'raydonians from V'ru, an all-knowing, eleven-year-old MystiK in the Sphere. Based on his records, it was believed that I had been born over eight decades into the future.

My people would eventually live here.

And they would all die here, leaving no one.

Longing hit with the swift strike of a sharp arrow, for a

family I couldn't remember and a life beyond the reach of my mind. I had nothing. No one.

In the brief, grueling days I'd been here, I'd formed a connection with Gabby and Tony back at the school, plus Callan and the MystiKs trapped on the Sphere.

And now someone wanted to take even that from me.

I continued sneaking through the town. No life stirred.

When I finally found the main road leading away from here, my feet picked up speed with each step toward the desert. Freedom was within my reach.

The road dropped off at a steep angle. I embraced the adrenaline pushing me to go and ran all-out through the moonlit night, using the broken white lines on the center of the road to navigate.

How long could I hold this pace?

I didn't know, but at least I had a trail to follow and, at this hour of night, no one would hear my sneakers slapping the hard surface.

Would this route lead me all the way to the school?

Breathing hard, I'd been on the desert level only a few minutes when I heard thunder.

I looked up. Not a cloud disturbed the vast sky.

The noise grew louder.

Not a storm, but the thunder of hooves pounding the ground.

I looked over my shoulder. Four men on horses raced toward me.

"No!" I pushed my legs harder and spun my feet, looking all around. Where was a place to hide or a way to lose them? Nothing. I stared at nothing but a vast ocean of sand interrupted by an occasional juniper tree.

I raced ahead with all the speed I could beg of my legs and feet. My side ached. I clutched it and kept running.

"Rayen, stop!" Takoda shouted as he closed in on me.

I was gasping for air. There was no way I'd outrun horses. Slowing down, I stumbled to a stop and spun to face him.

I raised my hands and begged the power to come forth.

Energy buzzed beneath my skin and hummed in my chest, but nothing reached my hands.

The horses pulled up hard, sending a cloud of dust boiling

around me. When it cleared, Takoda climbed down and walked up to me. "You can't leave."

Tears would do me no good. I blinked them away and pleaded. "Please let me go back. Cal . . . a person's life depends on me returning."

"Your people need you." His voice gentled. "You are special, Rayen."

How could I tell him that *my* people lived eighty years in the future and all of them were doomed to die because of a virus? I'd found out the C'raydonian race *had* descended from the Navajo and tribes intermarried with the Navajo.

But the people Takoda was talking about were not *mine*.

My throat was dry from running and the dust didn't help.

I coughed and croaked, "I can't ... save anyone here."

Takoda said something to one of the riders who tossed him a bottle of water. He handed it to me. "Drink."

I grabbed it and guzzled down the cool liquid. When I wiped my mouth, I asked, "Why won't you let me go back? I don't have any family on your reservation. I'm not from here."

He studied me for a long moment. "Where *are* you from?"

If I told him, he'd think I was insane. "You wouldn't know the place."

"You were sent by the spirits."

Just when I thought I had the exclusivity on being strange, he one-upped me. "I, uh, don't know what you mean."

I had a bad feeling that I just *might* know since I'd met a few spirits yesterday while I'd slept. Callan had held me during the night, consoling me after the spirits had told me they were my ancestors, that I had a destiny, then disappeared before I could get answers.

That seemed so far away now.

Takoda spoke in a calm voice as if he were trying to cajole me into doing as he wished. "Come with me, Rayen. I have someone you must meet."

I considered the situation I was in and wondered if I could draw on my energy again if I envisioned Callan being hurt. But I knew in my heart that I would not harm this man and his friends. Not if he didn't threaten me first.

What was I going to do?

I felt a new presence join us and glanced to my left, then closed my eyes for a moment, searching for patience.

The glowing image of an old man, in a seated position with his legs crossed, floated above the ground. My annoying ghost was back.

He was also Acheii, my great-great-grandfather.

Acheii said, "You must listen before you can be heard."

I curbed the urge to give him a biting retort about how he always showed up at the worst time, with unwanted advice, and never helped me out. Such as during the dream when I met the other spirits. Acheii was the one who'd cut me off and kept me from asking questions.

I wanted to convince Takoda to return me to the school. That might be hard to do if I started talking to the wind since no one else could see the old guy but me, so I ignored Acheii.

I looked at Takoda. "What time is it?"

The ghost answered, "Time for you to learn more of your destiny."

I refused to even glance in his direction.

Takoda looked at his watch. "The new day began four minutes ago."

Just past midnight.

Licking my dry lips, I asked, "How far away is this person you want me to meet?"

Takoda pointed to his left where a tiny campfire light burned bright as candle in the sea of darkness. "Not far."

"If I go with you, will you take me back to the school?"

"I will do what our shaman decides."

So they wanted me to see a shaman and that person had final say. I couldn't get away from four men on horses. If I convinced this shaman to let me return to the school, horses or a vehicle would be faster than on foot.

I asked, "How far is the drive to the school? I wasn't awake for the whole trip."

"Sixty five minutes."

That meant I had to be out of here by two-thirty to have enough time to return to the school and still have about thirty minutes to find Tony and Gabby before our four o'clock deadline to leave. Heading to the school sooner would be better.

"You waste precious time," Acheii said with brusque impatience.

"Don't you think I realize that?" I snapped at the space where Acheii had floated. The space was now empty.

And Takoda had witnessed the whole thing.

As did the three silent men on horses.

I didn't want to see the wariness in his eyes, but I rarely got what I wanted these days so I turned to Takoda.

No wariness. No questions about talking to myself. He waved his hand to his horse. "We should go."

Once I was seated behind Takoda, he made a clicking sound and the horse flew across the desert.

Wind blew hair loose from my ponytail. A memory swirled in my mind of riding at night through a desert. I reached for the memory, dragging it to me with anxious fingers, begging my mind to give me something from my past.

The memory slowly unfolded. My father and I were on horses.

He'd ridden with me to see someone he said would protect me.

I could see it all so clearly now.

A beast was after us. Red demonic eyes had glowed. The same type of sentient beast that had chased me two days ago when I'd awakened in the desert.

That deadly thing had come from the future, too. It had followed me here, to this time.

The vision wavered like a reflected image disturbed by ripples in a pond. I focused all my attention again, desperate to mine more of this one memory. My father yelled at me to keep going and to do as the elder told me. I would never disobey my father, but when he'd turned off to lead the beast away from me I'd panicked momentarily.

I pulled around hard to change direction and go help my father fight the sentient killer.

But a second beast appeared, charging hard toward me.

I ran my horse hard toward the opening between two sheer rock walls where my father had told me the elder waited in a narrow canyon. When I passed through the rock gap, the beast was close behind, but it crashed against an invisible force. It backed up, changing its form to a giant bird with a six-foot-wide wingspan, long talons and a vicious beak, watching me with the glowing eyes of a predator.

I reined in my horse, stopping before I ran down the elder on the other side of a small fire.

He wore faded colors of the sunset woven in geometric patterns on a robe that brushed the ground. For a frail man, his voice was strong. “You are Ashkii Dighin and you have a duty.”

That was the same name the spirits in my dream had called me. It translated to sacred child.

His eyes were two milky orbs incapable of seeing me.

Smoky air teased my nose.

The bird-beast charged, once again slamming up against some invisible field that prevented it from passing through the stone opening into the small area. The elder’s wrinkled brow furrowed at the bird’s screech. In one hand, he lifted a scuffed and battered gourd with faint black-and-red images of warriors fighting. He told me, “You must hurry. My magic will not hold the protective wall long. Come closer.”

Every detail of that next minute roared to life.

I slid off my horse and walked toward the fire. The elder began chanting and allowed sparkling granules of sand to sift from his hand into the fire. He shook the gourd that rattled like the tail of a deadly snake. The fire rose into a cyclone of swirling blue and green flames that moved away from the elder and toward me, engulfing me.

A scream rose in my throat, but the flames didn’t touch my skin. I was slowly mesmerized by the strange sensations flooding me. My body stretched and pulled.

The elder shouted a warning.

I couldn’t grasp what he was saying. I was lifted off the ground inside the cyclone as it picked up speed. I could feel the power pulsing through the whirling funnel, spinning faster and faster.

The elder’s voice boomed, but I couldn’t grasp his words.

I pivoted in slow motion, suspended as the world warped around me. The sound of a thousand voices chanted a melody that blended into a kaleidoscope of colors. As I came around to face the narrow opening for the canyon, I realized what the elder was shouting.

The sentient bird slammed the invisible barrier once more, bursting through this time. It flew at me, beak opened to rip me to shreds. Then it dove into the cyclone and—

"Rayen! Rayen!"

Takoda stood above me with worry etching his face.

I was lying on the ground, staring up at him and the moon that hung over his left shoulder. "What happened?"

"You passed out the second we stopped and I couldn't catch you before you fell to the ground. Does anything feel broken?"

I sat up, gave the dizziness a moment to diminish, then shook it off.

Bending my knees, I rocked forward and pushed off the sandy ground to stand, dusting myself. I murmured, "Nothing broken. I don't know what happened."

That was a lie.

Fear at being attacked in that fire cyclone had been too much. I'd blacked out. But now I knew how I'd ended up here in the past with that same sentient beast chasing me. It had gotten sucked into the same cyclone firestorm.

"Are you all right?" Takoda asked.

I would never be all right.

My life and family lived almost a hundred years in the future. I'd grown attached to Callan who had been born fifty years after my entire race had disappeared from this planet. Plus, I was running out of time to save him.

But if I could convince Takoda's shaman to allow me to return to the school, I still yet might save Callan.

When Takoda nodded, I turned to find his shaman standing on the opposite side of a small fire.

We were in a narrow canyon, like the one in my memory.

That wouldn't have been so disturbing if the shaman had not been the spitting image of the elder in my dream, right down to the painted gourd in his hand, the milky eyes and his next words.

"You are Ashkii Dighin and you have a duty."

I started backing away.

No, this couldn't happen again. Not now.

Chapter 2

"He won't harm you," Takoda told me, anchoring his hand on my shoulder.

I couldn't decide if it was to comfort me or prevent me from running. No one could reassure me at the moment and with my level of adrenaline reaching a new high, I doubted anyone could prevent me from running, either.

Looking around, I saw the other three horsemen still mounted and waiting a ways back.

Were they positioned in case I took off again?

Sweat ran down the side of my face and pooled at my neck. My fingers fisted and I was alert to every sound as I turned back to the shaman.

"Do not fear me, Ashkii Dighin," the shaman said in a voice gruff with age. "I only wish to speak with you."

I found my voice. "How do you know who I am?"

"I have seen you in a hundred dreams. The last one was yesterday. That is why Takoda came for you."

Finally someone who might have answers.

If I could trust any of this. The spirits in my dream had also called me by that name, but this shaman couldn't even see me.

The shaman must have taken my silence as disbelief. He asked, "Do you have the blue-green eyes of the sea?"

Hard to deny that with Takoda standing here. "Yes."

"Do you have magic that comes from within?"

Takoda didn't know about my powers so he couldn't have told anyone. My palms dampened. I was feeling excited at just how much that this shaman did know, so I said, "Yes."

"Do you come from another time?"

That caused the skin on my arms to prickle with warning.

How should I answer that one? Instead, I asked, "Why would you think that?"

A smile formed on the elder's lips. "This is the one, Takoda."

"Wait a minute," I complained. "I didn't say I was from another time."

Takoda said, "But neither did you deny it."

This was getting stranger than being dropped at the Byzantine Institute and finding a laptop that opened a time travel portal to another world. My hand had gone into the monitor.

Into. The. Monitor.

I'd survived that and time travel to the future and back. This shaman couldn't be any more scary than facing monsters in the Sphere so I admitted, "Yes, I'm not from ... this land." I chickened out at the last minute when I was going to say, not from this time period.

No one reacted, so I added, "If you know so much about me, maybe you can tell me who exactly my family is, because I have no memory other than pieces that fall together sometimes."

The elder nodded. He started chanting and opened his hand.

"*No!*" I shouted and raised my hands even though he couldn't see me. Or could he? "Stop that."

He paused his chanting and angled his head as if he *could* see me. "What is wrong, child?"

What wasn't wrong?

I ran my palms over my wind-blown hair and dropped my hands. "I will tell you the truth and answer your questions if you promise to return me to the school by three this morning." In the ensuing silence, I added, "And don't use your magic to send me to another place."

"I can not send you home, Rayen."

I hadn't really considered the possibility of going home until he said that, but the reminder that I had no way back to my family tore a piece of my heart open.

Everyone belonged somewhere. Except me.

The only place I'd felt as though I belonged at all had been in the Sphere with the MystiKs.

And with Callan.

But that was temporary. Hoping for more was a fool's dream.

"You do not have much time, Rayen," the shaman warned.

"For what?" Everyone kept telling me what I could and could not do, and that time was running out, but none of that made sense to me.

"You have a destiny to fulfill."

I kept hearing that, too. "To do what?" I asked.

"To save your people."

My eyes stung. "I can't."

Takoda had observed silently with his arms crossed. He asked, "Why do you say that when you have yet to hear what the shaman has to tell you?"

I was too weary to keep pretending that I was anything except what I was—a seventeen-year-old girl sent back in time who had been stripped of her family and her memories.

Lifting my hands to ask for a moment, I said, "This might be hard for you to believe, but I'm going to tell you the entire truth and hope that you will let me save the people that I can. I came awake in the desert just a few days ago with a beast chasing me that was capable of changing forms. It wasn't a live animal. I escaped it, but then I was arrested with other young people who the law enforcement called runaways. They couldn't find any identity for me here, because I haven't been born yet in this time. I *am* from the future."

The shaman had lowered his gourd and kept his cloudy-eyed attention on me, so I continued.

"They dropped me at that private school where I met two students. The three of us accidentally found a portal to the future. We landed in a place called the Sphere where other young people known as MystiKs are imprisoned by SEOH, a man who is the leader of all the TecKnati in their world in the future. In the Sphere, I found out that I am a C'raydonian, that—"

Rattling erupted from the gourd the shaman stabbed toward the sky. He stared up and chanted softly.

Words froze in my throat.

Did he see someone up there like I sometimes saw my old

ghost man, Acheii?

I was terrified of saying the wrong thing and he'd flash me out of here to another time period. He'd said he couldn't send me home, but that didn't mean he couldn't send me further back in time.

After several long seconds of the elder shaking his gourd and singing a chant to the heavens, he calmed down and lowered the gourd to his side where it quieted.

He said, "You *are* the one."

Clearly, what I'd just shared had not influenced his thinking one bit.

Trying again, I said, "I really think you have the wrong person. My people are C'raydonians and while they *are* descendants of the Navajo, their group broke off to live in solitude. They were killed almost a hundred years from now, wiped out completely by a virus."

The MystiKs believed the TecKnatis had brought a deadly virus back from space explorations of the future. After the virus killed much of the world, pockets of reclusive people from spiritualists to dedicated scientists and researchers who hadn't been infected by the virus came together in ten cities in this country called North America. From what I'd learned, the C'raydonians hadn't been so fortunate and the virus ran rapid through their population.

Any who didn't die outright were hunted to extinction.

Both the MystiKs and TecKnati had killed C'raydonians to protect their fragile populations—the ones who had not been infected—but it seemed the TecKnati leader had taken a special interest in wiping out C'raydonians.

"You have a destiny that you cannot avoid," the shaman repeated. The man was still stuck on one track.

"If I listen to what you have to tell me, will you answer some questions *then* let me go?" I asked, just as determined to gain what I needed.

The elder's reply was to raise that blasted gourd again and began chanting. We were getting nowhere.

I decided to let him move ahead with his ceremony in hopes that once he finished I could leave. But if a cyclone blew up out of that fire, I wasn't sticking around.

The shaman sprinkled crystalized grains over the fire that poofed and shot a flame high in the air then died down. I wasn't sure he was still with us when he began talking in a strange tongue to no one in particular.

Then he spoke words I understood.

"The future is in the past ... One will seek and all will forfeit."

My blood turned to ice. I'd heard those phrases in the Sphere.

The shaman continued, "When three become one ... the end has begun. The gateway will open ... a path will close."

My ghost grandfather, Acheii, had said that to me.

As if I'd called him, Acheii appeared next to the shaman, who smiled and angled his head toward the ghost. Was he acknowledging the spector? The shaman continued speaking. "A friend enters as enemy ... an enemy leaves as friend."

These were words from the Damian Prophecy the MystiKs spoke of during my last trip to the Sphere.

I repeated the shaman's ramblings in my mind, determined to remember every word to share with the MystiKs. I'd heard only bits and pieces of the prophecy. This man's version might differ from the one I'd heard before.

If I ever saw them again.

I started to speak.

Acheii raised his hand, palm out and shook his head at me.

The shaman chanted another few seconds then lifted his blind gaze to the sky again as he spoke. "Day of birth as Red Moon rises ... Night of end when last moon sets. Three must unite ... for the scales to right. The last will lead when others cede."

He dropped his chin and those empty eyes stared at me and through me. I couldn't breathe, waiting for his next words.

"All turn to the outcast. The past speaks to alter the present ... a bond of two will set us free."

All turn to the outcast echoed in my mind.

I trembled at the push of power that rushed around me. Was I the outcast?

Acheii gave the shaman a nod of approval and vanished.

The night was deathly silent as the flame died down.

Takoda didn't speak or move an inch. We waited on the shaman's next words. He frowned and angled his head as if listening to some voice I couldn't hear. He nodded and seemed to listen again, then his hands trembled and his mouth opened in shock.

When the shaman's frightened face turned to me, he said, "Go now, Rayen, or you will miss the window you must pass through. If Callan dies, all is lost."

"How do you know about—" I stopped in mid sentence when what he'd said hit me. He was allowing me to leave.

No, the shaman had *ordered* me to go and whatever he'd been listening to had frightened him.

My skin chilled at realizing the prophecy was more than a bunch of words in the future. I was tied to it.

And so was Callan ... if he lived.

Chapter 3

I clutched a handhold above the passenger seat in Takoda's truck as it raced over the road.

He slowed only when we approached a turn I recognized from the first time I'd been delivered to the Byzantine Institute.

I'd ridden in silence, afraid to ask what Takoda believed, but I couldn't risk that he'd change his mind and come back for me or tell them what I'd said. "Do you believe what I told the shaman?"

"I believe in our people and the elders who guide us."

No answer there. I pressed my point. "So you believe that I'm from the future?"

Seconds passed on slow feet as Takoda weighed his answer. "I have witnessed some unusual things in my life, but I have never met someone who time traveled." His dark gaze swept over to me. "That does not give it less credibility."

All the way back to the school, my body had vibrated with worry over Callan, fear that the Browns, who ran the Institute, had sent Tony away or found Gabby, who should still be hiding. Her powers had begun evolving when she'd entered the Sphere, but she was having a tough time gaining control of them. The last time I saw her, she was having issues such as uncontrollable levitation.

I didn't know which one to worry about more—Tony or Gabby. Tony had been locked up yesterday for a crime he hadn't committed after another seventeen-year-old lied, and Gabby was hiding from staff in the Institute who wanted to sterilize her.

Gabby was only sixteen.

On top of all my concerns, I wondered if Takoda would hand me back to the Browns and declare me mentally unfit, or if he really accepted what the shaman had said.

In the distance, the school shimmered beneath security lights growing brighter as we approached.

Takoda pulled to the side of the road before reaching the gates. He parked and turned to me. "When you don't know what to believe, believe in yourself and be true to your heart. You can never go wrong if you do both."

"Are you leaving me here?"

"Yes. The Browns sent me a message last night informing me they were reporting you as part of the theft ring that your friend Tony is leading."

"What? Tony didn't steal anything. Nicholas, the Brown's boy, lied about Tony."

Takoda nodded with understanding. "If I enter with you, they will be alerted that you are returning."

What he was trying to say dawned on me. "I have to find my own way in."

"That would be safest for you. My shaman said that you would either find the passage back to the place where you will fulfill your destiny or that you would return to us."

I was not returning to Takoda's people. Because that would mean I had failed to reach Callan in time to free him. I put my hand on the door.

Takoda touched my arm, stopping me, and said, "You will always be welcome among your people no matter the year. If you come back to us, I promise that we will protect you."

The words were heartfelt and sincere. I reached over and squeezed his arm. "Thank you. But you cannot protect me from what I have to do. What time is it?"

"Two-twenty."

Smiling my thanks again, I slipped out of his vehicle and headed for the school, searching past the lights for any sign of someone on patrol.

One glance over my shoulder confirmed that Takoda was gone. His taillights were quickly turning into tiny red spots.

When I reached the school, I found it strangely amusing that I had fought so hard to escape this place the first day, and here

I was, planning to break in.

No one guarded the gate, but a current ran through the metal bars. I could feel the energy of it as I drew near. It felt like the same kind of power that had struck my body when I'd tried to leave with an ankle cuff strapped on. It had been even stronger than the stun gun the security people here had used on me when I'd tried to run from Takoda.

The cuff was gone—Takoda had made the school remove it—but I was fairly certain the current in the gates would burn me.

The gates were metal, but they were attached to a high wall that looked similar to the adobe pueblos. It had intermittent square columns of layered sandstone. Going over the top was the only way in that I could figure, but there were only shallow handholds in the and the columns soared twenty-feet high.

My palms started sweating.

I hadn't realized I feared heights until I ended up in the top of a tree after a battle in the Sphere. Callan had been there to help me down. No one could help me now.

I had to get inside this wall and every second counted.

Heart pounding at a wild beat, I studied each column and chose a spot for climbing over that would land me in the shadow of the two-story school. That area would put me near the access to the dorm side of the building.

If I could make it all the way up there then back down again.

What could be more terrifying? Facing my fear of heights or showing up too late to prevent Callan's death? Pretty equal when it came to my level of terror, but saving Callan won hands down. I could do this. Had to. Drawing a couple deep breaths, I reached above my head and sank my fingers into a recess in the column structure. I started climbing, proud of myself when I'd reached six feet off the ground in spite of trembling. All was going well until Gabby's voice shouted in my mind.

Rayen, where are you?

Shocked, I let go and fell, landing on my back with a grunt of pain.

I'd heard her telepathically once before here at the school, but I had yet to figure out how to answer her.

Standing up, I calmed my startled heart, rubbed my behind that had taken the brunt of the fall and faced climbing one more time. Now I had even more reason to be afraid.

What if I let go at the top and fell?

What if Callan faced the wraiths alone and with no way to use his power?

Got it. I told myself to shut up and just do it. I lunged to grip the stone structure again. From handhold to handhold, I made it to the top where the column had a flat surface two feet square. Struggling with my balance, I was in a half crouch, trying to catch my breath when Gabby called out again.

We're running out of time, Rayen!

I jerked at the sharp sound of her voice in my head and lost my grip, sliding sideways and grabbing at anything to stop my fall. I ended up draped half on and half off the top of the column.

We need to go, Rayen, Gabby's voice boomed in my head once more.

"I know it. Shut up," I snarled, trying to keep my mind on not looking down or letting go. Gabby couldn't hear my words, but it made me feel better to answer her.

A bird flew past me. It stank like the sentient beast.

Hugging the column, I twisted to look around, trying to determine where the bird was or which way it was flying. Wings fluttering, it dropped to the ledge of a window on the second floor. The window slid up just high enough for the bird to enter.

That was one of the forms the sentient beast had taken since I arrived here two days ago. It had also turned into a three-legged creature the size of a buffalo and just as fast, and a whippet-shaped animal.

Why had it not attacked me this time?

Phen must have trained the beast to perform on his commands, but Phen was a TecKnati from the future and liked me no more than that sentient bird did.

Especially after I'd refused to help Phen find a way to return home. SEOH had sent him here from the future, but the TecKnati knew how to time travel in only one direction—into the past. That was why they wanted the computer that Tony, Gabby and I had used to travel to the Sphere, forward in time.

I couldn't stay in this spot much longer. The muscles in my arms were screaming in protest.

Now would be a great time to have Callan's kinetic ability to slow my descent. But I'd also need his lack of fear over jumping to the ground. I wasn't entirely sure what my powers were capable of, but since they couldn't be depended upon, I was stuck with figuring out how to get down the normal way and without killing myself.

I moved my feet until I caught a toehold and carefully slid my fingers from one handhold to the next. If the fall didn't kill me, a broken leg would destroy any chance of finding Gabby or Tony. *Don't look down or think about how far it is.* Tediously, I kept moving lower and lower until I was close enough to drop to the ground. I landed on trembling legs.

I'd rather fight a croggle monster in the Sphere again than face another climb. Wiping my damp palms on my pants, I gave myself a minute to allow my breathing to calm down while I listened for the sound of guards running toward me. I heard nothing. Even the wind moved too gently to make a sound.

I rushed to an exterior door that led to the boys' dorm, the quickest way to get inside. The door had two sets of locks.

More locks?

Where was Tony and his lock-pick skills? He was the one who had taught me how to unlock a door, but I'd had to use my powers with his to make it work.

An exterior door swung open slowly.

I shifted my feet into a fighting stance.

Phen appeared, same wide forehead, dull eyes and twenty-something attitude, and held the door open. His cruel gaze swept over me with contempt. The black bird was perched on his shoulder. "What do you want, Rayen?"

"I need to get back inside the building."

"We all need something."

If Phen raised an alarm right now it would destroy any hope of finding Gabby and Tony. "I told you I'd think about helping you find a way home."

His eyes lit with interest, but he refused to admit how much he wanted that. "I don't trust you."

"I don't trust you either," I countered. "But we need each other. Let me in and I'll try to help you."

"Try? That's not good enough." He gave a casual look over his shoulder then glanced back at me with a sly smile. "Wonder what the Browns would say if they knew you were on Byzantine property."

I didn't like making an offer for something that I had no idea if I could deliver, but every second we burned here was going to cost Callan on the other end. "Fine. Let me in and I'll share our time travel secret with you, but you have to help me get to my friends."

For the span of two seconds, hope and longing bloomed in Phen's face. He pulled the momentary weakness back under control and stepped aside, holding the door for me to enter. "We have a deal."

I rushed past him and tried not to think about how I could possibly make good on my offer when the portal only worked between here and the Sphere. I reached the end of the short hallway from the outside access and pushed through the door, then took a fast right.

Phen was close behind and hissed, "Hey. Where're you going?"

I paused to tell him, "To the girls' dorm."

"Is that where the computer is?"

The laptop with the portal should be in the backpack that Tony had left with Gabby, but telling Phen would cause him to follow me when I needed to lose him. Instead of outright lying, I said, "The laptop is in Tony's backpack."

"You're screwed. He's still in detention."

That was actually encouraging news, but I didn't want to admit it to Phen. I nodded and gave him a concerned look. "I have to go find Gabby and see if she knows what's been happening while I was gone. I'll talk to you later."

I turned and raced away before he could stop me.

He wasn't supposed to enter the girls' dorm, but who knew what Phen would or would not do?

~*~

Phen watched that miserable MystiK-loving twit run into the girls' dorm. He'd gotten caught there once last night while trying to track down Gabby. It wouldn't have been a problem if the Browns had been here, but they weren't on site at the moment. When the Byzantine security found him in the wrong place, Phen had barely gotten away by acting totally confused over what area he was in.

They'd cut him a break since he was so new.

He pulled the bird off his shoulder and stroked its head. At one time, he'd been responsible for tending sentient beasts at a zootech in the future. They'd turned out to be simple to manage if you understood the hard coding in their systems. He gave this one an order and the bird rolled into a black-feathered ball in his hand. Bones poked out at odd angles and the feathers morphed into the smooth skin of a chameleon.

Phen squatted down and placed the sentient critter on the floor then ordered it, "Follow Rayen until she's with Tony and Gabby, then return to me."

He'd programmed the images of Rayen, Tony and Gabby into the beast's memory.

The chameleon took off, flattened itself to crawl beneath the door, and scurried down the girls' dorm hallway.

Chapter 4

I reached the second floor, hunting the room number that Hannah had given me before we'd all separated. Hannah agreed to hide Gabby as a favor for Tony, who had poured on the charm.

But that had been prior to Tony being accused of theft and locked up in detention.

Hannah was the perfect student who worked part time with the office staff. If she'd heard about Tony's detention, she might have given up Gabby.

That nauseating thought jammed me in place. Where would Gabby be if Hannah had turned her over to the staff?

Rayen, hurry up and get back here, Gabby called in my mind again. Louder this time.

My pulse pumped hard. I searched the numbers on the doors and found the one Hannah had said was hers. I tapped at the door and it whipped open.

"There you are!" Gabby launched herself at me, hugging me.

We'd never hugged before. My throat tightened with emotion. I'd found one of the two real friends I had in this world.

Gabby pushed away and backed into the room. She wore her yellow and purple hair in multiple ponytails that jutted out all over her head in a signature Gabby style. On the last trip to the Sphere, she'd started having issues like dancing hair and her feet leaving the ground involuntarily.

Still wearing the heavy backpack Tony had given her, she ushered me into the room. "I'm so freakin' glad to see you, Rayen. Where'd you go?"

"Takoda took me to a place out in the desert, one of the reservations, and I just now got back." I looked around. "Where's Hannah?"

"I told her I couldn't explain, but that I needed to get to Tony. It's three o'clock already. We're running out of time."

"You still haven't told me where Hannah is."

Gabby lifted her shoulders. "She took Tony's hoodie and went to see him."

"We have less than an hour to open that portal." Of course, that would do Callan little good if we didn't have a computer to hand over to the TecKnati. "What about computer parts?"

"I don't know what parts Tony needs."

I clutched my head where a stabbing pain had camped out. "Do you have a way to reach Hannah?"

"She gave me her phone number, but she said she might not answer if she didn't feel it buzzing, because she didn't want to risk having the ringer on while she was sneaking into detention."

"Let's go find computer parts then we'll break Tony out of there and get back to the Sphere."

"I have doubts about breaking him out," Gabby admitted.

I was herding her out the door and toward the computer lab. "Why?"

"They put an ankle cuff on him."

"Like the one I had?" I was *so* glad mine was gone.

"Yes, but yours was programmed to stop you if you tried to step off the property."

"I remember." Hard to forget after I'd gotten a nasty load of electricity when I tried to walk out the front gate. "What's the deal with Tony's ankle cuff?"

"His is programmed to set off alarms if he steps out of his detention room."

How were we going to get him out of there?

Chapter 5

Tony ignored the food they'd brought him in the windowless basement room the Byzantine Institute designated as their detention facility.

How had he screwed up so badly?

He'd left everything he'd ever known in Jersey to come to a freaking desert school for a chance to get into MIT.

Right now, it looked like he was headed to juvie. Or worse.

Callan was in a bigger jam in the Sphere. Rayen was probably going postal by now. Those two had something going on that had no chance of working out, but that was between them. Tony had no desire to play the fatal messenger role. He'd do what he could to help save Callan, *if* he got out of here in time. Right now that wasn't looking promising at all.

Everyone would lose.

All because of Nicholas Brown, that lying sack of—

"Tony," a voice whispered on the other side of the door.

He walked over and leaned against it. "Who's there?"

"Hannah."

The sound of a key jangled, because security didn't trust Tony not to figure his way past an electronic lock.

When the door opened, Hannah stepped in, quickly closing it behind her. She usually wore prim skirt-and-jacket suits that carried an air of authority. In truth, that perception was more about *her* than the clothes. He'd thought she was an ice queen, but changed his evaluation when he'd gotten to know her.

She was sweet and smart, and looked adorable right now wearing pink flannel workout pants and a grey hoodie like one he owned. The girl could rock anything from business suits to cut offs.

Her hands trembled, causing the ring of keys to tinkle.

Dark auburn hair hung straight to her chin and swayed with her slight head movement. She speared him with an ice-blue look he couldn't read.

Had she come in friendship, or to ream him out for screwing up their chance to win the Top Ten Competition? She'd convinced him to partner up with her yesterday and he wouldn't blame her if she sorely regretted that move.

"Tony." She said his name with a breathlessness that had his brain short-circuiting, but she might just be nervous about seeing someone in the school equivalent of death row.

"Hey, Hannah. Why ya here?"

Her face fell.

What had he said wrong?

She stared away from him. "See if I come to visit you in detention again."

"Whoa, babe. I'm glad to see you. I just ... figured you're pissed at me."

"No. I'm worried about you."

"Really?" He scrubbed a hand over his face and stepped over to her. "How'd I get lucky enough to find someone like you?"

Her eyes twinkled and he knew all was forgiven.

He didn't deserve it because he'd let her down through no fault of his own, but he'd still let her down. He ran his knuckles up along Hannah's smooth cheek. "You're the sweetest thing I've ever met."

Surprised glowed in her. She unconsciously licked her full lips and the surprise shifted to a coy gleam. "Did you miss me?"

He couldn't resist the invitation when he might not ever see her again.

He pushed his hand into her hair and cupped her head, leaning down to kiss her. Man, she had amazing lips. He'd only planned to give her a quick peck, but he couldn't stop himself from indulging another few seconds. Hey, death row inmates got a last meal, right? He'd gladly take a taste of Hannah as his.

How had he spent so much time around her and not realized

until recently what a babe hid beneath that uptight exterior?

That's what happened when you assumed you knew someone.

Her fingers touched his shoulder then tentatively moved around his neck and the room got hot.

Lifting his mouth from hers, he smiled at her. In the middle of his entire life falling apart, just looking at her could make him happy.

This one was definitely a keeper. He sighed.

If only he could figure a way out of the trouble he was in.

The glaze over Hannah's eyes cleared and she blinked, snapping back into Miss On The Ball. "I came to tell you what's going on. When I found out who had fingered you for the theft, I did some checking. Nick must have heard about you changing to have me as your Top Ten partner, because I put the paperwork in before Mr. Suarez left yesterday. I heard Nick went to talk Mr. Suarez out of allowing you to drop Nick as your partner, but Mr. Suarez told him a little adversity built character."

Tony was touched that Hannah had enough faith in him to not jump to a conclusion that he was some lowlife thief, but Nick had done a number on him.

Stepping away from her, Tony cracked his knuckles then pounded his fist into the palm of his hand. "Suarez is wasting his time on Nick. His character is pretty ingrained at this point. He's got me in a corner. They're gonna expel me and throw me in jail. I can't even defend myself against his lies."

"I'm sorry, Tony."

"Not your fault, babe." Tony relaxed his hands and gave her a smile. "Thanks for finding out what you can."

Hannah pulled a hand from behind her and stuck a folded up sweatshirt toward him. "Here's one of your hoodies. I used my passkey to get into your room."

Tony took it and pulled the hoodie over his head. "Thanks. I was getting cold down here ... until you showed up." He winked at her.

She blushed and looked away. Cute.

He stepped close again and took her hand. "How's Gabby?"

That got him an eye roll. "Strange as usual. She won't take

the backpack off that you gave her."

Jealousy lurked behind Hannah's frown.

"Hannah, baby, that backpack is keeping Gabby balanced. She's having ... vertigo issues." Not really. Not unless vertigo included floating in the air. That backpack was probably the only way Gabby could keep her feet on the ground right now."Okay."

Girl-trouble bullet dodged. "Have you seen Rayen?"

Hannah stepped back, crossed her arms and scowled. "I'm the one who comes to see you and you want to know about other girls?"

For the love of St. Christopher. "I only asked because I promised to do something with Rayen and Gabby. We're just friends. Why would I be interested in them when I already have a girlfriend?"

"You do?" Hannah's pretty lips softened.

Tony would have laughed if not for fear of really ticking off Hannah. He touched his finger and thumb to her chin. "I hope so. I don't kiss just any girl. Only the *one* that matters to me."

Hannah was emotional, but she wasn't slow on the uptake. Happiness glittered in her eyes. She whispered, "I'm your girlfriend?"

"Of course you are, but I'm not sure you want to have someone who's headed to juvie."

"We have to get you out of here."

Tony held his breath a second. "Are you sayin' you're gonna help me break out?"

She looked defeated by the idea. "I can't. I accessed the security system. The alarms will squeal the minute you cross the threshold to leave this room."

"Crap. I thought this cuff was just programmed for if I tried to leave the property."

"Nick warned them that they couldn't be too careful with a genius like you."

Tony snorted. "The guy finally admits he's intimidated by me?"

She grinned. "Not exactly, but we both know he is." Her pocket hummed. She patted it and fished out her cell phone. "Who would be texting me at this time in the morning?

Actually ten minutes ago. Stupid cell service sucks here." Her eyes flicked back and forth. She clutched the phone in her shaking hand. "Oh, no."

"What, Hannah?"

Looking up, her gaze was full of concern. "You asked about Rayen. Security shocked her with a stun gun and —""*What?* "Hannah let him know with a look to not interrupt her. "Not now. Last night. I heard that guy from the Navajo council, Takoda, was in the office waiting for Rayen right after you were put in detention. She tried to run so they zapped her. The last I heard, Takoda was driving her to some reservation." Hannah looked at her phone as if it had lied to her. "I thought she was gone, but Gabby just texted me that Rayen's back and they're headed to the computer lab. What's Rayen doing here and what are they doing at the lab this time in the morning?"

He didn't want to lie to Hannah, but it wasn't like he could tell her he'd time traveled to a place 166 years in the future either. "I promised to do something for them and I'd tell you more, but if it goes bad I don't want you involved."

She didn't give him any indication of what was going on in her mind at first then finally said, "I'm going to trust that you're telling the truth."

"I am."

"Is what you need to do illegal?"

Insane maybe, but building a laptop to save Callan was not technically illegal since Tony had permission from Mr. Suarez to use parts to build a computer for their project.

Tony shook his head. "But it's hard to explain right now."

"Gabby and Rayen won't get into the science lab."

Tony recalled how Rayen had used her weird powers to unlock a door when they'd busted Gabby out of the clinic. "They'll get in. Rayen has a gift at getting past locked doors."

Hannah's lofty attitude surfaced. "But can Rayen get past a security system?"

"That area's not alarmed."

"It wasn't until Mr. Suarez reported a theft."

Tony sucked in a breath as if he'd taken a punch to his solar plexus. He grabbed his head. "Tell Gabby to stop. Please, Hannah."

Her attitude vanished and she tapped furiously on her phone screen. She stared at it a second then looked up. “It’s not going through.”

“They’re gonna get caught.”

Chapter 6

"Why can't you get the lock open?" Gabby whispered so close I jumped and my shoulder bumped the computer science lab door.

"I don't know." I put my hand back on the knob and tried to concentrate again, but my stupid power wasn't coming through. "I can't make the power appear the way you can just talk in other people's heads."

Gabby shifted the backpack that she had to be tired of carrying. "I do not talk in other people's heads without permission."

"You did in mine." The metal knob still hadn't changed temperature.

"I never know when you hear me," she argued.

I started to tell her that it didn't change the fact that I heard her voice in my head sometimes, but I caught sight of the clock above the door for this hallway. Two-forty-one.

I warned Gabby, "Stand back. I have an idea. I'm going to try something different to call up my power."

She stepped away.

The lock at the pueblo had sounded as if I'd broken it. I had to be careful not to destroy the door, but I closed my eyes and blocked out everything. I started imagining Callan being attacked. Blood ran down his face and—

My chest warmed.

Good enough. The knot in my stomach loosened.

I opened my eyes and took a moment to let the energy swirl then I focused on my fingers cupping the lock. Nice and slow, I felt the energy pushing out through my fingers and warming the metal.

Slowly this time. Don't push too hard.

An image of the tumblers appeared in my mind. Click, click ... the next one stuck. Maybe I had to put more power behind it. My hand trembled. I drew again on the power and it flooded my arm then my hand.

Click, click, *bang* then *pop!*

I released the knob and looked up at Gabby with a smile. "I think I got it."

She grinned, ready to move forward and enter with me. I'd just closed my fingers around the knob when I heard, "*Stop!*"

Hannah came running up to us.

What was I going to tell her? *This doesn't look like what you think?* Any idiot would realize exactly what I was doing.

I didn't get a chance to say anything, because Hannah said, "If you open that door, you'll set off alarms."

Gabby groaned. "What are we going to do, Rayen?"

"I don't know."

Hannah said, "Lucky for you two, I have access to the code. Stand back."

I looked over at Gabby who gave me an I-don't-have-a-clue-why-she's-helping-us look. I gave Hannah room and she slid a keycard into a slot next to the door that I had ignored because all the doors had those. I'd never heard an alarm set off by opening one in this area.

When a tiny light beamed green on the card slot, Hannah said, "Now you can open it, but you have five minutes."

Gabby asked, "Why?"

"Because I just saw Tony and he said you had to come see him before 3:00 AM. It will take me ten minutes to get you into his detention cell."

Hope surged so fast and hard through me it should have exploded my heart. "We'll hurry."

But the minute I stepped inside the room, the sheer volume of technical supplies against the wall overwhelmed me. I had no idea what we had to collect in computer parts. I was not the techno geek that Tony and Hannah were.

Asking Hannah for any more help at this point would open the door to questions I didn't want to answer.

I nudged Gabby in her side. "How do we know what parts

to take for Tony?"

"Select them the same way you chose the laptop that can—" Gabby looked over at the door and said, "You know what."

She meant the laptop computer I'd accidentally found that had a time-travel portal. I hadn't really chosen it. The computer had chosen me by pulling my hand to it as if the laptop was a magnet and I was made of steel.

Or had the laptop recognized the power inside me?

I followed Gabby to a wall of cabinets that were six feet tall and a foot thick. Plastic drawers started at four inches square at the top and grew larger with much wider ones across the bottom.

This was where I'd seen Tony grab computer parts the day we'd first met and he'd gotten stuck with me as a project partner.

But Tony was a technological genius who knew exactly what he'd needed that day.

Gabby held her hands up, palms facing the bins. She told me, "Hold your hands like this."

I did as she asked. Nothing happened. "We only have four minutes. Maybe we should just start grabbing—"

Fifteen drawers opened out toward us.

Gabby laughed and started pulling out odd little parts she handed me. "Put them in the backpack."

"That was bizarre," I muttered, carefully filling Tony's backpack.

Gabby spoke softly. "Is it any more bizarre than traveling to the future, meeting kids with all kinds of gifts and fighting everything from croggles to attack vines?"

She had a point.

She handed me a part the size of my fingernail and said, "That's the last one."

"Maybe we should grab some more."

Gabby was considering my suggestion when Hannah stuck her head in and said, "Let's go if you want to see Tony."

Speaking of Tony, he'd have a meltdown if he saw how we selected parts.

We hurried out the door that Hannah locked behind us then she swiped her card back through the slot. When the light turned red, I assumed it was alarmed again.

I wanted to ask her something, but she took off and we had to hurry to stay with her.

Gabby's shoulders were sagging from the weight of the backpack. I offered, "Want me to carry that?"

She gave me a pained look and shook her head. "I'd love for you to take this thing, but I'm afraid of going airborne without the weight."

I nodded and grabbed a strap to lift the backpack and lighten the weight some.

We had been lagging behind, but now Gabby and I were really moving. I glanced over at her and did a double take.

Gabby's feet were moving, but not touching the floor.

When Hannah finally stopped at an elevator and turned to check on us, I let go of the backpack faster than I'd intended.

Gabby stumbled under the sudden weight and glared at me.

I murmured, "Sorry."

Hannah might be pleasant to Tony, but with us she was abrupt. "I don't have all day. Hurry up."

While the elevator carried us down to the basement level, I asked Hannah, "Why are you helping us?"

Her mouth twisted up as if she'd eaten something sour. "I'm not doing anything for *you*."

This had clearly been for Tony, but that didn't explain why she'd take this much risk.

Gabby must have picked up on my thinking. She warned Hannah, "You better find a way to wipe your electronic trail out of security or they'll be questioning you on what you were doing in the computer lab this morning."

The elevator doors opened and Hannah's haughty smile came out. "I'm not *stupid*. I didn't use my keycard."

We followed her down the hall. I asked, "Whose did you use?"

"Nicholas Brown's."

Gabby grinned and covered her mouth to smother her laugh.

I found that funny, too, but was too worried about what little time we had left to open the portal for me to enjoy the moment.

Hannah paused at a door and pulled out the same keycard to slide into a slot, but it wouldn't open the door. "What the heck?"

She tried it a couple more times."Is that you, Hannah baby?" Tony called from the other side of the door.

Gabby made a silly face at the endearment.

Hannah said, "Yes, but I can't get Nick's keycard to work."

Sirens whined upstairs. An alarm had been set off on another floor.

Hannah said, "We have to leave. Security will be here in five minutes."

No. If we couldn't free Tony then Callan would die. I would not panic, but those sirens were sending my pulse into overdrive. Heat built in my chest and wicked out through every limb.

I pushed Hannah aside and called to Tony, "Back away from the door and protect yourself, Jersey." Gripping the knob, I called up my power and forced it into the lock.

The handle exploded and the door flew inward.

Tony stared at me then shook his head. "Daa-yam, Xena."

He rushed out and looked first at Hannah. "Can you get out of here safely?"

"Yes."Tony grabbed Hannah and kissed her in a way that should have set off the fire alarms. He broke apart from her, worry chomping in his gaze. "Go, Hannah. Get out of here first so if we get caught you won't be with us."

She nodded and started for the elevator.

Tony turned to Gabby and me. "If someone chases us, we separate, then once we're clear go to the computer storage room where we found the portal computer."

Sirens whined all around us on this floor and a mechanical voice shouted, "*A. Scolerio, return to your unit. A. Scolerio—*"

What if that storage room was alarmed?

We didn't have Hannah with Nick's card. We couldn't make it back upstairs and we couldn't access the portal computer and leave it anywhere that people would find it while we were gone.

Chapter 7

"We'll never reach the storage room," I told Tony and Gabby. "We've got to get out of here another way."

I thought Hannah was gone, but she'd turned around and ran back a few steps to shout at us over the sirens. "Take the stairs at the end to the next floor. Go to the door that says 111-B. The whole floor is for supplies and storage. Security will be looking for you on the street level above that floor."

Tony shouted, "Got it, now go."

Hannah ran to the elevator and we took off in the opposite direction.

We made it up the stairs and raced down the hall that was silent other than the muffled sound of sirens and Tony's name being shouted below us.

At 111-B, Tony opened the door.

I was glad not to depend on my power this time. I might blow up the whole room with all the adrenaline shooting through me. Once the three of us were inside, Tony closed the door and locked it by pushing a button on the knob.

The room was deep and had rows of wide shelves built of steel to support big cans and boxes of food stacked on them. I looked at the top of the closest shelf that stopped two feet down from the twelve-foot ceiling.

Gabby was red faced and panting from the run.

I pulled the backpack off her and slipped my arms through the straps. "What's in this thing? Feels heavy enough to be a dead body."

"Everything we need," Gabby said as her body rose a foot off the floor and stayed there. It was a sign of how much he'd been through in a few days that Tony didn't spare Gabby's levitation a second glance.

He was too busy looking around. "We need a place to set up the laptop."

I pointed above my head at the top of the shelves that were four feet deep and accessible on both sides. "We can go up there."

Tony gazed up at where I indicated. "Looks strong enough and wide enough for us to fit, but we'll have to lay down."

When Gabby stretched her neck to see what we were talking about, the movement caused her to float a little higher. "That's a great place to hide the laptop, but unless you two start levitating, I'm the only one who might reach it if I keep floating up."

I started searching around me. "Let's find something we can stack up for climbing." I ran through the room, hunting between shelves and found exactly what we needed. A folding ladder. Lifting it, I hurried back to them.

"Atta, girl, Xena." Tony took the ladder from me and set it up next to the shelves. "I'll hold it while you two climb up."

I told Gabby, "Just grab my shirt."

When she had a grip, I climbed and until I could move close enough for Gabby to crawl onto the surface. Then I had to stand on the very top of the ladder to hoist myself up to our hiding spot.

Tony took down two one-gallon cans of tomato sauce from the middle shelf and placed them next to the foot of the ladder as if someone had been interrupted while retrieving supplies.

Smart guy. I had the feeling this wasn't the first time Tony had been forced to evade someone.

He pushed himself up onto the top of the shelf and stretched out along one side of me. Gabby hovered on my other side. We were position the same way we'd always traveled through the portal.

That didn't stop me from having a moment of anxiety that it might not work this time. Gabby pulled out our portal laptop and that only lightened the backpack a little. Tony took it from her and opened the lid against the wall we faced.

I looked toward the door for this room and couldn't see it. Someone would have to climb all the way up here to find the laptop.

He powered it up.

Three circles of gold, silver and bronze formed on the screen, moving in and out of each other. It was time to go.

Tony slapped his hand down. "Oh, man."

"What?" Gabby and I shouted together.

"We don't have the extra laptop to take with us and give the TecKnati in trade for Callan." Tony sounded sick.

My stomach turned inside out.

Gabby said, "I have that computer."

"Where'd you get it?" Tony asked.

"Hey," I said. "We have a computer. We have parts. We have to go. Now."

Tony eyed both of us with suspicion. "How did you two know which parts to get?"

Gabby wiggled her fingers. "Rayen and I used touch."

"For the love of St. Christopher. We are so screwed."

"Listen, Jersey Jerk," Gabby growled.

The door jangled like someone was trying to open it.

We froze. I pushed my palm at the monitor and my hand passed right through. Gabby grabbed that arm and Tony latched onto my other one.

The door squealed open as my arm was sucked into the screen and my body stretched thin as a rubber band.

Chapter 8

I was jerked and bounced at warp speed.

Wait a minute. I knew what warp speed was? That thought flashed by while I spun in a twisting blur.

Just as I had revolved when I was in that fire cyclone.

I hated time travel. All of it.

Everything slowed at once and I had a whole second to prepare myself before hitting the floor of the transender. I bounced and forced myself to move because ...

Bam! Tony hit hard in the spot I'd left vacant, but he must have recalled last time, too, because he rolled away quickly before Gabby landed on his chest again.

I waited. No thump. "Gabby?"

Tony pushed over onto his knees. "*Gabby!*"

A ball of color rolled from the air and landed gently on the floor. Gabby sat there a moment then broke into a fit of giggles.

"Are you kiddin' me?" Tony grumbled. "How'd you do that?"

For once, I was with Tony. "Why didn't you land like a bag of rocks?"

Gabby caught her breath and stretched, pushing hair off her face. "I didn't actually do that on purpose. I panicked and curled into a fetal position, thinking that I didn't want to hit that floor or land on Tony again. The next thing I knew, I'd stopped. Then I was worried I wouldn't get here. I started moving and here I am."

Tony shook his head. "Only you would have auto-pilot woo-woo powers."

I struggled to my feet, wishing I had *her* powers. My body

had taken a beating over the past few days.

Red light flashed around the top of the round transender and a siren cranked up.

I stretched out the kinks in my body. "We know what that means."

Gabby said, "Time to get out of Dodge."

Had I heard that right? "What's a Dodge?"

Tony let out a painful sigh. "If we get out of this mess, we're puttin' you through Pop Culture 101, Xena." He turned to the end of the transender where we'd exited the last two times.

A purple glow shaped as an arch brightened then dimmed then brightened again.

Tony muttered, "And there's our blue light special." He lifted a hand. "Before you ask, I do know that glow is purple."

I tossed one of his usual replies back at him. "Whatever."

When we reached the end of the transender, I lifted my hands to rest on the humming wall. Tony and Gabby each grabbed one of my arms again just as the familiar sulfur stench began flooding the air.

I thought, *Please let us out*.

Then I held my breath because the last time we'd entered the Sphere it looked as if an apocalypse had hit.

And a ground fog had infected me to have hallucinations. I almost killed Callan because I thought he was a TecKnati.

The hatch that formed where I'd touched the transender wall disappeared and we landed on rock hard ground on our hands and knees.

Why couldn't one place have something soft to land on?

When I realized Tony and I were the only two on the ground, I looked around to find Gabby hovering upright again. She tried not to smile and failed. "I'm getting used to this."

A whirring sound that turned into a high-pitched squeal announced the transender was about to spin then leave in a cloud of red dust.

Tony and I jumped up. I started to run and Gabby shouted, "Don't leave me."

She was moving her arms like she tried to swim, but was going nowhere. I ran back and grabbed her shirt and dragged her along with me, getting away from the transender right before it spun furiously then disappeared.

All I could think was *please don't let anyone find that laptop in the supply room*. It was our only way back.

I watched where I stepped. The ground was still torn up from the prior destruction. Overhead, the red moon offered a weak light, but the vegetation glowed pink, orange and blue. Their pulsing added to the steamy heat, smelling a sweet sour.

Tony stopped and muttered, "Give me a break."

Gabby sucked in a breath.

I raised my head to see what was going on.

An oversized reptile had stepped from the woods.

Just once, I'd like to have an easy trip to this place.

When the creature turned its head toward us, it emerged from the broad orange palm fronds and where darker blue branches behind it had regrown since the last time. The thing was shaped like a huge turtle. It stood eye-to-eye with me when it lifted up on chubby legs and wobbled out into the field.

Then it fell down and fumbled around until it was up again. The head stuck out on a skinny neck that had a thick tuft of blue and white hair that resembled a chopped off horse's mane.

It made a chittering noise.

Gabby floated up and down next to me. "I think it's a baby something."

Tony wasn't as willing to downgrade the creature and reminded Gabby, "I remember Rayen fighting a *baby* croggle in this very spot, Sweet Cakes, that tried to eat us." He turned to me. "Think you can call up that crazy power of yours, Xena?"

I had no idea. Tony had a point, but I couldn't harm something that posed no immediate threat. "Not all baby reptiles are killers, Tony."

"Snapping turtles are dangerous back home."

Gabby whispered, "It looks pretty harmless."

At that moment, the critter angled his head to one side then the other, studying us. He yawned, exposing two rows of sharp pointed teeth.

Tony said, "If it's got teeth, it's got potential."

The baby turtle thing took a couple more tentative steps our way.

It wasn't often that I agreed with Tony, but I did this time. "Maybe we can scare it off," I suggested and raised my hands to wave back and forth.

That was the wrong move.

The turtle thing let out a blood-curdling scream, and dropped to the ground, sucking in its legs and head.

Something huge crashed around in the woods, making a loud grunting sound.

A head I wouldn't be able to wrap my arms around entirely shoved out from the woods. Way up. Another ten feet in the air. The eyes in that head zeroed in on the clammed-up baby and let out a screech of fury that forced us all to cover our ears.

Then it plowed out of the woods, heading straight for us.

Chapter 9

Power expanded and burned my insides then rushed up my arms and down my legs.

I jumped in front of Tony and Gabby, raising my hands again, ready to throw a blast of energy to stop that mama-turtle-thing from charging over to where we stood in the transender landing spot.

"*Ah-jeet!*" a deep human voice roared from the forest.

The mama-turtle-thing halted, but not until she squatted next to her baby.

"Do not harm them," another shout boomed as a guy making all that noise was coming closer to us.

Did he mean for me to not harm the creatures or for the mama to not eat us?

And who was he that I should care?

This might be nothing more than a TecKnati trick to steal the computer.

There was a sound of branches breaking as someone rushed through the woods then a tall young man with skin mottled a mish-mash of blue and brown splashes burst into the opening.

Kaz.

My whole body leaped with happiness. Only seeing Callan would have made me happier.

Kaz rushed forward, but halted next to the mama creature where he spoke soft words.

That mama dipped her head down and Kaz stroked the iridescent-colored skin covering her huge head. She had a full, blue-and-silver striped mane growing along her neck that gave her a regal flare. Her body was also shaped similar to a turtle except that her shell was flatter on top, more streamlined, and appeared furry. Dark-blue layers rimmed in a shimmering gold ran along the edges of the fluffy surface covering her shell.

The animal made soft grunting noises and lifted a paw instead of a foot to nudge Kaz gently. Silver hair flowed down over her paws and dragged the ground. Large round eyes with a blue center and gold iris looked down at Kaz with what I could only describe as affection.

But those curling horns with sharp tips that stuck out the sides of her head could do some major damage if she changed her mind about attacking.

Once he had her settled down, Kaz waved us over.

Tony didn't move and Gabby was stuck hovering above the ground unless someone pulled her along. Gabby had come a long way since I'd first met her. Two days ago she wouldn't allow anyone to touch her for fear of hearing another person's thoughts, but a MystiK healer name Jaxxson had taught her how to shield her mind.

"Come on, let's go," I urged and snagged the hem of Gabby's pink shirt to tow her along with me.

Following several steps behind us, Tony lifted the pendant haning on a chain around his neck. He kissed it then let the round disk fall back inside his shirt as he mumbled something about "St. Christopher."

When I reached Kaz, I let go of Gabby who remained floating a foot off the ground.

Kaz lifted an eyebrow at her, but anxiety rode his face in the place of his usual easy-going expression. "Why did you wait so long to come back, Rayen?"

After all I'd been through to even get back to the Sphere, I hadn't expected Kaz of all people to criticize me. "We got here as soon as we could."

"Callan is down to three hours."

Gabby had no trouble sharing her opinion. "Rayen was zapped with a stun gun and taken away from the school last night. Tony was accused of a crime he didn't commit and locked up. I had to hunt down a computer and parts while hiding this levitation problem, then we ended up breaking Tony out and had to make a run for it before they caught all of us." She put her hands on her hips and leaned forward, her mismatched eyes—one green and one brown—staring Kaz down. "Whatever's eating you must be suffering horribly."

Kaz reared back then scratched his head. "Sorry, but I've been here for four hours waiting when I should be back at the camp."

It didn't take much to appease Gabby. "Apology accepted."

I didn't care if Kaz was being short with us, because I was in the same mood and we needed to get going. "Tony needs time to build the computer."

Kaz raked Tony with an angry burst. "How long will that take?"

Tony moved forward, shoulders bunched and disgust peppering every word. "I haven't even seen the laptop we brought back and since Sweet Cheeks here picked out parts using your woo woo system, I have no idea how long."

I put a hand up between Tony and Kaz before they took any more steps toward each other. "We don't have time to argue."

Something bumped me in the back, knocking me off my feet.

Kaz grabbed me before I face-planted on the ground.

He swung me up by my arm and caught me to his chest. It's good to be an extra-strong MystiK warrior I guess. His skin had an interesting woodsy smell I hadn't noticed before, but then I hadn't been this close to him before now either.

He didn't need to clutch me so close against him.

I'd explained more than once that I wasn't interested in anyone but Callan. Kaz contended that Callan and I wouldn't work out. I knew all the reasons, but it didn't stop my heart from calling out to Callan, and only Callan.

I pushed away and stepped back, dusting myself off. If anyone asked me, I'd say that turtle creature had intentionally pushed me. Giving the animal my threatening look didn't faze her one bit. I asked Kaz, "What's with that ... thing?"

"She's a tortalone, not a *thing*." He was insulted on the creature's behalf?

Gabby leaned forward. "So that's what a tortalone is. Jaxxson said it would be easier to show me one than to explain it. I thought they were wild."

"They are." Kaz put his thumb and first finger in his mouth, took a deep breath and let out a shrill whistle.

Three more tortalones crashed their way out of the woods, moving slowly but on large paws that could push down small saplings. Three MystiK warriors rode on the toralones. The warriors appeared to be thirteen or fourteen and had splotches of color like Kaz's—Tony called it camouflage skin.

As they made their way over to us, Kaz explained, "We found a small herd yesterday and have come to an agreement."

Gabby quipped, "So you're a turtle whisperer?"

Kaz frowned at her then at me, waiting on an explanation.

I eyed him and the tortalone. "I think she was asking if you can talk to them."

"I told you my gifts were different than Callan's."

"Right." They were both warriors, but Callan possessed powerful kinetics where Kaz's were not as strong, but he had empathic ability. Kaz sensed emotions, which was another reason I had to be careful to keep mine locked down when I was around him.

He motioned with his hand and the mama tortalone dropped to the ground, leaving her legs out. "I don't actually speak the tortalone language," Kaz explained. "But this female leads the herd. She and I understand each other."

The animal made a gritty sound in her throat and the other tortalones dropped to the ground, too.

A MystiK warrior climbed off one animal and climbed onto another one, doubling up. Kaz pointed at the tortalone left without a rider and told Tony, "You and Gabby will take that one, because you only need to hold on. He will follow mine."

Tony sized up their situation. "You're telling me we're gonna ride something I can out walk and they're safe as long as you don't tick her off and she decides to have us for lunch."

Kaz's easy-going nature had come and gone. "If you were not needed for the computer, I would allow you to walk and learn for yourself who is quicker."

Tony raised his hands to ward off Kaz. "Chill, bro. I'll ride. How tough can it be to sit on a turtle hump?" He held his hand out to me. "Give me the backpack so you can be free to hold on."

I gladly passed off the heavy pack.

Kaz had already climbed up on the mama creature and sat on his knees. He leaned over and offered me a hand up. I had to step on her two-foot-thick leg to reach Kaz's hand.

I pushed up and stretched at the same time, extending my hand to Kaz.

Our tortalone scooped her head under my butt and pushed up, tossing me on her back. Kaz caught me around the waist and swung me around in front of him.

Had he somehow told the tortalone to do that?

Kaz made a strange chattering sound in his throat. The tortalone raised her head and dropped it straight back until Kaz leaned around me on one side to grip her mane.

He held her mane lightly. She curved her neck forward and lifted up on all four legs then made a sharp bark.

The little baby next to us came out of its shell and jumped up on springy legs, bouncing back and forth, squeaking happy sounds.

Mama tortalone took the lead, plodding across the long open field. Checking over my shoulder, I saw Tony holding the mane on his ride and Gabby sitting at his back, clutching his shoulders. The other two tortalones moved in sync with Tony's, all of them maintaining the same slow pace as the leader.

I was in agreement with Tony.

We could walk faster. How could Kaz snap at me for taking so long to come back, then bring turtles to ride?

This was going to make me nuts. "We have to get to Callan before his BIRG Day, Kaz."

"I know I said it was important to continue embracing our customs, but Callan turning eighteen is not the issue at the moment."

Yes, it was, but I couldn't tell Kaz about the wraiths that would come for Callan. Not unless I had no other choice. But we still weren't going to reach Callan in time to rescue him from the TecKnati. I tried to sound patient about our transportation. "Kaz, it has to be faster to—"

"Shh. Don't say a thing." He whispered close to my ear and wrapped an arm around my waist.

I tried to push his arm away. "I think I can manage to stay

on a turtle."

He just tightened his hold.

Our tortalone started moving faster.

I smiled. Kaz hadn't said she could run.

The shimmering gold-and-blue fur covering her shell swept away from each side and started flapping.

Feathers? Wings?

This thing could ... fly?Kaz chuckled as we took to the air. If he hadn't held me, I'd have fallen off out of shock.

Wind slapped my ponytail all around. It must have been beating up against him, because Kaz tucked his head next to mine, pinning my hair, and spoke words that were as disconcerting as the intimate feel of him behind me. "You must not go with us to free Callan."

"Why?"

"It is not my place to explain."

"Then I'm going with you."

"If you do, you will put his future back home in jeopardy."

How could that be? "What changed after I left?"

"I learned of another MystiK imprisoned at the TecKnati camp who is royalty from one of the Houses."

I recalled that the MystiKs had seven Houses based on different gifts or powers, but I was still confused. "I don't understand, Kaz. If the TecKnati have another MystiK I'd think you'd want my help."

He was slow to respond. "Normally, yes, but not this time. You are not able to hide your feelings for Callan from others, especially another empathic. And when you are near him, neither can he."

It was probably the wrong reaction, but hearing that about Callan made me happy.

Kaz ground out a noise.

Guess he caught my reaction.

He wasn't through warning me. "As Callan's best friend, it is my duty to protect him. Even from you."

That deflated my moment of pleasure. "Who's this other MystiK at the TecKnati camp?"

"I'm not sure how much Callan wants to tell you about her and it is his place to explain."

Her?

Chapter 10

Water hit Callan in the face. He jerked his head, slinging droplets from hair that clung to his neck.

He sat with his knees on the hard ground in an enclosed room. His arms stretched above his head, hanging from metal wrist cuffs attached to cables. Not just any metal, but one infused with an electronic component to interact with the grid outside that the TecKnati had used to capture him. After all these years, the TecKnati had finally designed something that would neutralize MystiK gifts like Callan's kinetic and healing abilities.

But the laser grid had to be powered up to full blast to completely shut down his kinetics and telepathy.

The thing had short-circuited once.

He'd either dreamed about a woman's voice or the cuffs were running so low on power they weren't preventing his telepathy. But when he opened his mind, the female voice he'd heard had been all wrong.

It wasn't Rayen's.

When Rayen spoke, Callan felt her rich voice all the way to his heart.

He might just be hallucinating at times. Sleep had been impossible and Thylan, the TecKnati in charge, had taken great pleasure in driving up the grid power when the urge hit him. That was only when Thylan was too tired to use his electric whip on Callan, striking him the minute Callan's head lolled from exhaustion.

Who knew if it was telepathy he heard or if he was slowly losing his mind? He hadn't been able to send or receive telepathy when he'd stood in the middle of the grid and the

TeK in charge had turned up the power to the point of frying Callan from the inside out.

He had burn marks on his skin that ached intermittently.

The grid was buried just deep enough in the ground to hide it, so when Callan had entered an enclosure to rescue a pair of MystiK children and Tony, he hadn't known it was there until the Tecknati activated the lasers in the grid.

How long ago?

He was losing track of time.

Icy water crashed into his head again.

He coughed and sputtered, slinging his hair like a soaked dog trying to shake off the excess. Water ran down his naked chest and pooled at the ragged skins he wore for pants.

When he stopped choking, he raised his head and looked through wet hair stringing over his eyes. His body hurt no matter how he tried to find a comfortable position and he couldn't heal the cuts on his chest while bound in these cuffs.

"You awake?" Thylan chided. "No sleeping on my time."

Callan said nothing, just as he had since being captured. This was the leader of the TecKnatis on the Sphere. Big man on a small pedestal. He was not SEOH, who ruled all the TeKs back home, but this one had SEOH's arrogance.

Thylan stood just inside the door of Callan's prison cell. He was decent size, but his soft middle bulged over the black belt strapped around the waist of his gray-green TecKnati uniform. Not a warrior. His blended alloy belt buckle had a holographic element that showed the ANASKO triangle emblem one moment and the name SEOH II the next.

Ah. Now Callan understood. This was SEOH's son. The II meant he was second born. This would be the middle son, the one often brought up on charges for abusive acts. A soulless predator.

SEOH's genes ran true.

Thylan smoothed a hand over black hair cut close enough to expose his pale scalp, then he twisted his thin lips in a cruel smile. "I haven't heard a word from your friends, or your girl."

Callan could only hope that Rayen had made it back to the past and stayed there. She was too headstrong for her own good. She would battle anyone and anything to protect an innocent or someone she cared for ... and she cared for Callan.

He'd tried to convince her that he didn't reciprocate her feelings, but he'd failed at that. More than failed. He'd climbed inside the kamara he'd made for her and spent the night with her. He was honest enough with himself to admit that he wanted to share *his* kamara with her, a major step toward bonding.

Regardless, he would be glad if she didn't return.

Never seeing her again would hurt, and that pain would cut deep, but he would be content with her being safe.

She'd given him memories he'd treasure for a lifetime if he survived this.

Thylan snapped his fingers. "Pay attention, warrior boy."

Callan lifted his chin. "Uncuff me and I'll show you who is the boy in this room."

A grin broke out on Thylan's flat face. "He speaks. And here I thought you were silent because I intimidated you."

"I would have to notice you first," Callan pointed out.

Thylan's thick black eyebrows drew together into one angry caterpillar. "You won't be so arrogant once we get that computer."

"She isn't coming back." Callan hoped. His chest felt empty without her nearby, but he didn't have much longer to live. He could endure until then.

"Oh, yes, she's coming back. I saw the look on her face. She'll return and she won't be empty handed."

It pained Callan to realize there could be truth in Thylan's words and, wrong as it was, a part of Callan admitted he would trade all his tomorrows for one minute to see Rayen again. But even if she came back, she wouldn't hand over the actual Genera-Y computer. She knew the danger of the TecKnati using that computer to destroy the entire MystiK population on and off the Sphere.

No one really knew what this Genera-Y computer could do, but it was supposedly a mythological computer built two millenniums ago that could travel both ways through time. Was that the computer Rayen, Gabby and Tony used to travel here? Callan didn't know and didn't care as long as Rayen stayed safely in the past.

He trusted Kaz to stop her from coming to this camp if Rayen did return. But that was the extent of trust Callan would allow when it came to Kaz being around her.

Kaz had better keep his hands off Rayen.

The one time Kaz had tried to gain her affections, Callan had considered skewering his best friend over a fire. But Kaz was still the friend that Callan would depend on and the one person who would do his duty.

Callan huffed a tired sigh he hoped sounded bored to Thylan. "Even if you get the computer, you won't be able to operate it without a MystiK."

Thylan leaned back on the closed door, overconfident at facing someone shackled. "You MystiKs have a high opinion of yourselves. We don't need you. By now, you should have realized that SEOH is far superior to your MystiK leaders. Your people don't even know how many of you are missing. They'd have to talk to each other to have an inkling of what's going on."

Shame flushed over Callan. He couldn't deny that claim. The leaders of their seven MystiK Houses had once been close while rebuilding their world. A world devastated by a virus they were pretty sure had originated in outer space.

The K-Virus had been introduced to Earth because of an aggressive space program the TecKnati were still pushing.

But somewhere along the way, the MystiKs created as many problems for themselves as the TeKs presented.

Thylan was on a roll, chuckling. "SEOH kidnaps the majority of future MystiK leaders, G'ortians no less, and your people won't realize how widespread it is until all your leaders meet to sign another treaty with us." He grinned and studied Callan with condescension. "You're one of those rare G'ortians with special powers, right? Look at you now."

This TecKnati needed to have a dose of reality.

Callan slung his hair out of his eyes so that Thylan had to stare into the eyes promising his death. In spite of the cuffs, Callan managed to summon enough power to shift his eyes from brown to a searing, glowing green. The ability to make that change had developed only in the past few days, along with many of his other G'Ortian powers. Even the powers he'd had for a while had grown stronger as he approached his BIRG day.

When Thylan paled, Callan nodded. "You would be wise to consider who you taunt. I *am* one of those. We are powerful, and when we join forces, we will destroy your dangerous space program and protect our world."

Thylan puffed up at that. "You think so? You people kill me." He thumped his chest as he spoke. "Our technology has created laser curtains to protect the ten cities where both TecKnati and MystiKs live. Our technology has created hospitals that are state of the art facilities for all citizens. *Our* technology continues to develop programs that better our world for *everyone*, even you miserable unappreciative MystiKs."

"I don't disagree, TecKnati. I can acknowledge that there are benefits to both MystiK and TecKnati skills, but you are too ambitious and risk bringing another virus back to our planet. What if you do that again?"

Thylan hunched his shoulders, acting unconcerned. "There's no proof we did that the first time."

"There could be, but your people refuse to work with ours to screen what you bring back. And from what SEOH has done here, there will be no treaties in the future. Only war. And we will win."

"You are so full of crap." Thylan was getting louder, the way a person did when he was frightened or trying to prove an indefensible point, or both. "You don't understand that you've already lost. You think the BIRG Con means a new treaty and the ascension of future MystiK leaders coming into power, but it doesn't. Instead of your symbolic end-of-childhood ritual, this year's BIRG Con will mark the death of all MystiKs. Why do you think we tested the grid on you?"

Callan hadn't felt real fear until now.

"That's right, warrior boy. We didn't test it here just to see what it would do. That baby holding your power in check is just a taste of the big one that has been installed back home for the BIRG Con." He snorted. "Basking In Reflective Glory Convention? Sounds like a summit for tarot readers."

Callan ignored Thylan's snide remarks. SEOH's spawn had actually shared important information, but there was no way for Callan to get word to the MystiKs back home.

The TeKs intended to use that grid on MystiK leaders? Callan had experienced the grid eating his power during the times he'd been exposed to the activated lasers. If Thylan hadn't backed off the power when he did, Callan was certain he would have eventually died as the grid continued attacking his gifts.

"Now you're getting a clear picture," Thylan chortled. "You people aren't very smart, you know that? You haven't even figured out that we have a hotline straight from your camp."

A traitor in our village. Just as Callan had thought.

Someone shouted outside the door.

Thylan called back, "On my way." Then he bent over with his hands on his knees, putting his face eye level with Callan's. "You're just a bunch of fanatics with a little power."

Callan lunged at Thylan, who panicked and stumbled back, landing in the water that covered the floor. He scrambled to get to the door. When he made it back to his feet, he snarled, "I was going to kill you after we got the computer, but I'm going to hold off. Killing would be too easy for you."

Callan vibrated with the need to get his hands on Thylan. He didn't think he could harbor any more rage until Thylan explained, "I don't want you to miss the show. Once your girl arrives and I capture her, I'm going to lay her out right here in front of you. Close enough for you to watch me take her."

Callan lunged again, straining and sounding like a furious animal. This time, the cables groaned. He spoke through teeth clenched hard enough to break a rock. "You touch her and I will kill you with my bare hands."

Thylan wisely rushed out and locked the door.

Callan fell back against a metal wall, breathing hard. His wrists bled where he'd punished them against the cuffs. His body shook, drowning in adrenaline and gut-wrenching worry over Rayen.

He prayed that she wasn't able to find a computer or return.

Chapter 11

The tortalone Kaz and I rode swooped low over the carpet of flourescent trees, a sea of peach, aqua and purple vegetation below us that gave way to dark blue and white. We landed in a large clearing and the tortalone trotted slowly across dark blue grass that would be shin-high on me. Black-and-white striped flower looked feather-soft, and darkened to coppers and reds in the shade. When we stopped, it looked as if we were in the middle of nowhere, but I knew better. Callan and a handful of the MystiKs around his age had used their combined power to create a ward that mimicked the surrounding woods to hide their village.

The cool air that had wafted over us while we'd been flying disappeared, and the sticky heat returned with a vengeance. But once that red moon vanished beneath the horizon, the air near the ground would chill.

I climbed off the tortalone and ran over to help with Gabby. Tony passed her down to me, and once more she floated at her normal space above the ground. I caught her shirt then the three of us followed Kaz. He could have passed through the ward easily since he was a MystiK, but we couldn't. So he paused and lifted his hands, then spoke an incantation for ten seconds before turning to us.

"You may pass through."

We did, and the other three warrior boys followed us.

While Kaz closed the ward, we continued in the direction I recalled as being toward the village, but we were quickly surrounded by a new group of warriors.

This bunch looked threatening even at six and seven years old, but that was because they were Uberons, part of an elite

MystiK Warrior division.

A young woman my age, known as Kenja, led the Uberons.

I'd had my share of run-ins with her.

Kenja appeared in our path, so fast and close we almost plowed into her.

Gabby shrieked and paddled her hands in the air, trying to back up.

Kenja smirked at Gabby and I wanted to strangle her, but Gabby wielded words the way Kenja handled a spear.

When Tony gave her shirt a tug, Gabby floated forward and used the advantage of her airborne height to rake Kenja with an imperial look. "Did you give up fighting your inner demons and just join them, Kenja?"

"Your sarcasm is wasted."

"It generally *is* on the ignorant."

In a blink, Kenja's expression switched from calm to the promise of retribution.

I didn't want a repeat of my last altercation with her. There was no time for it. "Either help or get out of the way, Kenja."

With a tiny move of her head, she redirected all her aggression at me. "You have less than three hours until my agreement to stay at this village has been fulfilled."

Then Kenja disappeared as quickly as she'd arrived.

Gabby muttered, "I've got levitation-itis, I just climbed off a flying turtle and we still don't know if that computer is going to work. She does *not* want to mess with me."

Kaz stepped up beside me. "Problems?"

I shook my head. "Nothing new."

He led us into the center of the camp where more sleeping quarters had been created from tortalone feathers hanging from poles and vines to form walls. Some of them had red tips as well as gold. Now I understood where someone would find a six-foot-long feather.

I caught the approach of another female. Headache number two. Zilya of the Governing House and senior pain in my backside.

Short, white-blond hair flared across her head, and a smattering of black and diamond jewels were embedded in her perfect cheek. She had that mix of haughty and exotic that would always cause male drooling. Her tunic-style gown was an odd yellowish, almost golden, material, not shiny, but elegant in its simplicity. Strange half-moon designs were sewn in a deeper burnished gold down the front. Callan had mentioned they indicated her status, but having her clothes speak for her seemed unnecessary. Her arrogance announced her status all on its own.

She stepped into our path.

What was with everyone wanting to get in my way right now?

Zilya spoke with the single purpose of commanding attention. "Do you have the computer?"

Tony sounded impatient. "We have *a* computer, but I don't know that we have *the* computer and until I get a chance to work on the one we have I won't know if we can use it to scam them."

She brought out her tone of superiority. "You were supposed to—"

"Hey, sister," Tony snapped. "We've had our own troubles. I need time and a workspace. If you can't provide that, then you're in the way."

Everyone was on edge.

Tony, Gabby and I had barely found each other and left before someone caught us. Kaz had been in charge of warrior duties that included keeping this group safe and alive. Zilya was a pain of the highest order, but she looked worn around the edges, too.

I raised my hands. "Can we all call a truce for a couple of hours until we free Callan?"

Kaz crossed his arms and addressed Zilya. "I will see to what they need." When she started to interrupt him, Kaz was quick to cut her off. "Where is Jaxxson?"

"In his healing hut."

"Take Gabby to him."

"I am not a servant." Zilya stomped off.

Kaz smiled at me. "Problem solved for now."

Jaxxson shouted, "*Gabby!*"

We turned as one toward the path that led to his hut. Jaxxson stepped forward, his naked chest showing above the skirt-like covering that reached just above his ankles. He was athletic, but didn't have Callan's sinewy build. His blond hair had a dark honey shade and his rich brown eyes were for Gabby only.

He rushed up and stopped short. "Gabby?"

She sighed. "At least I'm not sick this time and my power isn't trying to kill everyone, but I can't fix this—" She pointed her finger at her boots. "—or figure out how to move around when I'm up here."

Jaxxson smothered a smile, walked over and pulled her into his arms.

Red flagged her cheeks when she looked at me, then at Tony, who smirked. Gabby asked Jaxxson, "Can't you just pull me through the air? That's what Rayen does."

Jaxxson walked off, explaining, "I would never risk you bumping into a tree."

I doubted there was any real issue with drawing her along by her hand, but Gabby and Jaxxson had something special going on that had changed her over the past two visits.

I was happy for her, but I hoped she didn't end up with a broken heart.

Who was I to talk? I was in just as deep when it came to caring about Callan?

I wasn't backing away, but where Gabby had a life to go back to, I had nothing. I would take what little time I had with Callan and be thankful for it.

Kaz pointed across the clearing to a small structure. "That hut has a table and chairs. Callan and I have used it for planning sessions."

Tony was looking all around. Half listening, he said, "Sweet. Okay, I need V'ru."

Despair graveled in Kaz's voice. "V'ru has been in deep depression since learning of Callan's capture ... and since you left. He speaks to no one."

Nothing was deterring Tony. "Take me to him."

I followed Kaz and Tony to the isolated area V'ru had chosen for his kamara, the bubble thing that some MystiKs could create to use as personal quarters.

I didn't recall V'ru's kamara being this deep in the wooded

area. Maybe he'd moved it.

V'ru and Callan were G'ortians, some kind of rare MystiK that was more powerful than normal. Even though V'ru was only eleven, he was a prodigy who'd been born with his brain holding all the history of mankind up to the current year in his world.

Tony salivated to have the knowledge that V'ru held in one tiny finger, but he'd also grown close to V'ru, who reminded Tony of his own little brother, Vinny.

On the way to the kamara, Tony shook his head at Kaz. "You can't leave a little kid alone like that."

Kaz turned defensive. "We respect the privacy of others, particularly a G'ortian."

Tony turned on Kaz, fury rumbling in his biting words. "He's a freakin' kid. Little freakin' boy, not a G'ortian, not a future MystiK ruler, just a kid who's frightened and who just lost the one person he believes will take him home."

The look in Kaz's eyes hurt me.

All the MystiK children captured and sent here had suffered. Kaz had been one of their most fierce protectors. I touched Tony's arm. "No one meant to mistreat V'ru."

It took Tony a minute to pull himself back under control. He exhaled hard and spoke with compassion this time. "I'm not yelling at you, Kaz. I'm yelling at the way your leaders have treated him. V'ru has no identity. No sense of who he is beyond being a resource. All I'm saying is that it's up to us to take care of him. He's only a kid."

My throat swelled at the way Tony cared for V'ru. Tony had put everything at risk to help me, Callan and everyone else here. His little brother was in a foster home. Tony was determined to get into a school called MIT as soon as he could so that he'd eventually be in a position to bring his little brother home.

After what had happened back at the Byzantine Institute, Tony might not be able to do that for a long time, if ever.

Kaz reached over and gripped Tony's shoulder, looking him straight in the eyes. "You're right. We will do a better job of caring for V'ru."

"Thank you."

Another fifty feet into the woods, we found V'ru's kamara. I remembered the one Callan had made for me to sleep in on our last visit to the sphere. It had been more luminous than this one.

It was as though the energy fueling V'ru's had dimmed.

Tony put his hand on the kamara and called out in a cheerful voice. He must have pulled that voice out of his pocket because he was anything but cheerful right now. "V'ru Man, it's me, Tony."

No reply.

"Need you to come out and talk to me."

Silence still.

Shoulders down, looking defeated, Tony lowered his voice and said with genuine worry, "I'm concerned about you and Callan both, V'ru. I can't do anything to help either one of you unless you help me. Callan's depending on you and I am, too."

The kamara's glow brightened, and in the next instant V'ru stood beside Tony. V'ru's skin looked pale. "What can I do? I'm just an information vessel."

Tony sent a sharp look at Kaz who, to his benefit, merely gave a quiet nod of understanding.

Dropping down in a squat that put Tony closer to eye level with V'ru, he smiled at the boy. "Still got the hoodie on, huh?"

V'ru nodded. Tony's dark gray hoodie swallowed the kid and hit him at the knees.

Putting his hand on V'ru's shoulder, Tony said, "You're the most important person on our team. I can't even get the computer I brought to boot up without you."

V'ru's eyes lit up. "You brought a *real* computer?""Yes, sir. And I'm pressed for time. So if you—"

V'ru waved his hands around. "Where is it? Show me."

Tony stood and led the way back to the hut Kaz had pointed out. He spoke in a low tone the whole way, talking computer terms, with V'ru nodding enthusiastically.

Kaz walked beside me and leaned down to say, "He's right. None of us realized that V'ru is kept on a virtual pedestal and not allowed to be a part of this village. His knowledge is revered, but he is more than that and we should have noticed the hardship his position puts on him."

Finally, things were smoothing out. “Thank you for recognizing that Tony has V’ru’s best interest at heart.”

Shrugging, Kaz quipped, “Even a TeK has useful information on occasion.”

I turned to remind him that Tony was not the enemy here just because V’ru had determined Tony carried TeK blood markers, making him an ancestor of the people in Kaz’s world.

But Kaz’s lips twitched with a smile so I gave him a shove and he actually managed a chuckle.

Tony and V’ru had almost reached the hut when Zilya’s voice rang out. “You cannot share knowledge with him, V’ru of the Records House.”

V’ru froze. Poor thing was terrified of Zilya.

All the good Tony had accomplished by getting V’ru out of his bubble was about to disintegrate.

Tony wheeled on Zilya. “I thought we had this straight about not messing with him.”

“We have nothing *straight*, TecKnati. You will not access V’ru’s database.”

“Then Houston, we have a problem, because that’s exactly what I’m going to do.”

Chapter 12

I shoved my hands in my hair and growled to keep from throwing a blast of energy at Zilya. Pulling my hands down, I continued to where Tony and Zilya were facing off.

Zilya snarled at Tony, "I will not warn you again, TecKnati."

"You're always fightin' the wrong people, blondie. I'm trying to help Callan and your village. So is V'ru. So back the heck off and stay out of my way. And if I catch you trying to bully V'ru one more time, you'll regret it."

Zilya lifted her hands.

I warned, "Make a wrong move and I *will* fry you."

Shoving a shocked look my way, Zilya said, "You would not dare touch me."

"Yes, I would, and you won't like it."

"You are not more powerful than I," Zilya argued without conviction.

Tony chuckled, a dry nasty sound. "Bad move, blondie. You've never been present when Xena unleashed her power and cooked a croggle just by stabbing it with a spear. But, you know what? Go ahead and keep pushing Xena. I'd like to see you toasted."

I sent an arch look at Tony.

He opened his arms. "What?"

I squeezed out a sigh. "I'm trying to help so you can get moving on the computer."

"She started this crap." Tony put his hand on V'ru's shoulder. "Let's get busy, little man."

Zilya started, "V'ru, if you—"

Tony swung around and raised a hand so fast I was worried

that he had kinetic powers, but he only pointed at Zilya. "I've told you before and I'm only saying this one more time. V'ru is under my protection. Don't mess with him." Then Tony and V'ru entered the hut.

Kaz finally said something. "Zilya, this is the time to work together, not to fight. You should trust that V'ru will reveal nothing more than is needed to prepare that computer to trade for Callan."

She didn't acknowledge his words, merely replying, "When we return home, this will all have consequences."

Etoi, Zilya's assistant and closest friend, came into the clearing then. She wore ankle-high boots made of some kind of leather, and a muted burgundy tunic with a braided gold edge that stopped short of her knees. Swinging her blond-and-black ringlets at me, along with a full load of bad attitude, she warned, "If you threaten our Governing House leader again, you will not be allowed to remain inside the village."

"Says who?" Kaz asked.

Tagging him with her furious gaze, Etoi answered, "Says me if you're not willing to do your duty as a warrior."

I just rolled my eyes. "I'm tired of the threats. Do you or do you not want Callan to be freed?"

I'd said that just to break up the friction, but Etoi shrugged. "He's only a warrior, not a leader."

Now I wanted to strangle her for real. "Mathias left Callan in charge of this village."

Zilya lifted her nose. "*Then* Callan left me in charge."

Kaz interjected, "He left you and Jaxxson in charge. You have *joint* authority. We're done here. Return to whatever it is you do to fill your days and we'll deal with bringing Callan back."

Zilya's cheeks flamed, then she returned to her natural annoying self. "You have enjoyed too much autonomy here, Kaz. It will not go well for you when we are home again."

With that, Zilya and Etoi marched off.

Muttering to himself, Kaz said, "I'll worry about that if I ever see home again."

I wanted to comfort him and reassure him that he would go home again, but I was in no position to be making false promises.

Tony stuck his head out of the hut. "Need you in here, Xena."

I couldn't imagine why he'd need me with the computer, but I followed Tony as he ducked back inside. He had the keyboard off and V'ru stared at the electronics with a fascination I couldn't appreciate.

"What do you need?" I asked. "Didn't Gabby pick a good computer?"

"She did better than good," Tony said. "She got Nick's laptop, and he has state-of-the-art everything. This baby is loaded with every option available."

"I don't see what the problem is then."

V'ru looked up and his straight black hair fell over his huge brown eyes. He shoved a lock off his face, a futile effort when it fell again. "We made several alterations that emulate what Tony tells me your portal computer does, but this is not the same configuration."

The sound that came out of Kaz could only be called relief. "So we won't be giving the TeKs a computer they can time travel with, correct?""Correct," V'ru confirmed. "That's not the problem. This has to at least power up long enough to pull a fast one."

Kaz frowned. "What do you mean by fast one, V'ru?"

V'ru shrugged. "I don't know. That's what Tony said."

Tony chuckled and explained, "We're going to have to convince the TeKs to trade Callan for a computer that isn't going to do what they think. That's going to require some slick talking and sleight of hand to get him out of there, thus pulling a fast one."

V'ru nodded as if Tony had imparted a wisdom to be archived, then he said, "I was able to power this unit for only ten seconds with my residual power, but I'm not strong enough to keep it running very long. My power is focused on retaining information, not driving something physical. We need a super power."

Everyone looked at me.

What? "I couldn't turn the last computer on by myself. What do you expect me to do with this one?"

Tony pointed at one spot. “See what happens if you touch that. And don’t blow it up.”

Good advice if I had any control over my power. Half the time it wouldn’t even show up without someone being in dire straits. I hovered my hand over the spot and felt no tingle of energy, so I dropped my finger down to touch the part Tony had indicated.

Nothing happened. I looked at him. “I told you.”

Running a hand over his short hair, Tony stared at the laptop. “Kaz, you try it.”

He did. Nothing again.

Tony put the keyboard back in place and once the laptop was whole again, he handed it to me. “Try it again.”

I felt like an idiot standing there holding the laptop with nothing happening. “What do you want me to do? I can’t just call up my power.”

“Well I can’t do it,” Tony snapped back at me. “Your power is what runs the other one. Way I got it figured, we need this one to function for about a minute. That’s all.”

I gripped the laptop tight. “I have no control over the other one and this one is clearly not the same.”

“Just try harder, Xena.”

I had to make this work for Callan. I closed my eyes and pleaded with my power. Not so much as a flicker. Opening my eyes, I placed the computer back on the slab of wood they were using for a table and asked V’ru, “Can’t you wave your hands and make a computer work?”

V’ru held my gaze with a tolerant one and flipped one skinny hand without looking up. A holographic screen popped into view. “You mean like that?”

“Yes. If you can do that, why can’t you make this computer work?”

He sighed, sounding like someone a hundred years old instead of a stick-thin eleven-year-old. “That is like saying why can’t you use your power to fly or teleport. Those are two unique energy sources just as your power and mine function differently.”

Kaz looked out the doorway. “The moon will be setting in a little over an hour. We must leave soon.”

When would this day get any easier?

Tony crossed his arms. "Call up your power like you did to unlock the doors. That's all we need. Not croggle-killing level."

Frustration boiling inside me burst out. "Don't you think I would if I could?"

"I don't know," Tony argued. "How important is it to get Callan back? Or do you care enough."

I took a step toward him. "How can you say that?" Heat coiled and spun inside me like a whip of fire.

"'Cause you ain't makin' much of an effort." Tony lifted his shoulders. "Hey, if you don't care about him being tortured, that's fine by me."

I yelled at Tony, "Make that stupid thing work!"

"Not my problem."

"I'm going to make it your problem if you—"

"Look, it's working!" V'ru shouted.

I jerked my gaze to the table where the computer had three circles whirling on the screen. I started laughing out of relief. "It *is* working."

Tony scrubbed a hand over his face. "Getting you upset enough to power up is killing me, Xena."

"Oh, no," V'ru whispered.

The computer died again.

Kaz said, "That's okay. She'll make it work again. We have to go."

I caught the resignation in Kaz's face when he acknowledged that I had to return to the TeK camp with him. I'd do my best to hide my feelings about Callan once we were around the female captive. A royal.

Tony wrapped up the computer and started to put it in his backpack, then changed his mind. "I'm leaving my pack with V'ru. We'll just take the computer."

Tony, V'ru and Kaz were ready to walk out when Kaz turned to Tony. "I would rather you stay here and keep an eye on ..." He glanced down at the top of V'ru's head and said, "The village."

Tony looked to me and I nodded. There was nothing he could do once we got to the TecKnati camp if powering this thing was up to me.

"Sure thing," Tony agreed, though not looking all that happy. I didn't blame him as we were sticking him with Zilya, Etoi and Kenja.

I held Tony back when V'ru and Kaz walked out. "Tony, you said we needed the computer to operate for a minute. It only powered up for fifteen seconds."

"You weren't even focusing on the unit and the overflow of your power got it running. All you have to do is concentrate when you get there and you'll do fine, Xena. Plus you don't have a choice." Tony glanced outside and back at me. "Kaz said you have to leave now or you'll miss your window of time."

If my power showed up, I'd either make the computer work or take down the entire TecKnati camp until I found Callan.

If my power failed me ...

No. I couldn't accept the possibility.

With no other choice, I headed out with Kaz to the tortalones.

Chapter 13

Gabby had traveled the world with her surgeon father, and they'd stayed in five-star hotels where the staffs had catered to her every whim. Not one of those places had been memorable, not like Jaxxson's hut.

She'd missed the simplicity of his space with its dried herbs and tree stumps for chairs. Being back in his personal space filled her with a joy she'd never found in her own world.

Okay, to be honest, having Jaxxson carry her into said hut had a lot of influence on her frame of mind.

He still had the pile of blue-and-gold tortalone feathers on the floor where he'd placed them during her last visit.

Another reason to smile for no real reason.

She was officially an idiot. Over him.

But being with Jaxxson felt like coming home.

All semblance of home had vanished for Gabby after her mother had died in a car wreck. That death had been Gabby's fault. She'd been a small child, but even then she could hear a person's thoughts if she touched their skin. She'd blurted out something she'd heard in her mother's mind, a secret love affair that had been playing through her mother's thoughts. Gabby had terrified her mother to the point she'd raced away from her demon child and lost control of her convertible, rolling it.

In all the years since then, Gabby had isolated herself, refusing to touch or allow human contact. She'd gone from one location to the next with no urge to return or stay anywhere.

Jaxxson's hut had changed little since she was last here. Gabby had spent fourteen hours back in Albuquerque, but in that same time, two days had passed here in the Sphere.

Stopping in the middle of the room, Jaxxson lowered her feet to the ground.

But her feet refused to touch the ground, as if she wore anti-gravity boots instead of her scuffed black ones. Floating a foot above the ground was strange, but not a bad strange except for when she had to move around.

She lifted her hands. "What now?"

"You have to take control of your power, Gabby."

She would not bite Jaxxson's head off again about telling her to do something as if she could just snap her fingers and make her power perform. "Okay, let's take this one step at a time, Jaxxson. First, I don't feel that bright green power like I saw inside myself last time when you showed me how to find it."

He smiled. "You are annoyed with me."

"I was trying to not let it show."

"Your thoughts are hard to hide from a healer."

She cocked an eyebrow at him. "Then why don't you get busy healing and fix this?"

"Because if you recall, last time I made a mistake by tampering with your power and almost lost you. I will not suffer that moment again. You are the only one who should be controlling your power at this point."

She grumbled, "Then get ready for me to turn the village into a category-three weather event."

His smile slipped. "No, do not do that."

"It was a joke."

"You have a twisted sense of humor at times for such a pretty girl." If he hadn't smiled when he said that—and added the compliment—she might have been insulted, but Jaxxson would never say anything unkind to her. "Back to your power."

"What am I supposed to do to make this stop when I don't want to float? Why can't I see that green power inside me?"

"That's because the power is becoming one with you. When you're unfamiliar with it at first, the power feels like something added on or stuck inside you."

"I remember that feeling."

"Since then, your body has joined with the power so you do not have to go search for it, but you do have to *feel* it."

Gabby crossed her arms and stared almost eye level with him. She could get used to this floating thing if she could reverse it when she needed to walk. "Well I don't know how to *feeel* it."

Jaxxson crossed his arms now, which she read as impatient. Not a good sign. "Sit down on that stack of feathers, Gabby."

She gave him the stink eye, which turned out to be a wasted effort when he ignored it. Unfolding her arms, she flapped, trying to push herself down the way she would if she were in water. "Clearly, ordering me to sit doesn't work. Not that you'd miss that in your diagnosis, being a skilled healer and all. Just ignore me while I do what I've been doing since I left here. It's worked so well up until now. I only had to wear a thirty-pound backpack to keep my feet on the floor."

"There must be something wrong with me, because I have missed your caustic tongue." Jaxxson sighed. "You are not even trying to use your powers."

Gabby stopped flapping. She was not going to say another word until he figured out that telling her to just *do it* was not working.

His eyebrows jumped up. "Well?"

Nope. Not answering him.

"Let's try this. Close your eyes, Gabby."

She hoped this meant he was finally going to tell her something useful so she closed her eyes and waited on his next instructions.

"Now tell your body to breathe."

Her eyes flew open. "What? That's ridiculous."

"Exactly. You do not tell your body to breathe, just as you should not have to tell your feet to stay on the ground. Your body knows what it must do to keep you alive and your power will know what to do when you direct it. Close your eyes again and envision standing on the ground."

Here we go again.

She pictured her feet moving down and taking her weight again. She pictured weights dragging her feet down. She tried a couple mental commands. *Down, girl. Feet on the ground, now!*

When Jaxxson said, "Try picturing yourself sitting on the

feathers behind you," she instead pictured grabbing him by the neck and shaking some sense into Jaxxson.

Her skin chilled, then a voice whispered in her ear. *I told you I would help you if you kept my secret. Let go of your anger and I will move you to the feathers.*

Her neck muscles tensed.

She recognized that voice. It was Mathias, the former MystiK leader for this village. She'd seen him in ghost form last time she was here. Jaxxson hadn't seen the ghost and Gabby didn't tell him that she had.

Mathias had warned her not to, for one thing.

"Very good, Gabby!"

She opened her eyes and looked up from where she sat cross-legged on the feathers.

She whispered, "How'd you do that?"

"I didn't do that. You did." Jaxxson grinned at her and she felt like a star student, when she was anything but. "See how it works now?"

No, she didn't see. Mathias had moved her, but she couldn't tell Jaxxson about her invisible consultant. Like the rest of the village, Jaxxson believed that Mathias had left the Sphere and was being held in a TecKnati facility back in Jaxxson's home world.

She rubbed her eyes with the heels of her hands. When she dropped her hands and looked up at Jaxxson, he was still smiling at her.

But standing next to him was the translucent image of Mathias frowning at her.

Reacting to either expression was not going to go well since Mathias might take offense to her returning Jaxxson's smile and Jaxxson would question her glaring at Mathias.

Jaxxson's gaze strayed away from her, staring at nothing. She'd seen him like that before when someone called him telepathically.

He swung his attention back to her. "Zilya is calling for me, because Kenja is arguing with her. Those two are making me crazy. Stay here and practice using your powers. I'll be back as soon as I can. Sound good?"

She gave him a plain smile and nodded.

The minute Jaxxson stepped outside and the sound of his footsteps dimmed, she arched an eyebrow at Mathias. "Okay, time to start talking and tell me what is going on. What happened to you? Everyone thinks you're back home."

"I cannot stay long so listen closely."

"Do you really think you don't have my full attention by now, Math—"

"Silence!"

She scowled and crossed her arms. "Yelling at me is not a good way to gain my help."

His form wavered in and out. "I don't have much time."

Now she felt bad for snapping at him. "Sorry. Tell me what you came to say."

"The prophecy must be fulfilled."

"What's with this Damian Prophecy anyhow? All I hear is that it has to be fulfilled and time is running out and the world is coming to an end."

"You made that last part up. I heard nothing of the world is coming to an end."

She crossed her arms and rolled her eyes. "Okay, so no world is coming to an end part, but everyone acts like there will be dire consequences."

"That part is true. I did not understand the significance of the prophecy until I died. I have moments that things come to me, but I have not been able to relay what I learn to Callan."

Gabby perked up at that. "Does Callan know about ... you?"

"Yes. So does Rayen."

"Are you serious? And she didn't tell me?" Gabby was so giving Rayen a tongue lashing over holding out on her.

"She gave me her word. You should know by now that Rayen will not break her word no matter what."

True, but Gabby still intended to bust her on it. Friends told each other things. Like when someone freaking *died*. "Why can I see and hear you, but no one else can?"

"Because you are a Hy'bridt. Your powers are ancient and formidable. The Hy'bridts that live in our time are revered for their ability to move between worlds."

Gabby shook her head. "I don't want to move between worlds if you're referencing the one you're in right now. I have no control over my powers. I'd never make it back here and I might destroy your world at the same time."

"That is not necessary." Mathias waved her comment off with his ethereal hand. He moved across the hut, pacing back and forth, if you could call it pacing when his feet didn't move.

Maybe she should give him the "just put your feet on the ground" talk.

He paused and focused on her. "You must insure that the prophecy is fulfilled."

"How am I going to do that?"

"By following your heart when it comes to caring for people. You hide your feelings behind a sharp tongue, but you will not stand by and allow these children to remain trapped here."

"Are you saying I have the power to do that?" She shoved up to her feet, stomping over to Mathias. "Are you saying I could have gotten them out of here by now? If that's the case, you should have come to me sooner."

"It's not that easy."

"Why not?"

"I don't have time to explain things that you will not understand."

"So now I'm a moron?" she groused, hands on her hips, not backing an inch away from him.

His image shook with anger and the room vibrated around her. "How does Jaxxson deal with you when no one else can?"

"By not talking to me like I'm an idiot." Could he choke her as a ghost?

"I don't think you are a moron or an idiot, Gabby, but you are unfamiliar with all that goes on in this Sphere and in our world."

"Like I said, maybe if you'd have come to me sooner I would be more up to speed by now."

"I couldn't come to you before or I would have."

She grabbed a handful of her ponytails and growled. "Why not?"

"Because it is difficult to shield myself from the wraiths for long."

"What wraiths, Mathias?"

"No! Never say my name!" The terror that filled his eyes, bled through his body, shaking his form to the point it was hard to identify that wobbling mass as any version of Mathias.

Howling started inside the hut, but it sounded as if it was coming from somewhere beyond the Sphere. Mathias looked right and left, shouting at Gabby, "You must send the children home."

"How?"

"The prophecy. Fulfill it and ... "

Dark shapes flew into the hut, coming out of nothingness to form and fly around the room. Wind battered everything, slapping her ponytails against her face.

Gabby backed up, waving her arms. "What can I do? How do I stop them?"

"Nothing. They won't ... touch you," Mathias choked out before his head jerked back. The muscles in his face and throat were thick cords standing out. He clenched his jaw and groaned, struggling against an invisible force that yanked him right and left.

Her ears should be bleeding from the noise those things were making.

Mathias gutted out his next words. "V'ru ... has ... prophecy. Help him ... decode it. Bonding ... *must* happen—"

Black shapes flooded the room, swarming Mathias. He cried out, swinging his arms and fighting them until his arms were snatched behind him and he was dragged up toward the open roof of the hut, where the sky arched overhead.

The black swarm spun into a tight knot then ... poof. They were gone and so was Mathias.

Gabby's knees gave out. She hit the feather bed hard and looked up to see nothing but a sky losing light with every second that ticked toward moonset.

Ten minutes later, Jaxxson came walking back in. He glanced around at the hut, noticing herbs blown into a corner and gourds on the floor. "Did you have a weather event?"

I'm going to take one for the team, Mathias. Gabby nodded.

"Come on, Gabby. I thought you were going to practice. You shouldn't be intimidated by power. It is yours to control."

She moved her mouth like a guppy struggling for air.

Breathing wasn't a problem. She was trying to figure out what to say. "Did you hear anything while you were gone?"

"Like what?"

"Wind noise. Howling wind noise?"

Jaxxson's forehead creased in thought. "No, I heard nothing." He looked more closely at her. "Are you okay?"

No, she wasn't okay, but neither was she ready to talk about what she'd just witnessed. Poor Mathias had died a horrible death if those wraiths are what killed him.

And she was the only one who could hear or see him, so it was her job to do what he couldn't and make sure these children returned home.

She recalled what he'd said.

Fulfill the prophecy and the MystiKs would go home.

Plus something about a bonding that had to happen.

The only problem with what he'd told her was that she didn't have any idea how to unravel the prophecy. That meant she had to talk to Mathias again, but this time she wouldn't waste time arguing with him and she sure as heck wasn't saying his name again.

Finding a smile for Jaxxson, she asked, "Would V'ru have information on Hy'bridts?"

"Some, but he will not be able to tell you how to manage your power."

"That's not what I'm after. I want to know the history of the Hy'bridt abilities."

Jaxxson pondered that. "What exactly are you looking for?"

"You know, things like if they all have telepathy and if they all levitate." She let her words trail off, because what she couldn't tell Jaxxson was that she wanted to find out if she could cross over to another world and come back.

If Hy'bridts were so powerful and could walk between worlds, then why couldn't she go into the place where Mathias was caught and free him? It was the least he deserved after sparing Rayen, Tony and her on their first visit to the Sphere.

Chapter 14

Callan shifted his body, but there was no comfortable position with his arms shackled to the wall. His raw skin bled where the metal cut into his wrists and the room stank of rotted food he'd ignored.

Or maybe he was to blame for that obnoxious odor after all the time he'd been stuck here.

TecKnati scouts laughed and carried on outside. Someone shouted, "Red moon setting soon, warrior."

They'd been doing that for the past two hours.

Closing his eyes, Callan leaned his head back, determined to keep his wits about him no matter what they did. The minute it was dark, Thylan would be back with an army to hold Callan down.

Will Thylan cut off my fingers first? Or my hands?

He fisted his hands, shaking with the urge to break these chains.

Music pushed inside his mind. Someone was singing.

A girl.

Callan focused on the words that he'd heard sung at home. That voice was as sweet as any songbird's. Within seconds, his heartbeat slowed and he relaxed his hands. The lyrical sound curled inside him, soothing the fury that had raged for days. Exhaustion and pain left him. His body welcomed the relief.

His breathing dropped to a calm rhythm. The pain wracking him subsided for the first time in so long he just wanted to stay in this state of disconnect.

Something tapped on his mind.

"Hmm?" He drew a deep breath and let it out slowly, unwilling to disturb the tranquility wrapping him.

The second tap on his consciousness brought him back to alertness. He stilled and opened his mind a tiny bit, just enough to determine if this was friend or foe, but a TecKnati would not know how to execute telepathy.

He sent out a silent question. *What?*

I'm so glad you answered. I have tried to reach someone, anyone since I was captured two days ago. What House are you from?

I am with the Warrior House. And yours?

Creativity House.

Callan's mother was fond of the Creativity House and mentioned it often, hoping to pique Callan's interest in the females there. Now he was interested in only one young woman and she didn't live in his time, but if he survived this Sphere he'd be expected to choose a future mate when he returned home.

The Houses were big on long engagements. They still struggled to rebuild the population of MystiKs, and encouraged proliferation, but only after two people had made a true commitment.

He wished the Houses were big on allowing teens to have a life first. Some did, but not the MystiK teens expected to assume roles of leadership at some point.

To be honest, right now he'd take being home and facing that decision over sitting here worrying that his little village in the Sphere was vulnerable.

When he didn't hear from the girl again, Callan reached out to her telepathically again. *Were you singing?*

Yes. Her answer held a shyness that would be a rosy blush if sound had color.

His mother thought he would be content with a shy, accommodating woman. That just proved how little his mother knew about him.

Callan was attracted to a stubborn, argumentative female with eyes the color of a turquoise jewel and hair dark as midnight.

The songbird's voice poked at his mind again. *How long have you been here?*

On the Sphere almost a year.

Do you have any idea of how we can return home?

He hated the longing in her voice. It was no different from that of any other adolescent MystiK newly captured and delivered to the Sphere. By the time they were here a month, the longing changed to despair.

He had to give her an answer, but he stayed with the truth. *No, I don't have a way home yet, but that doesn't mean we won't find one.*

Her silence answered with more anguish than if she'd used words.

He'd like to give her encouragement, but he might not be here long himself. Now he knew how Mathias felt as his eighteenth BIRG Day neared. Callan had considered Mathias a close friend and respected him as the senior teen from the Governing House, which had given Mathias the authority to rule the MystiK village he'd created in the Sphere.

Governing had not gone to Mathias's head either.

He would have made an outstanding leader back home ... had he lived. The minute the red moon had set on the day Mathias turned eighteen, the deadly wraiths had dragged him away.

Callan clinched at the memory of his friend screaming.

He and Rayen had been the only two present to witness the hideous killing and had given a vow to keep Mathias's death a secret from the others in the village.

Mathias had good reason. He'd wanted the rest of the children in the village to maintain hope. He'd explained how it was best that they think SEOH had taken him back to their home world and locked him away until the treaty was signed again.

And now Callan faced that same fate. He could only hope that Kaz, Zilya, Jaxxson and the others believed the TeKs had killed him.

Turning eighteen hadn't seemed like a big deal when Jornn, his twin, had been alive and slated to be the next Warrior House leader, but SEOH had murdered Jornn. Callan had never wanted to lead a House. Give him an army of warriors any day, but politics and stuffy events had turned reaching eighteen into a monumental pain in the butt back home.

Or so he'd thought until he'd been captured while tracking down a lead to prove SEOH had been behind Jornn's killing. Then he'd been transported to this Sphere.

Now reaching eighteen equated death, because he doubted the MystiKs would find a way out of the Sphere before the red moon set on his BIRG Day.

He felt another bump on his mind and telepathically replied, *Yes?*

Are you feeling any better?

His chest didn't hurt as much as it had, and one of the gashes had closed up. It was no longer bleeding. *I do. Did you do that?*

I could feel your pain, she answered then added, *The TeKs don't know. I pretend I can't do anything and I scared the leader into thinking I'm crazy. Who are you?*

Callan of the Warrior House.

She didn't answer at first then she said, *I thought it was you. This is Becka.*

He bounced his head back against the wall and locked down his mental shields before she heard him groan. Was the universe bored and had no one better to toy with today?

Her gentle thump was back.

To ignore her would be a major breach of protocol. Even in this place. He carefully dropped his shields just enough to talk, but not enough to allow her music to pass through again, or she'd get the wrong idea.

Becka?

Oh, good, I thought the TecKnati had activated their laser grid again. I can ease more of your pain.

No. He shouldn't have replied so harshly.

Why not?

I'm fine.

I can feel that you are still hurting. Why won't you let me ... Her voice faded to silence then she came back. *Are you bonded with ... someone?*

The hurt in her voice radiated through their mental connection. Callan thunked his head back again and admitted, *No, I'm not bonded to anyone.*

Oh, good. You had me worried there.

And that would be due to his mother and her mother discussing a possible future alliance. Why couldn't parents stay out of things like that?

Becka's mother had three daughters and intended for every one of them to marry well. One was a year older than Callan, and lived to be served. The second daughter was a year younger than he was, and had always looked down her nose when they ran into each other, as if he were unfit to be in the same room with her.

As the youngest and two years behind Callan, Becka was the quiet one. She was the only daughter he could tolerate spending time around, but that didn't mean they were well suited.

He wasn't bonded, but to act as if nothing had changed since he had been captured would be a betrayal to Rayen and dishonest to Becka. He might not be able to bond with Rayen, but his heart was his own to give away and she held his in her hands. It mattered not that he'd never see her again. That was the way he felt.

Up until now, Callan had not actually admitted to himself that he never expected to go home, but he must have always doubted that he would. Otherwise, why would he have opened himself up to Rayen when he still had commitments at home?

Such as Becka.

She was the one his parents had encouraged him to consider. By the time she turned eighteen, he would be well on the way to taking his place in the MystiK hierarchy. His parents hadn't done anything archaic like demand he choose her as his future wife, but there were expectations that came along with responsibility.

They wouldn't understand if he told them he wanted to spend his life with someone else.

A C'raydonian no less.

Becka wouldn't understand either.

Callan could avoid telling Becka the truth since there was little chance that either of them would escape the TecKnati camp, but to allow her to think there was any hope between them would be dishonorable.

He took a breath and answered her telepathically. *Becka, I need to tell—*

Shouting erupted outside his door. He slammed his mental shields down and prepared for Thylan. The moon shouldn't have set yet.

What was going on?

Becka tapped again, but Callan needed to remove all distractions to face what Thylan had planned for him.

Thylan opened the door. Six beefed-up TecKnatis stood behind him. He grinned. "Time's up."

Then Thylan told his men, "Bring him outside."

Chapter 15

I climbed off the tortalone in a clearing barely wide enough to contain the two creatures. The heat here was thicker, with a dirty yellow hue and a smell like burning sulpher. Maybe it was because of the TecKnati presence, or maybe because the trees and shrubs in this area looked stilted, more bleached bones than soft foliage.

Kaz had maneuvered his mount to come in very slowly until it dropped vertically out of the air.

He'd shown me how to handle riding one by myself so that we could bring two for the trip back to the village. He said the creatures didn't mind several people, but they tended to become unstable with more than two riders of our size.

That was fine by me.

It meant Callan and I would be riding home together.

I was not leaving here without him. I could already feel his arms around me. He would hold me close when we rode back to the village and Kaz could fly on the second tortalone.

The TecKnati camp sat three hundred feet ahead.

Dropping down beside me with an easy move, Kaz pulled the laptop out of a shoulder sling. He'd carried it so that I could focus on handling my tortalone.

Once he handed the precious computer to me and tossed the sling on top of his tortalone, he whispered to the creatures. They immediately settled down and tucked inside their shells.

I asked, "Do you think any of the TeKs will come out here?"

Kaz shook his head. "They should keep all of their scouts in close to have as many as possible for when we return, but I do worry about the tortalones being here. They disappeared once on me yesterday."

If we had to return on foot, we'd just suck it up and do it. "Do you think the TeKs have hurt Callan?"

"Possibly, but they want this computer, or they want the one you traveled here through if that is indeed the Genera-Y. To harm Callan ahead of moonset would work against them."

I hoped he was right.

Speaking of moonset, I had made a decision on the way here so that Kaz would understand why we *had* to break Callan out before the red moon disappeared. "About Callan's BIRG Day—"

He scowled at me. "I wish I hadn't told you about that. It *is* important to MystiKs that we hold true to our ceremonies, but the celebration of his birth is trivial at this point. Stop obsessing."

I hoped Callan would forgive me, but I couldn't leave Kaz in the dark and expect him to be as committed as me to getting Callan out *now*. "You don't understand, Kaz. Callan's birthday is *not* trivial. He'll die when the moon sets unless we can find a way to protect him from another threat in this Sphere besides the TeKs."

That clearly surprised Kaz. "What are you talking about?"

"I gave my word to Mathias, but I think he would understand why I have to break it, given this situation."

"Mathias? You think I care anything about a leader of the Governing House who left our people here to fend for themselves?"

I understood his feelings since Kaz didn't know the truth, but I was about to enlighten him. "We don't have much time, so I need to tell you this quickly and explain more later. The minute the moon sets on any MystiKs celebrating their eighteenth BIRG Days while in this place, they will die a horrible death from these awful wraiths. *That* is what happened to Mathias. I saw it."

Kaz's lips moved with his struggle to form words. "Why would—"

"I'll explain later, but Mathias was the second one to reach eighteen and die in this place. Callan will be the third if we don't get him out of the TeK camp and give him a fighting chance. I don't know what it will take to stop the wraiths, but I intend to unleash all my power on them." I swallowed and still that lump of worry wouldn't go away. "I don't care what we have to do to free him now, but we're not leaving without Callan. Understood?"

The dark gaze of a ferocious warrior slid into Kaz's eyes. "Agreed, but we have to rescue *two* captives."

"Who is the other one?"

"Just as you said, we have no time. I will explain later. Let's get moving."

Something told me I wasn't going to like that explanation, but nothing could be worse than Callan facing death with his hands tied and no way to fight.

We hurried through the woods. My palms were damp. I clutched the computer tighter to prevent dropping it. When we reached the edge of the bone-colored trees, Kaz held up a hand and studied the terrain.

The fenced area where they'd captured Callan now stood empty, which explained why there were no guards around it. It was seventy feet wide and covered in fine-powdered orange dirt that had hid a dangerous grid capable of stealing power. I had to assume the grid was still in place. Between where I stood and single-story metal building at the far end of the camp, a series of tents had been erected in two rows that bordered the walkway to the metal building. The tents had been painted in colors that matched the woods, hiding them from the sky if we hadn't already known the location.

The TecKnati had removed trees, leaving a broad sweep of cleared ground around the camp with the widest open area at this end.

I saw little activity and, even at that, it was all down near the metal building where a handful of scouts moved around.

Kaz said, "They must have Callan locked inside the building." He eyed the sky where the moon dipped closer to the horizon.

"We need to go, Kaz."

He grunted, his gaze sweeping the TeK camp once more.

I was done waiting and started to move.

He caught my arm. "You must do as I say when we meet

with the TeKs. I know them better than you do."

My first thought was to remind him that I was not receptive to being ordered around, but there was no give in Kaz and Callan when they were in protective mode. "I understand."

"No, you don't. I shouldn't even be bringing you here, Rayen. Callan will be furious with me, but after seeing how Tony brought V'ru out of his kamara, I had to leave Tony to watch over him."

"That TeK Thylan is expecting me, not Tony or you, and Callan can't be angry unless he's alive. I'll smooth everything over with him, but if you try to tell me to leave before we have him back, I'm not going. Are we clear?"

"Yes, but—"

I didn't want to hear any more. "Callan doesn't get to make that choice and neither do you. Besides, we both know what I can do."

"*If* your power comes when you call to it," he pointed out.

He would bring that up when I was already worried about making this computer work. I ended the conversation by telling him, "The longer we wait, the less time I have to make this thing work."

He waved his hand forward. "Go."

As soon as we emerged from the woods and started across the open space between us and the structures around the camp, TecKnati scouts came out of the tents, following us on our way to the building that sat dead center. Ahead, more boys from age ten to older teens poured out of the camouflaged tents.

We moved through a sea of metallic gray-green uniforms and clipped haircuts so much like Tony's short hair, but that's where any resemblance ended.

Tony would never mistreat someone.

Several spun around and shouted for Thylan.

That was the arrogant TecKnati who had taunted me after he captured Callan. Thylan enjoyed telling me how he was going to cut parts off of Callan if I showed up after moonset today.

I hated watching that red moon. It drifted toward the horizon with little care about what was happening here. In another thirty minutes, it would be gone.

The scouts we approached jeered at us, and the ones

following behind picked up the mantra, lifting the noise to an angry rumble. There had to be sixty or more. Kaz continued walking, not giving heed to anyone or anything.

Of course, they all stood back from the menace emanating from both of us.

They wanted blood?

Harm Callan and I'd show them their own.

Fifty feet from the building, guards stepped into my path. "No further, MystiK."

Should I correct him and say I'm a C'raydonian?

Kaz would kill me. I said nothing, waiting for the all-powerful Thylan to make his way to me.

The men parted for Thylan and filled in behind him as he moved toward us with a cocky gait. He stopped in front of me, grinning and sweeping a slow look over me in a way that made my skin crawl. "I can see why Callan would want you, but not why you'd want him."

I hadn't seen *that* coming.

An arm bulging with tense muscles went around my shoulder. I looked up at Kaz who didn't spare me a glance. What was he doing? It looked as if he was staking claim in front of Thylan.

Did Kaz think I cared what this creepy guy thought? Or that I couldn't take Thylan in a battle? The mouthy TeK was slow and, in a fight with me, slow would lose.

I tried to ease away from Kaz, but he squeezed me tighter up against him.

Then Kaz pinned Thylan with a bold stare, making it clear who he was addressing. "She and Callan are friends. Just as Callan and I have been friends for many years. We're here to deliver your computer and take our *friend* back to the village." His voiced dropped with an edge of threat. "Just to be clear. She is mine. If you insult her again before our exchange is completed, you will regret your words."

Since waking up in that desert, I'd prided myself on assessing a threat situation quickly. I didn't understand what Kaz was up to, but he wouldn't be doing this unless he had a reason.

He must realize something about Thylan that I'd missed.

Was Kaz doing all this to prevent Thylan from thinking I was of value to Callan? If that happened, I *would* become a liability in this negotiation. That had to be the reason behind this posturing. Kaz was diffusing the notion that my presence had any particular value, so the Teks would focus on the exchange, which meant Kaz was protecting Callan.

Our goals were the same.

Thylan rubbed his chin, taking Kaz's measure with a long look. "Show me the computer."

"Not until we see that Callan is unharmed."

This commanding voice of Kaz's was one I hadn't heard before now.

Thylan laughed. "You do realize you're outnumbered, right?"

Kaz's gaze hardened. "You do realize that MystiKs sabotaged the last ANASKO space launch using only natural powers, right? Would you care for a demonstration?"

That wiped the attitude off Thylan's face.

I wasn't sure Kaz had chosen the right approach, considering we were at a disadvantage if we were standing above another grid.

"Show me how the computer works first," Thylan demanded.

"No." Kaz and I said that together.

I added, "You can't be trusted after what you did to capture Callan."

"Don't like getting outsmarted, do you?" Thylan laughed. "All I'd have to do is throw a switch to capture you two."

I wanted to use a blast of power to make Thylan think twice about that laser grid.

Kaz warned, "If you turn on that grid you risk destroying the sentient component of this computer. Now, where is Callan?"

Thylan gave me a taunting smile. "He's been out here the whole time."

Thylan's eyes lit with mean happiness. He kept his attention on me while he called over his shoulder. "Callan? Got your ... well, *not* your girl since she's with someone else, but she's back with the computer. You want to say hello?"

Forcing myself to remain planted in this spot was a battle when all I wanted to do was run to find Callan.

Someone thumped against my mind so hard it jarred me and I sidestepped to keep my balance.

Kaz jerked his gaze down at me. "What?"

Everyone else was watching, too.

I couldn't let Thylan misread the stumble as me reacting to Callan being near. I said, "Nothing," and shook it off, ready to negotiate.

Callan came blasting into my mind shouting, *What are you doing here? I told you—*

I slammed my mental walls down, shutting him out. There was no way I could handle these negotiations and Callan yelling at me at the same time.

He thumped again hard and I pushed back.

That silenced him.

Thylan's men cleared a path between where we stood and Callan.

When the crowd parted, I saw him and my heart thudded.

Definitely alive, but he was far from unharmed, with bleeding wrists and gashes along his chest and shoulders as if he'd been struck with a whip. One nasty cut had closed up, but none had healed entirely.

What was stopping him from healing?

The laser grid?

I didn't sense any such power operating beneath me at the moment. And based on the last time here, Callan wouldn't be able to contact me telepathically if the laser grid was activated.

Callan slung wet hair off his face and split his furious glare between me and Kaz.

It took a moment for me to realize how this picture looked to Callan.

I tried to step out of Kaz's hold, but he had an unyielding grip on my shoulder. I tugged again.

Kaz yanked me closer and told Thylan, "She'll show you the computer, then you will uncuff him."

Callan's fierce stare was all for Kaz and, after a moment, I had the feeling he was trying to communicate telepathically with Kaz, too, but Kaz must not be opening his mind either.

Growling like a trapped animal, Callan shouted, “Kaz, get her—”

Someone threw a bucket of liquid straight at Callan’s face. Energy crackled at his wrists and he jerked as if shocked.

I flinched, the urge to fight trembling through me.

Kaz slid one word at me through his gritted teeth. “Don’t.”

I hoped he knew what he was doing.

Thylan tucked a gadget in the pants pocket of his uniform before I could see what it was. He stepped closer to me and held his hands out, palms up.

I placed the laptop on them and lifted the lid. Flexing my fingers, I hovered my hand over the keys.

Every TecKnati gaze was locked on my hand.

Callan yelled, “Do not—”

More water hit him. Just hearing him choke and the sizzle of energy shocking him hurt me. I’d thought about how I would do this on the way here. All I had to do was make my power surge if I focused on envisioning them hurting Callan.

Holding the computer in one hand, Thylan yanked the gadget back out that was just big enough to fit in the palm of his hand. Silver and oblong shaped. He lifted it in Callan’s direction and Callan went silent.

What had he done to Callan with that small device? Energy stirred inside me and I snapped back to my task.

Callan thumped hard on my mind once more. It had to be him. Kaz wouldn’t interrupt me right now.

Calling hard for my power, I envisioned the TeKs taking a knife to Callan’s—

He bumped me again mentally, over and over.

I lost my train of thought. Poof. The energy settled down.

Thylan shifted his feet, getting antsy. “What’s the hold up? Does this thing work or not?”

“Yes,” I was quick to assure him.

Kaz stepped closer and questioned Thylan. “Why can’t the TecKnati build a two-way time travel computer?”

Good. He was distracting Thylan. I dug into my memory for more nightmares, such as Callan being attacked by the croggle.

But we had defeated the beast together.

Thylan said, “Who’s to say we haven’t built a portal

computer that will time travel in any direction?"

"I'm saying that must be the case if you need this antique," Kaz pointed out. His foot nudged mine that I took to mean hurry up.

I changed my mind on searching for a vision of Callan and started thinking about Tony and Gabby attacked by the deadly vine.

Heat stirred inside me once more. Thank goodness.

Energy balled and twisted, churning.

Tony warned me not to feed too much power into the computer and blow it up. I pulled the power slowly toward my arms and into my hand.

The monitor flashed on.

I wanted to shout and let Callan know we were close, but I kept all my attention on the three circles moving in and out of each other across the monitor. The blue, green and red colors weren't the same as the image on the actual time travel computer, but no one here would know that. The only people to see the real time travel computer besides me were Tony and Gabby.

When scouts behind me saw the monitor come to life, they started murmuring.

Now was as good a time as any to turn it around and make our swap.

Kaz's gaze tracked the monitor screen, but he kept up his conversation with Thylan. "We told you it requires a MystiK to operate this computer. What are you going to do when you take it back to SEOH?"

Thylan found Kaz's question amusing, but then he found everything about the MystiKs amusing. "You think my father doesn't have MystiKs on our payroll?"

What? This was SEOH's son? And they had MystiKs working for them?

I lost my focus in that one second.

Thylan had just looked down at the screen when it flashed twice and blinked off.

One of his guys shouted, "They're trying to trick us."

"No, I'm not," I lied. "It'll come back on in a minute."

For the first time, Thylan was not amused. He slapped the

lid shut. "Lock these two up."

Kaz jerked me back and shoved past me. He lifted his hands in front of his chest and behind him, shoving a fast kinetic blast in a circular arc to stop scouts in front and those who surged toward our backs.

They slammed into the invisible wall and bounced off.

Thylan yelled, "Blast them."

Callan roared and lunged. Metal screamed as the chain mounts started ripping away from the wall.

I screamed inside my head, begging my power to come back. Nothing. What good was the stupid power if it couldn't show up when I need it most?

The noise of Callan struggling snatched Thylan's attention and offered me the perfect opening.

I shot past Kaz, snatched the computer from Thylan's hands and spun around to stand in front of Kaz, holding up the computer. "Shoot us and you'll lose the Genera-Y computer. Then who's going home?"

Everyone stilled.

Kaz whispered, "Smart, but give it to me and get behind me."

"Not going to happen," I murmured. Keeping my gaze on Callan, I spoke to Thylan. "The computer works. I can prove it, but I'm not even going to try again unless you release Callan."

"Then he dies."

That was a greater threat than Thylan knew, because that blood red moon was sinking faster every second. "If you harm him, I will destroy this computer."

"Do that and SEOH will destroy this Sphere."

Kaz shouted, "Have you forgotten the counter measure bespelled in the Amity treaty? SEOH wouldn't risk killing a MystiK child and lose a TecKnati youth of equal standing. The majority of MystiKs in this Sphere are future leaders, the highest ranked in our Houses."

"That's the thing, MystiK. There has been no loss of TecKnati children from all the deaths here, so SEOH *would* destroy this Sphere."

Kaz answered, but confidence was absent from his statement. "Yes, but none of these deaths have met the requirements of the treaty."

"Or so you think," Thylan said, not the least bit concerned.

Callan had shared the details of the current treaty with me. It was signed every five years between the TecKnati and the MystiKs. Due to a spell infused by the leaders the last time, if a TecKnati intentionally killed a MystiK child younger than eighteen then a TecKnati child of equal political stature would die immediately, and vice versa. Callan said SEOH's oldest son had died the minute Callan's twin had been murdered, proving the treaty had teeth.

Thylan said, "I'll make you a deal."

I'd trust that as much as making a pact with a wraith. "What's that?"

"I'll trade Callan now for the computer ... and you."

Kaz and Callan shouted, "No!" Callan lunged against the chains again.

Bolts holding Callan's chains squealed.

Another bucket of water hit Callan. I was going to hurt whoever held that bucket as soon as I had the opportunity. There had to be an evil reason for keeping him wet.

Thylan held up his hands. "I'm trying to be reasonable."

If Kaz got Callan away from here, Kaz knew about the wraiths and would help Callan fight. That would only happen if Callan was free to use his power.

I stepped forward. "I accept the deal."

Kaz's hands landed on my shoulders, pulling me back. "I said no."

Callan drove his body hard against the chain mounts. Metal twisting against metal screamed. "Get her out of here, Kaz!"

Driving forward hard again, Callan forced the supports to give another inch.

Looking panicked, Thylan fished his gadget out quickly and pointed it at Callan's wrist cuffs that glowed blue.

Callan arched up and back, shuddering against power being activated by Thylan's remote controller.

I yelled, "Stop or I won't trade."

Thylan held the button down an extra second then clicked the device off.

Callan fell to his knees and hung forward, his arms pulled

back against the chains that were stretched tight.

He was hardly breathing. Unconscious.

Thylan erupted into laughter, a nervous one, but his scouts joined in.

The noise covered my words to Kaz. "Let me make this trade. Keep Callan alive, then come back and get me out. I trust you to help him fight off the wraiths and for you both to come back for me. You trust me to deal with Thylan."

"No."

"It's my choice, Kaz. I'm doing it with or without your help. If you don't help me, we're going to all end up captives. Or dead."

I yelled at Thylan, "Make up your mind. Deal or not?"

The laughing died down. Thylan ordered Callan unchained and carried to just short of the tree line.

I stepped out of Kaz's grasp. When I turned to look at him, sick disappointment stared back at me. He was worried for me. I wished I could return Kaz's feelings, but my heart belonged to Callan. I mouthed the word *please*.

Kaz inhaled deeply and followed the men carrying Callan.

I hoped I would see them both again.

"Bring the girl and the computer," Thylan ordered.

I swung around and jerked my arm away from the first scout who reached for me. When Thylan snickered at my reaction, it occurred to me now that Kaz's protective attitude might have been entirely for my benefit.

If that was the case, I would need my power for more than lighting up this computer.

Chapter 16

"Wake up!" shouted so close to Callan's face he jerked away.

Pain clawed up his arms, dragging him back to consciousness as much as the loud voice and someone shaking him. He opened his eyes and saw the sky peeking through branches.

"Get up!" Kaz stood and pulled on Callan's arm that sent a burning pain racing up it.

Callan snatched his arm back. "Do you want to die?"

"No, but you must if you're not going to get up and fight. You have only minutes until moonset."

Callan shoved himself up to a sitting position and looked around. The woods surrounded him. Kaz was here. The TecKnati camp ...

He launched to his feet. "Where's Rayen?"

"She traded herself and that computer for you," Kaz snapped, eyes accusing Callan of the trouble Rayen was in.

Callan shoved up into Kaz's face, his voice threatening to maim. "I told you not to bring her back. How could you leave her in that place?"

"If you had told me the truth about Mathias I might have had a chance of talking her out of it." Kaz shoved him back.

Callan didn't retaliate. Something was seriously off with this conversation. "What does Mathias have to do with anything?"

"Rayen told me what happened to Mathias and that you two were sworn to secrecy, but *you* should have told me that Mathias hadn't abandoned the village."

Callan shoved both hands over his face then back over his

wet hair. Thylan liked to zap him with a charge of electricity when he was saturated. "There was no reason to tell you until the right moment."

"And when would that have been?"

Callan had never seen Kaz this angry. "Tomorrow. I was going to take you with me when the time came so you would see what happens just as I had to watch Mathias. Then you would understand why I have held his confidence."

Kaz raised his fists, shaking them at the universe. "Tomorrow? Have you lost all track of time? We'll talk later. The wraiths will be showing up any minute now."

"No, they won't."

"Is this not your BIRG Day, moron?" Kaz shouted at him.

"Today? No. My BIRG Day is tomorrow." Callan put it together and fury ignited. "You told Rayen it was *today*? That's why she traded herself so I wouldn't be defenseless against the wraiths?"

Confusion wiped the anger off Kaz's face. "It's not today?"

Murdering your best friend was generally frowned upon, but Callan had never cared about what society thought before so why hold back now. "You get the date wrong every year. Jornn was born today at midnight and I was born six minutes later."

Kaz muttered, "I don't recall you correcting me."

"I did when we were little. Later I stopped, because it didn't matter to me. Jornn and I celebrated together."

"Then it's your fault I told Rayen the wrong date," Kaz spat back. "If anything happens to her, the wraiths will have to stand in line behind me."

Rage blinded Callan so fast he just reacted and lashed out a kinetic hit that slammed Kaz back twenty feet into a tree. "I want her out of there now! You I'll deal with later."

Kaz banged into the tree and groaned. Then he dropped to his feet, rolled his shoulders and came walking back over. "I'm not done with this."

"Neither am I," Callan made clear.

"How do we get to her?"

"That's not going to be easy."

"Why?"

"Because the TecKnati have run a narrow grid around the

perimeter of that metal building. Thylan doesn't trust putting the grid beneath the floors of the building."

Kaz snorted. "Doesn't trust their technology? I'd say he was intelligent if Thylan wasn't SEOH's son. What do you think they're going to do with the computer?"

Callan stared off at the camp in the distance. "SEOH wants the computer sent back to ANASKO so he can destroy it, but Thylan thinks he can make it work for time travel in both directions. He's determined to outsmart his father on this."

"Rayen says it's just a computer with no special ability."

"That will keep Thylan from harming her for a while, but not for long." Callan's hands trembled with just thinking about her inside there, subject to that animal, Thylan. Getting Rayen out of that camp and to safety came before all else.

Callan forced his emotions into the hole where they stayed out of his way so they didn't distract him. "We've got to find a way to enter the camp without them knowing so Thylan doesn't turn on the laser grid."

Chapter 17

2179 ACE, in ORD/City One

SEOH's office faced the east. From the hundred-and-seventieth floor of the ANASKO building that towered above Lake Michigan, he could see reflections created by the last glimmer of sunlight dissolving into the calm water. Very soon, the MystiKs would no longer be a problem. He leaned back, smiling.

One more day until the BIRG Con.

The moment of reckoning for those furkken MystiKs was finally approaching. Furk, that worthless old board member who had died *after* he'd made the tiebreaking vote *for* the treaty, deserved to have his name live on in posterity as a favorite curse.

A light on the control panel built into SEOH's desk glowed, then a hologram of his female AI assistant appeared. Leesa announced, "Vice Rustaad will arrive in your office in eight seconds."

SEOH replied, "Acknowledged."

The holographic woman disappeared and Rustaad entered, silent as a killer in the night, a role he'd performed exceptionally well from time to time.

Before Rustaad began his report, SEOH asked, "How close are the leaders of the MystiK Houses to arriving in our city for the BIRG Con?"

Holding himself with the posture of one born to money, Rustaad considered the question, never rushing to answer until he had the exact words required. "Based upon tracking the vehicles we sent for the leaders, none should arrive prior to noon tomorrow, but all should be on site by an hour before sunset. However, two H'ybridts have arrived already, early and within thirty minutes of each other, which I find odd."

"Everything about those people is odd." SEOH waved a hand, dismissing the issue. "I detest them personally, but they're not an issue for us. Even their own people treat the Hy'bridts as reclusive wackos. It's the G'ortians we need to keep an eye on."

Rustaad inclined his head. "Agreed."

"Any news on the remaining five to capture?"

"Some," Rustaad admitted. "We had a small bit of fortune. A Hy'bridt went to the Creativity House and, from what I've gathered from our snitch in that House, the Hy'bridt raved that Callan was at the center of the prophecy and must bond to see it fulfilled."

"Callan?"

When Rustaad nodded, SEOH stood and leaned forward with his hands on his desk, speaking softly. "We killed the wrong twin? Because if that's so, my son died for no reason."

Anyone other than Rustaad would be shaking in his boots, but Rustaad was cut of the same shark cloth as SEOH. The TecKnati leader might regret losing his first-born son, but he had a natural indifference to things like having possibly murdered the wrong MystiK teenager.

Rustaad said, "There is no way to know for sure until tomorrow and even then it may all be a moot point. At the time that you ordered Jornn's death instead of Callan's, everyone was of the belief that Jornn represented the greatest threat to TecKnatis if he managed to do what no one else had and unite the fragmented MystiK Houses."

"I know why I had him killed," SEOH snarled.

Rustaad remained silent for several seconds, the equivalent of a sigh from anyone else. "My point is, had Jornn not been killed he would still be a threat because so many were willing to follow him when he took over leadership. But even if Callan is central to the Damian Prophecy, he is no longer in a place where he can influence change."

"But he's a G'ortian," SEOH argued. "You're the one who finally convinced me to take the G'ortian power seriously.

Now you're dismissing it."

"No, I'm not." Rustaad continued in a calm voice. "As long as the G'ortians we've captured stay on the Sphere, we shouldn't have an issue here. If their powers transcended that Sphere, they would have been able to contact someone via telepathy by now, especially a Hy'bridt, but they haven't. The Hy'bridt who spoke at the Creativity House managed only to further your plan."

Settling back into his chair, SEOH asked, "How's that?"

"Becka is the youngest of the Creativity House, but she has been singled out as Callan's future mate since she's also G'ortian." Rustaad's lips slanted up a tiny degree, just enough to televise his pleasure at what he was about to share. "She felt it her duty to inform Callan, so she—"

SEOH started chuckling, seeing where this was going."—rushed to tell Callan," Rustaad finished.

"And we caught her, right?" SEOH added, enjoying the moment.

"Absolutely. We now have three G'ortians with Callan, V'ru and Becka. Plus Thylan is holding Becka captive and away from Callan to prevent their bonding."

"That's right. You said the Hy'bridt mentioned them bonding." SEOH studied on that. "I wonder if we can feed her to a croggle to keep her from Callan."

"That would be dangerous, SEOH. We've been fortunate to have no loss of TecKnati children when the MystiKs died on their own in the Sphere, but intentionally feeding Becka to a croggle would—"

"Constitute murder." SEOH waved him off. "I won't risk my youngest son." SEOH had Bernardo surrounded by guards and medical professionals twenty-four-seven, but his firstborn had died of asphyxiation in front of several people. He just couldn't trust that furkken treaty not to kill his prodigy.

Rustaad picked up where he had paused. "There have been reports of Kenja and Callan battling, so sending in a group of Uberon warriors is turning out better than we'd hoped. If she kills Callan, we don't risk losing a TecKnati child."

SEOH hadn't believed in any of this mumbo jumbo until his son died, but he acknowledged the risk now. He asked Rustaad,

“What about the other four G’ortians still at home?”

“They are all kept within their respective compounds and protected by heavy security, but my resources tell me none of those G’ortians have a desire to lead, nor are they being groomed for such. It appears that as long as we keep the powerful ones segregated in the Sphere until tomorrow night, we will eliminate the threat of MystiKs joining forces.”

Propping his elbows on the chair arms, SEOH steepled his fingers. “Any news on deciphering the prophecy?”

“Nothing new from our technicians working on it, but the Hy’bridt who spoke to Becka’s family confirmed the prophecy will be fulfilled when the red moon sets tomorrow.”

SEOH pushed an eyebrow up. “You told me our sun will set at the same moment the red moon sets in the Sphere. Did the Hy’bridt specify the location of the red moon referenced?”

“No, and we aren’t due to have a blood moon for another four years. That’s the closest we would come to a red moon here, which leads me to believe the Hy’bridt meant a red moon somewhere else. If we’re to give credence to their powers, we must assume she meant the Sphere’s moon even if she does not know the Sphere exists.”

“She couldn’t know about that,” SEOH argued, then leveled Rustaad with a don’t-go-there look to cut him off before he reminded SEOH, again, that the MystiKs supposedly had psychic perception or *visioning* powers as well. “Let’s move on to things that we know we can control. The laser grid must be ready to activate city wide tomorrow, but only after all MystiK leaders are inside the boundaries of our city. I don’t want any MystiK leader to become suspicious and remain outside the power grid.”

“They won’t turn back,” Rustaad said, planted as still as a statue in the middle of SEOH’s office. He rarely sat. Everything about him was contained, as if Rustaad held his body in constant readiness for any situation. “As long as the MystiKs continue to be distrustful of each other and paranoid that every other House is a threat to their power bases, they’ll be too busy watching each other to worry about us. I’m only concerned about the grid performing consistently across such a massive area. We haven’t tested as much—”

SEOH slapped a hand down on his desk. “The grid was tested successfully in the Sphere, based on the report from the last scout brought back.”

Patient to the point of being annoying, Rustaad blinked slowly in the face of SEOH’s anger, then said, “The scout said that Thylan had turned the grid sample up to eighty-percent to neutralize Callan’s power. The grid he created covers an area the size of a basketball court. Our grid is over twenty miles square. We can’t just run it up eighty percent the first time it’s powered across the city.”

“If our engineers say it’s safe, then it’s safe. I have faith in technology.”

“I do, too, SEOH, but you’ve used a skeleton crew of engineers to do this secretly. Every project designed and built as a prototype requires more beta testing than we’ve executed.”

SEOH rubbed his forehead and sat back, considering how much nicer life was going to be once he was the only ruler.

Rustaad made a valid point, but a miniature example of this laser grid had been tested in one of the cities with a majority population of MystiKs over TeKs. SEOH’s MystiK snitch in that city had helped carry out that test. Sure there was always a chance of a misfire with any new project, but the element of surprise was far more important than worry over one section of the grid not functioning properly.

He crossed his arms and reminded Rustaad, “Based on what our engineers determined, we need only sixty percent of the grid functioning to contain the power of the MystiK leaders.”

“True. As long as that sixty percent of the grid is in direct contact with the BIRG Con meeting hall.” Rustaad paused and touched his lips with a finger while in thought. He pulled his finger away before adding, “There is still a certain amount of gamble to all of this. I don’t like that we have no Plan B in place.”

Grunting his acknowledgment, SEOH lifted a hand and a hologram appeared at his left shoulder displaying a map of the ten cities left in North America. “Oh, I have Plan B.”

For the slightest moment, Rustaad’s eyebrows flinched with surprise before his indifferent mask slid back into place. “Would you care to elaborate, SEOH?”

"If the grid doesn't work, we send word to the past immediately to destroy all MystiK ancestors' eggs being stored in the female research center at the Byzantine Institutes across the world and order the K-Virus to be released."

Rustaad argued, "But you were going to wait until you were sure we had the MystiK power under control before unleashing the virus."

"Not anymore. This is Plan B. No need to wait once the MystiK population is reduced to a fragment of what they have now."

"That would be almost a month ahead of schedule. How would we know our people in the past have located the genetic ancestries for *both* of us?" Rustaad asked, his voice tight. "Plus, based on the schedule we set and assuming they're on track in the past, we would still lose a third of our TecKnati population by releasing the K-Virus too soon."

"Stop worrying. They were told to find the DNA link for both of us first. Nothing has changed with the orders we gave our people sent to the past. Unless we send another person back with new orders, our people will continue on track. But you wanted a Plan B, so there it is."

SEOH waited for Rustaad to ask what SEOH had told Phen before sending the TecKnati scout to the past days ago, but Rustaad's ruthless control exerted itself. His rigid posture relaxed only enough for SEOH to notice, and that was only because SEOH had spent years watching for those rare tells. Rustaad had been SEOH's right hand of justice for over ten years, the one person he trusted with many of his secrets.

Not all, but many.

Switching topics, SEOH asked, "Has Thylan gained the computer yet?"

"His last report indicated he would have it by tomorrow." Rustaad's unruffled demeanor had returned. "Thylan may surprise you yet, in a positive way."

"That'd be a welcome change after years of fixing his screw ups. Why couldn't the MystiK treaty have targeted Thylan instead of my oldest?"

"One of life's mysteries," Rustaad muttered. "Speaking of Thylan, he did mention something odd about those three intruders in the Sphere."

"What's that?"

"The traitor said the girl called Rayen claims to have no memory and that she only recently arrived at the Byzantine Institute in the past."

Shrugging, SEOH, said, "Why should that matter?"

"Because this Rayen also claims to have been hunted by a sentient beast." Rustaad's cool gaze studied SEOH. "There were no sentient beasts recorded during that period of history. The technology wasn't developed until after the K-Virus infected our country. With the exception of a few that have been de-programmed and reside in the zootech, no others should be roaming our land. Correct?"

"Yes. You're not one to be subtle, Rustaad. Make your point."

"If we have a sentient beast that has *not* been decommissioned, but is in fact active and traveling through time, the ANASKO board will turn on us."

"Of all people, I know that." SEOH held Rustaad's unwavering gaze. "If you're asking if I've got one on the loose, I'm insulted you think I'm reckless enough to risk my freedom, and life, by hiding or activating a sentient beast."

"I would never insinuate such, SEOH."

"Good, because that would put a cramp in our relationship."

SEOH's holographic assistant appeared, saying, "Vice Rustaad, you are wanted in R&D."

When Leesa disappeared, Rustaad gave a slight dip of his head as his way of saying goodbye, and left.

SEOH sat back and pulled up his online vault of private information no one else could access.

Rustaad thought SEOH had a rogue sentient beast, huh?

The board turning on him would be the least of his worries. Possessing sentient beasts or shielding knowledge of their existence could earn someone convicted of the crime a lifetime in prison.

Transmission from six security videos surfaced on a holographic screen that could be seen only from SEOH's side of the display. When he tapped keys on a holographic keyboard, one of the vid feeds doubled in size. Three sentient beasts growled and pawed the ground. A four-legged jungle cat prowled across one cage, then paused and morphed into a bird of prey that had a sickle-shaped beak.

Chuckling, SEOH pointed a finger and the screen disappeared.

Rustaad didn't think SEOH had a viable Plan B?

That was understandable since Rustaad had no idea that Plan B was to inject a body with the K-Virus and ship it into the past day after tomorrow, regardless of whether they found Rustaad's genetic origin or not. SEOH knew *his* had been located because the uncle he'd never liked just disappeared eight months ago, along with his entire family.

SEOH had sent his first TecKnati team back to the past with orders of locating his specific DNA lineage, separating out his mother's side that led to the uncle he hated and destroying that line.

SEOH hadn't told Rustaad any of that for the simple reason that Rustaad would have focused too much on his own survival and not on doing his job.

Rustaad's only living relative, a cousin, had died in an explosion at one of their test facilities. That left no specific indicator to insure Rustaad's ancestry had been located.

More important to SEOH had been insuring he did not lose a TecKnati engineer who had played a part in creating the ANASKO Empire to this point. Every leader of ANASKO since the onset of the K-Virus in their world had hand selected engineers from eight specific families.

SEOH had seen confirmation that his people in the past had located the ancestors of those families.

Plan B was definitely in place.

SEOH even had one more play to make.

Once the laser grid was activated in this city and these furkken MystiK leaders were out of SEOH's hair, he was transporting three sentient beasts to the Sphere and programming them to attack anything that was not TecKnati.

Chapter 18

I sat in a twelve-foot square metal room of the same building where the TecKnati had held Callan captive, but it didn't appear to be the actual space where they would have put Callan.

This room was too clean, sterile feeling and cold.

Thylan had brought me here and he now stomped back and forth in front of the dull silver table. I sat on the opposite side of the table, studying the laptop that stared back at me in total silence.

"Why isn't it powering up?" Thylan asked as he crossed in front of me for the fiftieth time.

"It takes concentration to make something electronic come on with power derived from a human." That sounded pretty good for being totally made up by someone with zero electronic knowledge. I was no technical whiz like Tony and knew nothing about this computer, but the flat screen monitors at the Byzantine Institute had seemed familiar so I wasn't completely clueless. I hoped.

On the other hand, the only real memory that my mind had given up had involved horses in the desert, not buildings and equipment.

"I suggest you start concentrating a lot harder or I'll have to motivate you." Thylan's words slid and shifted, viscous as thick slime.

"*Threatening* me interferes with my concentration." I moved my hand over the keys, ignoring him as best I could.

"It wasn't necessarily a threat. You might enjoy yourself."

I paused my hand and took a closer look at Thylan.

He hadn't stopped moving since he walked me into this

room. His eyes were bright, too bright. Everything about him said he was agitated and nervous, but in an intense way. His last words settled into my mind, warning me that Thylan might be mentally unstable.

My skin prickled with the way he leered at me. Thylan had more on his mind than just what I could do to make this computer operate. Did he intend to force himself on me?

The room and Thylan blurred, then all my senses sharpened.

I could hear his watch ticking with loud clicks. He shifted his stance, scuffing his boot heel over the gritty floor. It

sounded too loud to be natural. He smelled of hate and fear.

My skin heated from the inside out.

I warned him, "Don't underestimate me."

He turned rigid. A muscle jerked in his jaw. "You do *not* give me orders. The last girl who tried regretted it."

I didn't want to kill anyone here, but I wouldn't allow him to assault me. I warned softly, "If you touch me, *you* will be the one to regret it."

I heaved one breath after another. My body fed off the tension, preparing to fight.

Thylan unbuckled his belt.

Images on the buckle flickered between a triangle design and letters, then he started pulling the belt through the pocket it had been threaded into. "You're clearly not motivated, but I'm going to fix that."

Energy stabbed through me like a lightning bolt.

In my peripheral vision, the monitor flickered, but I kept my eyes on the predator in the room.

He whipped his belt out of the last loop with a snap.

I flinched.

Thylan smiled, pleased at my reaction.

My heart beat faster.

The monitor flashed bright, drawing my attention. I caught the flick of the belt being swung and put an arm up to protect my face. A sharp sting slashed across my arm.

Clearly, my power had no loyalty or it would rise to the surface and protect me.

Thylan raced around the table and grabbed for me.

I shoved him back, but he didn't fall. The belt flew over and over in a chaotic attack, biting my shoulder, then it popped my face.

Slamming a hand down on the keyboard, I pushed up and grabbed for the belt on the next swing, catching it before the whip slapped me again.

Light exploded from the computer.

It screamed at a high pitch. Out of instinct, I clamped down my mental shields, which thankfully muted the sound.

Scouts started yelling and running with their hands over their ears.

Thylan released the belt that I yanked away and tossed to the ground. He doubled over, cupping his ears and screaming, "*Shut it off*!" Blood trickled from his nose.

I grabbed the computer and slapped it shut. The thing kept screeching. That worked for me. It was incapacitating the TecKnati. I raced out of the room.

When I entered a cramped hallway, narrow strips of light shone a green glow on scouts fighting each other at the end.

That was the only way out I knew about.

But then it dawned on me that the scouts were actually jerking around, still holding their ears.

Not really fighting.

All at once, bodies flew backwards, hitting each other and the walls before they fell into piles. It was as if a giant arm had swiped across them.

Two figures rushed forward through the cleared space.

Not a giant arm, but one with powerful kinetics.

Callan stormed toward me. When he reached me, he grabbed me to him in a fierce hug with the screaming computer sandwiched between us. He cupped my face in two hands and pulled my head back so he could look at me.

Warm liquid trickled from where the belt had cut my cheek.

Callan growled, "I'm going to kill Thylan."

I was both glad to see him and wanting him gone from here. "We don't have time, Callan. I don't know how long this computer will keep making noise and they'll probably turn the grid on as soon as it stops."

Callan kissed my forehead and stepped back. "Go with Kaz. I'll be right behind you."

I grabbed his arm. "No. I'm not leaving you here again."

"Just go outside and give me a minute."

"Why?"

"I have to free another MystiK."

That's right. I forgot about the second one. "Hurry."

As Callan vanished through the hall, Kaz stepped into view and yelled over the sound blaring from the computer. "I was ordered to take you out of here even if I had to use my powers."

"I'm coming." I gave him a hand motion to get him moving. We ran past bodies of unconscious scouts. A few were groaning and shaking their heads against the torturous noise. I had a hard time feeling sympathy for them even if some might not have wanted to be here in the Sphere.

None had raised a hand to help the MystiKs.

Or to help Callan.

When we stepped outside, I searched around us. Dark was choking off the last hint of twilight. Scouts had fallen to the ground, gripping their heads. Some rolled around as if that would stop the noise.

I looked up in the sky and realized... "The moon is gone, Kaz." My gaze snapped to his face. "What happened with the wraiths?"

"They didn't come."

I searched his eyes for the truth. "Are you joking?"

"No, I'm not." Kaz sounded grim enough to be serious.

How could he be so unhappy? I was thrilled that Callan had survived. I wanted to run around shouting and dancing. Callan would not die.

And now he would be free from the TecKnatis, too. Where was he?

Callan shouted, "Get moving. I'm coming out."

I turned with a huge smile breaking on my face until I saw who Callan had gone back for. A young woman held his hand and looked up at him like he was her world.

The same way I would look at him.

Callan slowed only long enough to shout, "Why aren't you running? Let's go."

I suffered a rush of embarrassment I couldn't explain and

took off in the direction of the tortalones. Kaz caught up and fell into stride next to me.

Tossing a glance over my shoulder, I noticed that Callan was falling behind us because that girl was slower. And he was still holding her hand. Swinging my attention forward again, I asked, “Who is that, Kaz?”

“It’s not my—”

“Stop telling me it’s not your place.”

Kaz lowered his voice as we reached the edge of the forest. “He can hear every word you say. So can she.”

Heat blossomed in my cheeks and it wasn’t from my core energy. I was making a fool of myself. Callan had told me not to come back, but I’d thought that was for my safety.

Maybe I was just dense and missed the fact that he had been trying to tell me our time was over.

It didn’t matter. I would have still come back for him.

Fool that I was, I still cared.

In the forest, Kaz turned his hands palm out and a glow pulsed on the ground ahead of us or I’d have fallen over roots and downed trees. The computer under my arm continued to pretend it was some kind of siren.

We reached the tortalones first. Kaz walked over to the one he’d ridden here and put his hand on her shell. Nothing came out of the holes of his tortalone or the male I’d ridden.

Kaz frowned in my direction. “Turn that squawking thing off.”

I opened the laptop and colors flashed repeatedly. Holding my hand over it did nothing. I tapped keys. Still nothing.

Kaz stepped over to me, lifted his hand to shed light on the keyboard then he pressed a button and everything went silent.

I asked, “How did you do that?”

“I pushed the power button.”

When he returned to his tortalone, a head slowly came out followed by a long, snaking neck. Kaz whispered something and the head nudged him in a sweet way.

The female tortalone then swung her head over and bumped my tortalone’s shell. Another head emerged.

I could see the glow of Callan’s hands coming through the woods. He was still a ways back. I caught Kaz by the arm to gain his attention.

"What?"

"Don't snap at me."

He dragged his fingers through his hair. "I'm sorry. What?"

"Just tell me who she is. Please."

"Her name is Becka. She is the youngest of three daughters in the Creativity House."

"Thank you." That wasn't what I'd specifically been after, but the friction between us seemed to be dissipating so I pushed for a little more. "But who is she to Callan?"

"Not now."

At this point, Callan and Becka were approaching and Kaz was silent again. I stood there, watching the pair illuminated by the glow Callan was generating. He held branches out of her way and guided her carefully as if she were fragile.

Kaz took the laptop from me and slid it into the sling he'd once again strapped across his chest and back. Once he had the computer loaded, he pushed the thing around to his back. Then he shined light from his hands on the tortalone I'd ridden here and told Callan, "That one is yours."

I waited for Callan to hand Becka off to Kaz and ask me to ride with him.

But Callan lifted Becka up on his tortalone.

Shock rolled over me.

Callan was so busy getting her settled that I was invisible to him. Or was he ignoring me on purpose?

I stood there like an idiot with no clue what to say or do.

Kaz's light disappeared then his hands hooked around my waist and lifted me up on his tortalone before I could protest. I was not fragile. I could climb up on my own.

He jumped up behind me and grasped the mane with one hand, hooking his arm around my waist.

I started to tell him that was not necessary either but then I felt a bump on my mind.

Callan was paying attention after all.

My heart raced at the contact I'd missed so much, but I did not want to do this mind to mind. If he wanted to talk to me, he could do it in person and to my face. Plus, I wasn't sure I could hold back all the hurt banging around in my head if I opened my mind.

I told Kaz, "I'm ready."

He clicked with his tongue and the tortalone rose up on all four legs.

Callan said, "Be careful with—"

Kaz cut him off. "I've got, Rayen. You worry about your passenger."

Our tortalone flapped its wings rapidly.

"What's your tortalone doing, Kaz? I thought she needed enough area to run and take off."

He kept an arm tucked securely around my middle and when he spoke he was right next to my cheek. "It's more difficult to lift straight up, but she can do it. She knows it is important."

What had Gabby called Kaz? The turtle whisperer? That fit.

Why couldn't my heart beat for Kaz? He'd made it clear that he liked me and he had no obligations back home that mattered. We could enjoy the time we had left here.

But that wasn't how I was built. I had opened my heart to Callan and the stubborn organ didn't want to give him up.

Turning enough to look over to where Callan and Becka flew maybe fifty yards away, I could only see them because Callan continued to shine a soft glow from his hands.

He had his arms around each side of Becka, holding the mane of his tortalone.

The words came out before I realized I was speaking. "Why are his hands still glowing?"

"I sensed that Becka was afraid of flying on the tortalones when she first saw them. Callan is talking her through it and keeping enough light available that she doesn't feel lost in the darkness."

Who could feel lost with Callan's arms around her?

Maybe Becka was a friend and he was just protecting her as he would any defenseless female. He knew that I could handle myself in a fight where Becka looked ... delicate.

And pretty. I hadn't missed the fall of blond hair that hung like long strands of corn silk, or the smooth skin on her perfectly sculpted face.

She probably had fine hands that were soft, where mine

were rough from the gritty work of staying alive.

A wave of a dark emotion plowed through me. Jealousy. It dug deep and twisted my feelings into a warped animal that howled in pain. After a bit, the sound quieted and there was nothing left but me.

Alone. Just as I'd been when I woke up in that desert and just as I'd be when this last trip was over.

Kaz hugged me. "Stop feeling so sad. It's killing me."

I'd forgotten I was with an empath. "I'm not sad."

"And now you lie to me."

Kaz had been here for me when I needed his help to meet the TecKnati and he'd managed to get Callan out of the camp when I asked him. I would not weigh him down with my self-inflicted misery.

I swallowed my sinking pride and admitted, "I'm being silly, sitting here feeling like I've been rejected when Becka is just another young woman captured and sent here. Right?"

We flew in silence for a moment, the chilly wind whistling past my ears. I couldn't say that I was cold with Kaz's heat so close to my back.

His chest moved against my back with a deep breath. "When Callan's brother was killed, the Warrior House was in an uproar until Callan accepted that he had to take his brother's place. To do that, Callan will be expected to make an acceptable choice. Based on how things were left back at home, many Houses will be watching for an indication of Callan's decision by the BIRG Con."

Blood rushed too loud in my ears. "When is the BIRG Con?"

"Tomorrow. Becka is the G'ortian Callan's parents expect him to choose and Callan will not shirk his responsibility. Nor will he humiliate Becka. I have tried to warn you off him so you would not be hurt, but I was unsuccessful."

In other words, that was the woman Callan would spend the rest of his life with and I would not have even one more moment with him.

I blinked back tears. I would not cry, but it hurt worse than

any physical wound I'd suffered.

This one would never heal.

Chapter 19

Callan crushed his jaws together, watching a glow Kaz shined for a moment, illuminating Kaz and Rayen while they flew too far away for Callan's peac of mind. Then the glow extinquished. Had Kaz done that to hide any actions from Callan's view?

Was his arm still around Rayen. She was clearly no wilting female like Becka.

Callan was not being fair to compare Becka that way.

She'd been raised in a sheltered environment, the baby of the family. He wasn't sure how Rayen had been raised, but she had fighting skills and he had no doubt she could live off the land. Two completely different women. For example, Rayen must have ridden one of the tortalones here for there to be a pair of them waiting.

If that was the case, then Kaz had no reason to be wrapped around her for the ride back. Callan glanced over and now ground his teeth at not being able to observe the pair.

Becka's grip tightened on his arm, drawing his attention back to her. She'd slipped from side to side when they first lifted off and latched onto him in terror, so he'd been forced to wrap an arm around her and hold her against him.

But this wasn't the body he wanted to hold.

She had her long hair clamped in one hand, holding it to the side. Her hair was such a bright gold color it should glow. Any man would want her for his wife.

Any man but Callan.

If she had not been so terrified by the time they reached the tortalones, he would have handed her off to Kaz. But Kaz and one of Becka's older sisters had a falling out last year. Becka had tensed the minute she noticed Kaz and he hadn't been any more hospitable. He'd pointed out which tortalone belonged to Callan as Kaz's way of saying not to stick him with Becka.

"How will we escape this Sphere, Callan?"

Her words flew past him in the whipping air. He could pretend not to hear her, but that would be wrong on his part. "I told you before that I don't know. We haven't found a way back yet."

"This is your time to lead. They need you at the BIRG Con tomorrow."

"There's always someone else to lead." Taking over his brother's position was the least of his concerns.

Becka twisted to look at him over her shoulder. "The Damian Prophecy must be fulfilled."

"Then it may have to happen without me," he said only halfway listening.

"No, it can't."

He finally paid attention to her. "What are you talking about, Becka?"

"A Hy'bridt came to our House. She's precognitive and explained things about the prophecy she'd seen that included you."

"Did she see that I would be captured by the TeKs?"

"No," Becka admitted.

"Then she must not have gotten the entire picture in her visions."

Becka was shaking her head. "This Hy'bridt has never been wrong and she did say that MystiK children were at more risk than normal."

Astronomical understatement. "Did the leaders of your House tell mine what she said?"

"You know our leaders do not talk."

Callan didn't shield his bitterness. "And that is something they will regret when they walk into the BIRG Con tomorrow evening only to realize they have no future leaders ready to move up in the ranks."

Becka turned back to face forward.

Had he somehow insulted her? She had to realize that the future they both had expected was not going to happen. No one even knew the timing of the prophecy. Oh, sure, many had speculated that it was intended to happen at this BIRG Con, but that could have come from someone's wishful thinking that turned into rumor and eventually became a concrete belief.

The only thing Callan believed in right now was that his days were no longer numbered. At this point, his hours were numbered. He would do all in his power to protect the village and insure that Kaz and Jaxxson were ready to take over after the red moon set tomorrow.

Until then, Callan wanted only one thing for himself. Rayen. That shouldn't be too much to ask of the universe.

He looked at the back of Becka's head, feeling a twinge of guilt, but only for the sake of their families who were pushing them together. There was no chemistry between him and Becka, only responsibility. She was too subservient for her own good. Before tomorrow night, he would explain to her that if they both managed to get out of the Sphere, she deserved to choose the person who made her heart beat fast and someone she missed when he wasn't nearby.

For him, that person was Rayen. They had no future, but they had right now.

After what Becka had just gone through, Callan could give her until tomorrow morning to adjust before he explained how she should accept nothing less than someone who truly loved her.

When Callan's tortalone began descending, he realized it was following Kaz's and allowed the animal to continue.

Becka leaned right with the slant of the downward shift. She turned to look at him again. "The Hy'bridt knew much about the prophecy and she did say that I would have trouble finding you, but that I would find you."

Anyone could say that, but Callan kept his thought to himself.

Becka wasn't finished. "Our Hy'bridt said it was imperative that you know the details she shared about the prophecy."

"How did she expect you to tell me when we weren't going to see each other again until the BIRG Con ceremonies?"

"She said that we all must make decisions and it was up to me to decide if I would tell you in time or not."

Callan realized how she'd been captured. "Did your father take you to my father's House?"

"No. He refused. That's why I snuck away and went to find you and how they captured me."

She was here because of him. Callan closed his eyes, wishing the world would give him a break. He shook it off and opened his eyes, listening to the soft flap of large wings.

Becka turned her back to him again as the tortalone slowed to land with a walking trot across the open field leading up to their warded village.

Callan was glad to be back, but it was hard to rejoice when he was bringing Becka here and she'd been captured while trying to reach him.

As the tortalone stopped and dropped to the ground, Becka released her fall of hair. Her tense shoulders relaxed. She'd been terrified the whole ride, but she hadn't cried or carried on. He was thankful for that. It wasn't that he didn't like Becka. She was nice enough, but ... she wasn't a raven-haired beauty with eyes the color of a tropical sea.

He leaped off and reached up for Becka as she slid down. When he started her forward, she jerked around and said, "One more thing. You have a traitor amongst you. I heard the TecKnati talking about it."

"Did they mention a name or if the traitor was male or female?"

"No, but whoever it is believes they are leaving this place with the TecKnati. You must be very careful with what details you share about the prophecy."

"I will." But he was thinking more about finding the person who aided the enemy and making that person pay. Children had died and the traitor had opened the ward around the village to the TecKnati once already.

When Callan got Becka moving, they walked over to where Kaz and Rayen had dismounted from their tortalone. Kaz was shining a glow from his hands that illuminated a twenty-foot wide circle.

If Callan could get Kaz to just escort Becka to the village, then Callan could have a moment alone with Rayen. He was still seething over her injuries and wanted to hold her, to know she was definitely safe.

He tried once more to reach Kaz telepathically, thumping his mind.

Kaz finally answered, *What do you want, Callan?*

A little help with Becka for one thing.

Why? She is your intended. Not mine.

She's not my intended yet. I've made no formal claim and right now I want to see Rayen. Do me a favor and walk Becka to the village, okay? Callan had just pushed that thought back when he reached where Kaz and Rayen stood.

Kaz replied telepathically, *I'll try, but no promises.* Then Kaz spoke to Becka. "Let me show you where the village is."

She looked at him then at Callan, waiting on Callan to say something. When he didn't, she huffed a weary sigh. "Fine. Show me."

Rayen said nothing the whole time she observed the exchange. The minute Kaz and Becka started toward the village, she turned to follow them.

Callan sent a thump to her mind. She hadn't answered him the last several times, but there was no danger here that would prevent her from replying.

He felt the moment she lowered her shields, but she said nothing so he sent her, *I want to talk to you.*

She replied, *About what?*

Why are you not talking to me?

Rayen stopped walking and turned around, returning to him.

He opened one hand and allowed a soft light to glow.

This time Rayen spoke her words. "I understand that you didn't want me to come back, but I couldn't not come back and free you from the TecKnati. That's done. Now that you're free and the village will be safe again, I'll be gone tomorrow."

Callan hadn't wanted her here where she was in danger, but neither did he want her gone right now either. That was so messed up, but he blamed it on two days with no sleep.

She was here for one more night.

He wanted to share this time with her.

She'd seemed thrilled to see him when he returned for her at the TecKnati camp. Where had this indifference come from that he was sensing now?

He lifted a hand to touch her cheek and she stepped back so quickly the air turned brittle between them. "What's wrong, Rayen?"

"Kaz told me who Becka is. I have no right to be spending time with you"

Now he understood. Callan would have a talk with Kaz about keeping his mouth shut, because although there was truth among those words, that was not the entire truth. He'd deal with Kaz once he sorted this out with Rayen. "Becka and I share no commitment."

Rayen's gaze drifted away from his face and he feared she was drifting away from him as well.

When she finally looked back, her eyes hid emotions that churned and struggled to be released. She said, "I'm not supposed to be here or in the past with Tony and Gabby. I don't belong anywhere, but you do. And Becka does and all the other MystiKs do, but not me. Everyone should just pretend that I'm not here, because soon I won't be. You have a responsibility and it doesn't include me."

She turned and walked away, dragging chunks of his heart in her wake.

Chapter 20

I passed through the opening Kaz made in the warding and ignored the way his eyes searched my face for answers. When I put my hand out, he handed me the laptop, then I continued on.

He'd told on my last visit that I was stepping between Callan and Becka, interfering with the natural order of the MystiK world.

It took a while to sink in, but now I accepted the truth.

Callan was not mine to feel jealousy over, or this deep wrenching loss that I couldn't make stop. Yes, I accepted that, but it didn't mean I had to be happy about it.

When I reached the central area of the village, children were eating and arguing and running around.

Gabby and Jaxxson stood in the middle of the chaos, handing out food and keeping peace between Kenja's Uberon Warriors and the kids of Callan's village, some warriors and some from other Houses. With the exception of their missing leader, not one of the Uberons was over the age of thirteen, but they were a deadly lot that had to be kept under control.

Kenja strode into the scene, at least six feet tall and strongly muscled. She surveyed her warriors as one would look over an army at rest, then her gray-green eyes swept over to me.

We'd had our differences, one that had ended with me sending her flying across fifty feet to slam against a tree. She hadn't tested me since then. My power was hiding again, but the look on my face should warn her against crossing me now. I would do what was right and honorable, but I couldn't be held responsible for any reaction to someone's bad attitude.

While I'd watched her, Kenja crossed the village common area and stopped in front of me. "So? Were you successful or not?"

Callan chose that moment to walk up. "I'm back, if that's your question, Kenja."

"Then I have fulfilled my duty and will take my Uberons away from here."

"The TecKnati are going to attack."

Kenja's tone dismissed Callan and his claim. "I am not worried about my people. They are skilled in ways the TecKnati will never understand or be able to combat."

Tension sheared off Callan. I wasn't empathic like Kaz, at least I didn't think I was, but I could feel Callan's anger seeping out with every harsh breath.

He made a rough scoffing sound. "You know what? Fine. My duty is to my people, the ones who trust me to protect them. My people believe me when I tell them the TecKnati have created a laser grid that can neutralize your powers, and you witnessed it being used on me."

Kenja's eyes flared as if insulted, but even if she had wanted to speak up, Callan wasn't done.

"If you're so independent you can't see past your nose and realize that we're stronger as a unit, then take your Uberon children and lead them to their deaths. As they die, remind them what a powerful leader you are and how they should feel honored to die for you, because the TecKnati are coming for all of us. All. Of. Us. You step outside the ward around this village and you're on your own. I'm not risking *any* of my people to come after you, because *my* duty is to keep the MystiKs in this village safe."

Zilya and Etoi had just walked into the common area when Zilya noticed Callan and changed direction to join us.

Just great.

I found a tree to lean against so that I could stand to the side and not fall on my face from lack of sleep. I was growing more tired as the adrenaline rush subsided, too tired to interfere in whatever was going to play out between Kenja and Callan.

Kenja hadn't liked what Callan said. From the fire in her glare, I wondered if we were going to have a replay of their last battle. Unlike that time, when Callan pulled back to keep from harming Kenja, he might not be so considerate right now with her threatening to take children from this village.

He would do anything to protect these children, even fight Kenja for real this time.

Zilya stepped up between Kenja and Callan. "What's going on? As senior leader from the Governing House, I—"

"Shut up!" Kenja shouted and Callan snapped, "Stay out of this."

Zilya took a step back as if she'd been hit. Her mouth dropped open. Etoi gripped her spear in a tight fist, but wisely held her tongue for once.

Kenja turned to Callan and one side of her mouth curved up with a ... smile? Yes, Kenja found something humorous about all this tension. She told Callan, "I may have judged you too quickly. Your brother was groomed to be the next leader, but I would never have followed him into battle. I will stay and we will defend this pitiful village together, because that is what warriors do."

Callan let out a long breath and after a moment he extended his hand. Kenja gripped it, and they shook.

When she released him, she swung to face an audience of children and called out, "Silence."

Quiet fell over the rumble.

Kenja said, "Uberons, when you finish your meal, which will be in no more than six minutes, you will meet me at the west wall for our evening drills."

A resounding "Yes, Doyen!" shouted, then the kids returned to eating.

The term *doyen* bumped around in my mind until I brought up the meaning as one of respect.

Before Kenja walked away, she told Callan, "If the TecKnati bring the weapons they had the last time, your ward may not hold."

I heard a noise of someone moving up to the group and Becka appeared. "The TecKnati complained that equipment they used as weapons was taken out of the Sphere, but I heard Thylan speaking to his scouts about taking the grid components apart and turning it into a weapon to use against you ... if he didn't get the computer."

Everyone looked at me right then.

I had the computer tucked in one arm. "They can't have this. Thylan believes this computer is something called the Genera-Y computer, but it's not. Until he figures that out, he isn't going to risk destroying it, but the minute he realizes he's been played he *will* attack this village and destroy everything. He's insane."

Zilya found her voice. "Who is Thylan?"

Callan answered, "SEOH's son."

Zilya shook her head and sounded appalled. "Attacking us would be the height of insanity. If the TeKs could kill us outright, SEOH would have done that already. If they wipe out this village, an equal number of TecKnati children die at the same moment back home."

Gabby and Jaxxson were heading over as I told Zilya, "I understand the whole treaty thing and Thylan probably does, too, but I'm not sure he cares. I really don't think he's mentally sound."

Callan's gaze had strayed to mine while I spoke. I could feel him staring at the cut on my cheek and wanted nothing more than for him to come over and hold me. No matter that I could defend myself, the memory of Thylan's attack was an ugly blotch that lingered in my thoughts.

But then I caught Becka looking over at Callan with big round eyes, begging him to notice her.

Or was she looking past Callan to where Kaz had quietly joined us? No, that was a bad case of wishful thinking on my part. She and Kaz apparently disliked each other, because she'd obviously not wanted to ride his tortalone.

Etoi shouted, because that was her only volume, asking Becka, "Who are you?"

For all of Becka's delicateness, she whipped a haughty glare at Etoi. "I am Becka of the Creativity House and you are not to speak with that tone to anyone at my level."

Etoi surged forward, but Zilya touched her arm and that produced the same result as giving an order to a well-trained animal. Etoi glowered at Becka, but she backed down in the face of Becka's arched eyebrow daring her to speak.

Lifting her chin with regal arrogance, Zilya said, "I'm sorry you were captured, but you are welcome in our village. You are G'ortian, correct?"

"Yes, I am."

"I am Zilya of the Governing House. We have food and will find you somewhere to rest tonight."

"Thank you. I would like a bath as well."

A bath? To be honest, I'd like a bath, too, but since I didn't recall anything resembling the bathroom back at the

Institute, I was out of luck and so was Becka.

Kaz had refrained from speaking until now, but Callan must have spoken to Kaz telepathically because Kaz jerked around to Callan and shook his head.

Callan said nothing and moved no muscle. He just stared at Kaz until Kaz took a deep breath and called out, "Zilya." When Kaz had her attention, he said, "Once Becka bathes, let me know and I'll create a kamara for her."

Becka swung around and tossed a look from Kaz to Callan, then back to Kaz. "You? That's inappropriate."

Callan finally said, "Things are different here, Becka. We do whatever it takes to survive. I'm too drained to build one. Zilya's power is for the children first. We assume you'd like privacy. So it's either a kamara by Kaz or you sleep outdoors."

She looked as though Callan had suggested running naked through the village. "I must have a kamara."

Callan told Etoi, "Get with Kenja and fortify the perimeters." When she opened her mouth, he added, "Don't give me a reason to discipline you. I'm not in the mood. Push me, and you won't like the way it turns out."

Gabby came over to me and touched the cut on my cheek. "Are you okay?"

No, I wanted to find a corner to curl up in and sleep, but that wasn't happening yet.

Callan started toward me.

Kaz sent me a condemning look as if I was pulling Callan's strings.

I straightened from the tree and told Gabby, "I'm fine."

"No, you aren't," Callan said, contradicting me. "I saw a cut on your arm. Where else are you hurt?"

"Nowhere that you need to be concerned about."

"Rayen—"

"Don't." That was the only word I could get out between the painful thumping of my heart. That single word managed to cut off whatever Callan was about to say.

If he comforted me right now I'd forget about my resolve to do what was best for everyone.

Well, everyone but me.

Kaz stepped up, clearly trying to draw Callan's attention. "We need to talk about the warding."

Callan kept his eyes on me. "What's the problem?"

"The ward isn't going to hold. We have to redo it, but we need more power."

That broke my and Callan's staring match. He asked Kaz, "How do you know it's weak?"

"We had a dugurat get inside last night."

Gabby exclaimed, "You found some more dugurats?"

Only Gabby would miss the point about the weakness in the perimeter and focus on an animal that was similar to a dog, but with some peculiar hair and a brain that never grew beyond puppy stage.

Jaxxson put his hand on Gabby's shoulder, smiling at her. "*One* dugurat and I have her locked away for now because they can be aggressive when expecting."

"She's pregnant!" Gabby's smile took over her face. "We have more pupples coming."

"Yes."

I had to laugh at the thrill in Gabby's voice. If only we could all be that happy in the darkest of times.

Gabby's ponytails bounced with her animation over the news. "When can I see her?"

Her question interrupted something going on between Kaz and Callan, who were exchanging murderous looks again.

Breaking away from Callan, Kaz replied, "I have to inspect the ward with Callan then ... take care of Becka, but Jaxxson will be able to take you to the dugurat once he's free. Don't go without one of us, because she's not friendly at the moment."

Gabby waved the issue off. "That's fine. I want to take care of Rayen's injuries first anyhow."

Callan whipped around at the reminder that I'd been hurt.

I was done with all this tension and told Gabby, "I'm not

hurt that badly." At least not physically. "But I'll let you do your healing thing if you can find a place away from ... everyone." Before I turned my back on him, I reminded Callan, "V'ru needs to see you and know you're safe. He was deeply depressed while you were gone and wouldn't leave his bubble. Tony got him to come out and help us. I think V'ru is better, but he's still a scared child."

"I'm on my way to see him next." Callan held himself still, but I could tell he wanted to say more. If I had given him any encouragement, he would've, but I didn't.

"Follow me," Gabby walked away, turning her head toward Jaxxson, whose eyes were only for her. Gabby returned the look with a flirty one.

She waved at Jaxxson and nodded, another silent conversation. Two happy people in this place, but for how long? Gabby had to go home and so did Jaxxson. I wanted everyone to be able to go home.

In fact, I wanted to go home. I wanted to be somewhere that it mattered whether I lived or died.

The vision of riding across the desert at night with my father had replayed through my mind all day. Had he sent me to the shaman knowing I would be spun away to another time?

"Here we are," Gabby announced.

With being so lost in my thoughts, I hadn't realized where I was going. Six-foot-tall blue tortalone feathers strapped together formed the walls. They were attached to some rough posts, something the MystiKs had created by hand. I dropped my head back to look up. There was no roof.

Turnning to Gabby, I asked, "Whose place is this?"

"Jaxxson's healing hut."

"Does he care if we're in here?"

"No." To prove her words, she went about picking up bowls and a woven piece the size of two hands. Pointing at a slab of blue-ish gray wood supported by two tree stumps, she said, "Have a seat."

I did, and watched her carry a container over that she set in front of me. It was a scooped-out piece of wood, the size of three hand widths, with a carved exterior, and full of water, or whatever they had here that passed as water. "First, why don't you clean up?"

She handed me a rag and a chunk of something that smelled floral. I used it to scrub the dirt from my arms and face. Gabby kept herself busy while I washed under my shirt and anywhere I could get to without stripping off all my clothes since Jaxxson might walk in at any moment.

When I was done, Gabby came over carrying a stump. She positioned it across from me and plopped down on it. She opened her hand and I held my arm out for her. She carefully turned it, studying the gash on my arm. "It's not bleeding any more. What'd you get hit with?"

"Thylan thought he was going to force himself on me. When I told him it was a bad idea, he pulled off a wide belt and started hitting me with it."

Her lips scrunched up with a bitter twist. "What a coward." Then she placed her fingers over my cut and whispered a jumble of words.

Whatever she was doing soothed the aches everywhere I'd been hit. When she let go of me I could still see where the cut had been, but now it was a pink scar. I touched my cheek.

Gabby said, "That will be better tomorrow. I focused my attention on the ones that I sensed were more painful. You should be able to heal yourself."

"I can, or at least I did one time, but I needed Callan to show me how to direct my power. You've figured it out though. Thanks."

"You're welcome. I only wish you'd have made that slime ball pay."

"I did when my power finally showed up. It has a mind of its own sometimes. But when it did come through, I had my hand on the computer. My power turned the computer into a screeching animal. Thylan's ears and nose bled. I got him back." *The computer!* "Where are Tony and V'ru?"

"Tony said he was going to help V'ru with the prophecy and to do some geek therapy. I heard V'ru laughing a little while later. Jaxxson called it a miracle. He said no one had been able to get through to V'ru after Callan was gone."

"I'm sure Callan stopped by to see him."

"Let's forget about them and the computer for now," Gabby

suggested. "Let's talk about Mathias."

What could I tell her without breaking my word? "What about Mathias?"

"To begin with, he's dead."

I held my breath, trying to think of what to say. Who'd told her? Callan wouldn't have, but he and I—and now Kaz—were the only three who knew. Had Gabby told anyone, like Jaxxson? "Uhm..."

"Hold it, Rayen. I know you gave him your vow that you wouldn't tell and although I think we're close enough friends by now that you should have told me, I'm not holding you to the friend rule."

I let out my breath. "How'd you find out?"

"Mathias told me."

That was not what I thought she was going to say. I opened and closed my mouth, struggling to find any words that would be right in this situation. I gave up and said, "You're going to have to explain this to me."

She sat with her hands clasped between her knees and lifted the most serious look I'd ever seen on Gabby's face. "Mathias came to me. I can see him, but Jaxxson can't. He's telling me things." She waited for me to say something. When I didn't, she said, "You must see a ghost of someone, too. You've talked to someone at times that Tony and I couldn't see or hear."

True. My grumpy ghost. "Yes, I have an ancestor who shows up from time to time, but I have no control over when he appears. What about Mathias?"

"He appeared briefly before we left the Sphere the last time."

"Why didn't you tell me?"

"I tried, but we were a little busy if you recall."

Yes, we'd been rushing to make the transender so we could find a computer to bring back. "You're right. We haven't had time to talk about anything. So, uhm, do you know how Mathias died."

Gabby's eyes were shiny with unshed tears and her voice came out raw. "It was awful. The wraiths that took him came and found him when he was talking to me. I screwed up the first time I saw him on this trip and said his name." She swallowed. "I didn't make that mistake again."

"Again? How many times have you seen him?"

"Three. The first time was on our last trip and twice today. He's trying to tell me about the prophecy, but he gets dragged away. His spirit is weakening all the time. We have to save him. If he doesn't cross over soon, he'll be stuck forever with the wraiths and his spirit will remain a shadow of himself for eternity."

I grabbed Gabby's hands. "Tell me what we have to do and I'll do it."

"Mathias says we have to fulfill the prophecy."

Dropping her hands, I sat up and ran my hands over my face. Why couldn't the answers ever be easy? When I lowered my hands, I asked Gabby, "How are we going to fulfill the prophecy with Callan and the other MystiKs stuck in this place? I don't see any chance of them going home before that BIRG Con ceremony tomorrow and it sounds like all the prophecy has to happen there. I have no idea what to do. It's taking all everyone can manage to keep the MystiKs alive while they're here."

"Mathias said he's watched V'ru search archives when V'ru thought translating the prophecy might save Callan from the TecKnati. Mathias said there was a legend about an ancient analog computer that had been created by the first TecKnati sent back in time, which didn't make sense at first."

"Why?"

"Because the first computers we know of back home were built in the mid 1940s."

I did a quick calculation. "So the ancient analog one would have been created long before your time."

"Right. A TecKnati was sent back over two-thousand years ago as the first test for time-traveling, but he ended up much further in the past than expected. He landed in ancient Greece."

"How did he build a computer back then?"

"It wasn't one with components like the computers we have today or—" Gabby waved her hands around. "You know, not *today* as here in the Sphere, but current day in the past where I live." She took a breath and muttered, "That sounds so screwed up, but whatever."

Then she continued. "The story Mathias told me was that this TecKnati sent back in time picked a name from the era he landed in. He called himself Antonis because that was the day he arrived in Greece."

"You mean like the day of the week?"

"No, the Greeks actually named *every* day of the year back then and, based on that name, Antonis arrived on January 17. Weird, but whatever. Antonis was not thrilled to be sent back to primitive life in Greece, but it wasn't so bad once he fell in love with a woman called Lysandra who had unusual powers."

"Was she something like a MystiK?"

Gabby shrugged. "Maybe. That's how it sounded to me. Anyhow, when Lysandra showed her powers to Antonis, he told her about how the world was headed toward destruction in the future. She convinced him it was their duty to fix things so that technology and natural gifts could coexist in a balanced world, and she showed him how to live in peace with someone who had natural gifts. So this Antonis decided he would create a computer that would send him and her far into the future. He figured out what had gone wrong during his first time travel and believed he could travel forward in time until just before the K-Virus shows up that kills so much of the population in the future."

I wasn't the person to argue computers or technology, but even I knew that didn't make sense. "How was Antonis going to make this computer work two-thousand years ago with no power source?"

"That's what I asked. Mathias said the computer had to be a sentient machine, which meant that Lysandra would have to power it using her gifts."

Call me impatient, but I was exhausted from no sleep last night and dealing with Thylan, and I was having a hard time following Gabby. "How does all that have anything to do with figuring out the prophecy?"

"I'm getting there and jumping ahead is only going to confuse you."

I was already confused. "Please continue."

"One of the fetial came to Antonis and his wife to warn

them about—"

"A fee *what*?"

"I knew you were going to ask that." Gabby scratched her head in a spot between the multi-ponytails. "From what I gathered, a fetial was a group of twenty Roman officials, sort of a cross between priests and peacemakers. They worshipped the god Jupiter, but that was acceptable at that time. Anyhow, one of them was not quite like the others. His skin was darker than most Romans and he had the sharp cheekbones found on those from Eastern Asia. He had shamanic-like powers that the others didn't, so they tiptoed around this guy."

I held up my hand and counted as I pointed out what I knew. "Antonis was a TeK sent back two-thousand years ago to Greece. He met a MystiK woman name Lysandra and built a sentient computer. What did the fetial-shaman-priest warn Antonis about?"

Gabby gave me a look she usually saved for Tony. "I know your day probably sucked more than mine, but have a little patience Rayen. I'm trying to explain this."

I hadn't meant to sound so irritable. "Sorry. I'm just ready to fall over and I have a bad feeling this story isn't going to end well."

That would have been a great time for Gabby to smile and tell me to have a little faith, too, but she didn't and my sense of impending doom expanded, threatening to suck the air from the room.

I nodded at her. "Go on."

"It took Antonis almost two years to build his device out of cyprium, their name for copper. The shaman guy shows up one day and tells Antonis that rumors were flying about Antonis building a war device. Antonis denied it and this shaman guy believed him, but that didn't change the fact that Antonis stood to have his head cut off or die some other horrible way. He finished the device, but he and his wife had not been able to get it to work so when the shaman came to tell them they had to flee, Antonis packed up his wife and device. They joined the shaman, who smuggled all of them onboard a ship leaving port that day."

As if a switch had been thrown, Gabby stopped talking, sat

up straight and stared at nothing.

I whispered, "What's wrong?"

She held her index finger up for me to wait then nodded to herself and returned to me. "There's a problem with the ward. I have to go help Jaxxson and the others, but I want to tell you this first."

"Did you just talk to Jaxxson telepathically?"

She smiled and her cheeks pinked with embarrassment. "Yes."

"That's amazing." I smiled back at her, glad to have Gabby and Tony with me. I hated for them to be subjected to all this, but I couldn't ask for better friends right now.

Gabby got serious. "Listen up. This is pieced together from spoken history, myth and MystiK visions so I'm just going to tell you what Mathias told me. As the ship Antonis was on left the dock, his wife had a vision that they wouldn't survive the trip so while Antonis and his wife hid below deck, he tried once again to make the device work. Nothing happened until the shaman came down and told Antonis that he would change the course of the world, but not the way Antonis thought."

That sounded like the shaman I'd spoken to in the past who made no sense. Why couldn't people just say what they meant? But I kept my thoughts to myself, letting Gabby continue.

"Antonis ignored the Shaman, but his wife suggested combining their power for the device. The details get a little vague at that point, but someone on the Greek island of Antikythera saw the water spinning up around the ship, then an explosion of light and the ship sank. That sunken ship was discovered in the early 1900s with copper gears and engineered parts that has since been called the Antikythera computer."

My mouth fell open. "How is that any help?"

"I had the same reaction, but Mathias said the point is that it's believed they overloaded the power and the device blew a hole in the ship instead of activating the time travel."

Gabby stood up, floated a moment. The muscles in her face showed the strain as she came back down to the ground.

"You figured out the levitating?"

"Jaxxson thinks I did, but Mathias actually showed me how to get control of my power."

"You didn't tell Jaxxson about seeing Mathias?"

Gabby hit me with a sharp stare. "No, just as you didn't tell me about Mathias. I gave my word."

Point taken. "Is that all you have to tell me about the prophecy, because I'm still confused."

"No, but I have to hurry. I can tell Jaxxson is getting anxious waiting on me." Before I could ask how she knew that, Gabby finished explaining. "The prophecy supposedly originated with that shaman named Damianus who received the words in a vision and told the prophecy to Jupiter before leaving on the ship. Jupiter has since passed it on to others through visions. Mathias is convinced we need a sentient computer with MystiK power sources to fulfill the prophecy and once that happens the MystiKs will be sent home."

I jumped to my feet. "Gabby, there's no way to bring the real computer we travel through here and this one—" I held up the laptop. "—wouldn't work today. It *isn't* sentient and all I managed to do was shove so much power into it that I almost destroyed it."

She swatted loose hairs out of her eyes, a motion more about frustration than her hair being a problem. Gabby's voice was thick with emotion. "If we don't figure this out, Mathias will never cross over. But that's not why he's coming to tell me all this. Mathias continues to lead this village even from death. He said if the prophecy is not fulfilled by the time the red moon sets tomorrow, everyone still on the Sphere will die."

Chapter 21

"I only asked you to help with Becka," Callan said, hacking at the vines that had grown in the two days he'd been gone. They needed to keep a path inside the ward cleared for the warriors to move quickly between security points.

And for the children in case they had to run for their lives.

Kaz retorted, "I did help. I walked her through the ward. That should be enough."

Why did he sound so surly? "I'm not asking that much.""Yes, you are, Callan. You want me to handle Becka completely while she's here."

"What's your problem with her? You told me you and her sister had an issue, not that you and Becka did. Can't you two let whatever happened back home go while we're in here?"

Kaz grumbled, "That doesn't matter. Becka is not *my* responsibility. I know my duty and she isn't part of it."

Meaning Callan was shirking his duty? When had he not given his all for everyone here and back home? What else did they want from him?

"She's not—" Callan stopped before the whole village heard them and lowered his voice. "She's not *my* duty either."

"What of the betrothal?"

"There isn't going to be one."

"Because once you're betrothed, you have to—" Kaz caught himself. "What did you say?"

Callan raked his hand through his still-damp hair. He'd visited V'ru then swung by to wash off in a trough of water fed from a spring they'd magically tapped when they created this village. "I knew my mother was planning with Becka's, but my mother has been so depressed since Jornn's death that I didn't have the heart to say anything. Right before I was captured, I told my father I didn't see this as a wise union. I told him I didn't want it."

"Why not?""Becka gets on my nerves."

"What's wrong with her?"

Callan cut his eyes at Kaz's sharp tone, but he tried to explain. "She's too ... "

"Too what, Callan?"

"Give me a minute. I'm trying to tell you."

"Fine." Kaz cursed under his breath.

"She's too neat and tidy and looking for someone to be the perfect husband. I'm never going to be that. She's too proper."

"More like she's too perfect," Kaz murmured.

"What'd you say?"

"I said you're being overly picky. She's a nice girl. You should be glad to end up with one that is pleasant and pretty."

"She's boring."

Kaz turned on him. "She is not."

Callan finally grasped something that was going on with Kaz and poked at him. "She's not even that pretty."

"Are you blind?"

"She talks too much."

"Because she has something to say," Kaz argued, shoulders up and defensive.

Callan crossed his arms and leaned back. "If that's so, why don't *you* date her?"

Kaz snapped his lips shut and stalked off.

Oh, no, he was not getting off that easily after busting constantly on Callan. After catching up to Kaz and jumping ahead to block his path, Callan said, "I thought you didn't like her either."

"I never said that."

"Then what *is* the deal between you two?"

Kaz inhaled long and slow then let out the breath. "I wanted to date the middle sister in her family. She had a reputation of being wild, probably because she wasn't expected to marry the head of a House. All I'd heard about Becka was that as the baby, their father doted on her and treated her like a princess. I took that to mean she was a brat. When my mother visited friends in their city, I met Becka's sister at a party and asked her out. That was a mistake." Kaz grabbed a dangling limb and yanked it out of the way with more force than was necessary.

"What went wrong?"

"Her sister told me she would never date a half-bred warrior, but if I wanted to mess around she'd meet me in secret as long as I promised to never tell anyone." A sound of disgust came from deep in his throat. "She acted as if she was being magnanimous to make me her dirty little secret."

Now Callan felt bad for pawning Becka off on Kaz. "That was cold."

"Unfortunately, I was not as mature a year ago and told her if I was looking for someone to breed with it wouldn't be the useless middle daughter of the Creativity House."

Cringing, Callan asked, "How'd that go over?"

"About as good as you'd expect. I was banned from the Creativity House permanently."

"Sorry about pushing Becka off on you. I didn't know you despised them so much."

Kaz was silent a moment then he lifted sad eyes. "I don't despise Becka. I saw her for the first time as I was being thrown out of their House. She tried to stop her father's men from tossing me down twelve stone steps. When they ignored her and did it anyhow, she came down to see if I was okay. I was seeing stars. By the time I could speak and my eyes focused, her father's men were escorting her back inside."

"Then I don't understand why you're avoiding her."

"Becka didn't know what I'd done to provoke her sister and end up thrown out, but I'm sure she's been informed since then that I'm the closest thing to a demon that she will ever meet."

Callan had found little to smile over, but he grinned now.

Kaz lifted an eyebrow. "I will have to reconsider my basis for choosing friends if you find my misery amusing."

That brought a chuckle from Callan and it felt good to laugh. "I do find this humorous, but not for the reason you think. None of Becka's family is here."

"For that I'm grateful, but what's your point?"

"I'm not interested in her. When we finish with the ward, go spend time with her. If you have to, tell her I ordered you to watch over her."

Kaz's eyes lightened at the notion. "She may still shove me away anyhow."

"If that happens, then you aren't as good as your reputation, Kaz."

"I'm better than that." Kaz got a wicked gleam in his eyes then frowned. "What about Rayen?"

"You mean what about how bad you messed it up for me with Rayen?"

"She can't go home with you, Callan."

"I know all the reasons she's wrong for me." He studied the ground.

"Don't misunderstand me. I don't care that Rayen is C'raydonian, but if we ever figure a way out of here, you two can't travel to our world or to the past together. I just ... don't want to watch your heart get ripped to pieces over something you can't change."

It was too late for that.

Callan tried to explain what he'd figured out while he was in the TecKnati camp. "I've always accepted my responsibilities, never backing away. I stepped in when Jornn was killed even though I've never wanted to lead all the Houses, and still don't. I tried to make Rayen stay in the past, but she came back and I'd be lying if I said I wasn't thrilled to see her." Callan searched Kaz's face for judgment, but there was none, so he told him, "I've done everything I had to do and by this time tomorrow I'll probably be dead unless by some miracle we find a way home."

Kaz stopped walking and his eyes filled with disappointment. "I'm not much of a friend. With all that's happened, I'd forgotten you still face turning eighteen in this place. Rayen asked me about the wraiths when you were freeing Becka from the TeK camp. I didn't have time to explain so she thinks you *survived* the wraiths. You have to tell her the truth, that your BIRG Day is tomorrow."

"I'll think about it." Callan didn't want her to come back to him out of pity, but because she wanted to be with him.

It had been a long time since he'd felt wanted instead of needed and he longed for that from Rayen.

He had no future to look forward to, but there was still hope for the rest of this village and his duty would always come first.

Thylan and his TecKnati scouts were no doubt planning an attack if not already heading this way.

Rather than address new questions cropping up in Kaz's face, Callan said, "Show me the weak spot in the ward. We need to figure out how to reinforce it by ourselves."

"You, Jaxxson and I don't have the power required to strengthen the ward."

"Jaxxson is bringing Gabby to meet us. We can't risk anyone else helping until we find out who the traitor is, because he or she will leave a spot in the ward that we won't know about until it's too late."

Kaz stopped close to the invisible wall protecting the village and lifted his hand until the ward hummed softly. "Any idea who is contacting the TecKnati?"

"No." Callan lifted his hands to feel the energy from the ward. The humming grew stronger as he neared it, energy swirling in preparation of parting to allow him to pass through. When he stepped back, Callan looked around, considering the entire compound. The ward had been created so that it was a hundred yards from the closest structure.

He took in the area around him. "I have an idea of how to flush out our traitor once we restructure the ward."

Kaz's mouth fell open. "Rebuild the ward? You have to be joking. We'll be lucky to just strengthen the one we have."

"That's not what I'm thinking about doing."

Dropping his chin to meet Callan's gaze, Kaz's eyebrows cinched together with curiosity. "I don't understand."

"You will when I show you how we can catch the traitor."

Chapter 22

I didn't want to sit around Jaxxson's hut being miserable alone, so I went searching for Tony and V'ru. Those two were our best hope at figuring out what to do with this computer and the prophecy.

At V'ru's kamara, I lifted my hand and stalled it in mid air when I heard V'ru shout, "Yes! I win."

Tony's deep voice chuckled. "You would be a legendary gamer in my time."

What had happened to the mouthy Jersey boy I'd met only days ago? It felt like eons since I'd first walked into the Byzantine Institute.

"Would you like to enter, Rayen?" V'ru called out.

Lifting an eyebrow at him that V'ru couldn't see—or could he?—I answered, "Yes."

"Put your hand on the exterior."

I did and the next thing I knew I was standing inside his bubble. From the outside, it appeared the size of the room I had in the girls' dorm back at school, but inside made a liar of the exterior. "How is it that your kamara is so much larger on the inside than it is on the outside?"

V'ru and Tony sat cross-legged three strides from me with a holographic screen hovering between them displaying some game. V'ru tilted his skinny chin up. "Can you comprehend multivariable calculus?"

"No. Never heard of it."

"Then explaining the interior of this kamara would be impossible with your limited intellect."

Just when I think I'm going to like this kid he spits out an insult that I can't even counter.

Tony's failed attempt at hiding his snort only annoyed me more. Pinning a gaze in his direction, I said, "When you finish enjoying yourself at my expense, let me know because you two can use all that intellect you're so proud of to solve our problem."

Coughing and clearing his throat to wipe away his humor, Tony said, "Sit down and tell us what you need."

I squatted down and debated on sitting. That was only one step from stretching out on this cushy floor that looked like the surface of a cloud.

My body cried to sink into it, but I persevered and ended up cross-legged, too. "We have to figure out the prophecy and make that computer work."

"What have you been smokin', Xena?" Tony clearly thought I was out of my mind.

V'ru scratched between his eyebrows for a moment then explained, "I have spent many hours researching the prophecy. I know more than anyone here and *I* am not able to decipher all the meanings behind the words."

That didn't mean someone else couldn't even if V'ru might find that unimaginable. "We have to search until we find answers."

Tony watched me with a little more concern. "What's the computer have to do with anything?"

"The prophecy came from a shaman named Damianus in Greece two thousand years ago. Isn't that correct, V'ru?"

"That was the belief. Damianus was a fetial."

"But he was possibly a shaman, too, right?"

V'ru eyed me suspiciously and explained, "Damianus appeared physically different from other Greeks. He was thought to have come from what was later known as Siberia on the Asian continent."

I'd meant to ask Gabby about Greece, but we ran out of time. "Is any of that near Albuquerque, Tony?"

"Uh, no. Asia and North America are separated by an ocean."

V'ru waited patiently then continued. "During the twenty-first century, a discovery about North American Indians was made based on the oldest human genome possessed at that time, which supports a theory that a major number of North American Indians originated in the same area as Damianus, so that does support the idea that Damianus could have been a shaman."

I took that information and turned it around in my mind. "I met some men in Albuquerque this morning before we left. I was told they are Native Americans. I think at least one is Navajo. Are you saying they came from another continent, V'ru?"

V'ru sighed and I knew it had to be in direct relation to the confusion that was inhabiting my face. "I cannot share what came to light years later after the discoveries made in Tony's time, but to put all of this in simple terms, the genetic makeup of North American Indians originated in the Siberian region and they were believed to have crossed the Bering Sea over a land bridge that later disappeared."

I wondered if Takoda knew about this.

"Regarding Damianus," V'ru said, getting us back to the root problem. "There is no way to absolutely confirm the history tied to the prophecy as it was supplied by verbal and written word plus visions, but Damianus supposedly shared the prophecy only with Jupiter who then passed it to worthy record keepers through visions and dreams."

Tony's eyebrows crawled up his forehead at that. "As in the mythological god Jupiter?"

V'ru nodded solemnly.

"How'd we end up with it called the Damian Prophecy, V'ru Man?"

"Over time, names and terms shorten or morph." V'ru lifted his shoulders. "As centuries passed, the Damianus name in society shortened to Damian. Someone interpreting a vision or dream was susceptible to altering the name to one that was current or familiar."

When V'ru spoke with such authority and knowledge, it was easy to forget that he was only eleven, but the return of his confidence was a good sign that he was feeling better.

I hoped.

He lashed a suspicious look in my direction. "How do you know so much about those details?"

How did I explain this without giving away where Gabby got her information? Then it dawned on me that I was an unknown to V'ru so I should be able to manufacture my own truths. "I speak to those who have crossed to the other side."

For the first time since meeting the kid, V'ru's eyes widened and he appeared impressed.

Tony's widened, too, but I think it might have been apprehension. "Is that what happens when it looks like you're talking to yourself, Xena?"

The old ghost hadn't been the one to tell me the information I'd gotten from Gabby, but he *had* shared parts of the prophecy so I wasn't lying when I answered, "Yes."

"What can you tell us?" V'ru asked, completely convinced that I had a direct line to information since I knew about Damianus.

That was the problem.

I had all kinds of information from Gabby and even from my ghost, plus references to the prophecy mentioned by the shaman back in Albuquerque. "I'll tell you what I know then we all have to figure this out. One person can't do this alone. If they could, you'd have come up with the answers by now, V'ru."

The kid squared his little shoulders, pride coloring his face.

But it was true. If anyone could have sorted out this puzzle by now, he would have and the fact that he hadn't was evidence of just how much trouble we were all in.

But I was not going to tell this child that the lives of everyone on this Sphere depended on solving the prophecy. He carried enough weight on those slender shoulders as it was. Tony had been right to bark at everyone over how they'd forgotten to treat V'ru as an eleven year old.

He was brilliant and certainly special, but at the core he was still a child who had been through enough.

I explained everything I'd learned from Gabby. When I finished, I asked, "Do you have a way of displaying the prophecy so we can see what we've figure out and what's still missing?"

"Of course."

While I rolled my eyes at the superiority in his tone, V'ru

moved his hands in the air and the hologram that he and Tony had been playing a game on disappeared. In its place was something similar to the white board that Mr. Suarez had written on back at school.

Guilt pinched me hard at the reminder that every minute here was putting Tony in more trouble back home. And Gabby.

Me, too, but nothing in the past mattered to me since that wasn't my world. If I ended up there when this was all done, I faced a life where I might be sent away for good and never see my only two friends in that world again.

When V'ru sat back, the prophecy appeared on the holographic screen.

The future is in the past
One will seek and all will forfeit

When three become one
The End has begun

The gateway will open
A path will close

A friend enters as enemy
An enemy leaves as friend

Day of birth as Red Moon rises
Night of end when last Moon sets

Three must unite
For the scales to right

The last will lead when others cede
All turn to the outcast

The past speaks to alter the present
A bond of two will set us free

Tony ran a hand over the stubby hair on his head. "I don't understand how someone two thousand years ago wrote that and knew something would happen now."

His lack of belief was an obstacle we didn't need. If Tony wasn't totally committed to this, he wouldn't be much help.

I suggested, "You didn't understand how we could travel through a computer to land here either, Tony. Or how I could use only a power inside me to burn a croggle inside out. Or how V'ru makes a holographic screen appear in thin air."

Pushing his bottom lip up hard against the top one, Tony studied the hologram then said, "You're right, Xena. Let's get busy figuring this out."

V'ru pointed a finger at the prophecy and my name appeared in brackets at the end of the line *One will seek and all will forfeit*."

"Wait a minute," I complained. I hated that part about *all would forfeit*.

Tony defended V'ru. "He's right. You're the only one looking for answers, because you don't have your memory."

Blowing out a puff of air, I said, "Okay. What else?"

V'ru lifted his finger again. "Prophecy" appeared at the end of *The future is in the past*.

That made sense in a strange way. The prophecy was telling us that we had to understand the past to figure out the future.

I ran down the list and told V'ru, "Put Callan's name next to *The last will lead when others cede*."

Nodding and smiling, V'ru made that addition.

Tony suggested, "Put Rayen's ghost next to *The past speaks to alter the present*."

Technically, that wasn't correct, but I couldn't tell them words from the past should be attributed to Mathias. On the other hand, my ghost *had* mentioned parts of the prophecy. When I'd met with the shaman this morning, I'd thought the outcast was me, but I didn't want this to be about me since the prophecy belonged to the MystiKs so I didn't suggest adding my name again.

But that brought up a question that had been nagging me.

Why would my ancestors know anything about this prophecy?

No ghost appeared with an answer, so it would just have to continue nagging me.

When V'ru added *traitor, Tony* and *three powers,* I reviewed the hologram:

The future is in the past [Prophecy]
One will seek and all will forfeit [Rayen]

When three become one
The End has begun

The gateway will open
A path will close

A friend enters as enemy [traitor]
An enemy leaves as friend [Tony]

Day of birth as Red Moon rises
Night of end when last Moon sets

Three must unite [three powers]
For the scales to right

The last will lead when others cede [Callan]
All turn to the outcast

The past speaks to alter the present [Rayen's ghost]
A bond of two will set us free

"I still don't get why this has to be figured out by tomorrow," Tony mused, studying the hologram.

"Oh!" V'ru lifted his finger and Callan's name appeared at the end of both "Day of Birth when Red Moon rises" and "Night of end when last Moon sets."

I gave V'ru an understanding smile, happy that Callan had been spared from the wraiths, but V'ru was wrong. "If it's tomorrow, then that can't be Callan because his birthday is today."

V'ru angled his head, a small line forming across his forehead with the frown. "No. He turns eighteen tomorrow."

"But Kaz said it was today."

V'ru laughed. "It's a joke in Callan's House that Kaz has gotten Callan's birthday wrong for the past six years."

Air backed up in my lungs as I mentally rewound the conversation with Kaz outside the TecKnati camp when we were escaping.

I'd asked, "What happened with the wraiths?"

Kaz had answered, "They didn't come."

That was because they would come tomorrow for Callan.

I forced the anxiety behind a calm front and told V'ru, "There is nothing Callan wants more than to take all of you home. If that part of the prophecy does relate to Callan's birthday, then let's surprise him by figuring this out by tomorrow."

V'ru came alive with hope. "We could ... we could go home?"

Mathias had told Gabby that. If that wasn't correct, this child didn't need to know the only other possibility. "That's right."

Tony's expression darkened, which I understood. He thought I was giving V'ru false hope, but I wouldn't be able to explain what was going on until I had Tony away from V'ru.

And right now I needed both of them working on this.

I pointed at the computer. "That is key to all of this, Tony."

He reached for the laptop and pulled it over to him. "I can't make any promises, because I'm not going to paint fake rainbows." He paused to slam me with a judgmental gaze. "But I'll see what we can do."

"Thank you and I'll explain more later." I emphasized later, hoping Tony would stop condemning me with every glance my way and give me a chance to explain.

He dipped his head in a short nod.

I'd been given a reprieve for now.

Standing up, I asked V'ru, "Would you please put me outside?"

"Are you coming back?"

The apprehension in his voice twisted my heart. "Yes, but not right away. I need to talk to someone else first. Send for me if you need me, okay?"

V'ru nodded and waved a hand.

I was standing outside in the cold again. How did this place go from suffocating heat to bone-chilling cold so easily?

Probably an extra torture treat from SEOH.

I wanted to find that man and make him pay for what he'd done to these MystiKs, but that wasn't my main concern at the moment.

Of all the people I worried about right now, Callan topped that list, which was saying something since I would put my life on the line for Gabby or Tony.

I had to return them to the school before the red moon set in this Sphere tomorrow, but Callan and all the MystiKs also had to be safe before I left.

Less than a day from now everything would change forever.

I had one last day with Callan and I couldn't stand the crushing pain of spending it away from him. Every second we'd been apart was killing me.

But Becka was here and Kaz claimed she was part of Callan's future. When Callan had tried to talk to me once we'd arrived at the village, I'd thought he was going to tell me that he didn't care for Becka. That he'd sent her with Kaz so he could be with me.

Then I'd chastised myself for imagining what I wanted to hear. I'd been too angry and hurt to listen. *Had* he been trying to tell me goodbye or that he still wanted to be with me?

I should have given him a chance to speak his mind.

There would never be another person who meant as much as him to me. I knew that with ever fiber of my being even without knowing any more than I did about my past. I couldn't get back to my home and I couldn't control my future.

All I had was right now.

Pointing my feet toward the glowing common area, I took a step toward what I wanted.

Callan.

Chapter 23

"It doesn't work that way here, Becka," Callan said for the third time while he stood in the village common area. Or was it the thirtieth time? Darkness had fallen long ago and he did not want to spend his last night dealing with Becka.

What did Kaz see in this girl?

She was high maintenance on top of being too contained to the point every move seemed thought out with a plan in mind.

Kaz had called her too perfect.

Callan called her a pain in the—

"Regardless of where I am, I can not allow a male to create my kamara unless he is my *intended*," she argued on and tossed her hair over her shoulder. Again.

Did she have some affliction that caused her to constantly sling that mane around?

He held his patience by a thread that threatened to snap any second. Hadn't he instructed Kaz to build this kamara? Where was he? "You've got it wrong, Becka. It is not acceptable for you to *share* a male's kamara unless you're committed to each other."

"My point exactly. I should be sharing yours."

Callan bit down to keep from shouting that he didn't want her within a solar system of his kamara. He lowered his voice. "We have no commitment and we have not bonded. Sharing a kamara requires one of those."

"Not necessarily, because we could share an kamara *then* bond."

She would argue with an empty room. Bonding was the last thing on his mind.

He took a breath, admitting to himself that wasn't entirely true. He'd been thinking about bonding since returning from the TecKnati camp, but it had nothing to do with Becka.

Zilya and Etoi drew his attention to where they huddled on the far side of the common area, whispering as they watched. Were those two joined at the hip? At least the children were all bedded down. Neelah, her strawberry-colored cornrows bouncing with each step she took, carried a bowl of fruit as she crossed the clearing. She paused to glare at Etoi then moved on.

Callan had to get Becka settled and out of his hair pronto. "Where's Kaz?"

Becka waved her hand in the direction of Zilya and Etoi. "Last I saw of him, he was a little bit that way."

A little bit that way? Becka would be of no use outside the village or searching for anyone. She might end up lost *inside* the village.

Sighing, Callan said, "Let's go see what he's done."

Becka let out an undignified noise.

He took her gently by the arm to get her moving. When he reached the other side, he slowed long enough to ask Zilya, "What time does Kenja have you and Etoi on guard duty tonight?"

Fury rolled through Zilya's eyes. "You will not bully me into that again. We have been on our feet all day. Must I remind you that I am of the Governing House and abusing one of my standing is punishable by MystiK law? Continue to harass me and you will be brought before our leaders when we return. You have others to place on guard duty."

Was that last shot directed at Becka?

Or maybe Rayen.

Callan was not going to ask Rayen to do anything else for him or this village. If he asked her for anything, it would be to take down the walls she'd thrown up the minute she'd encountered Becka. Callan would have explained their convoluted situation, but Rayen hadn't given him the chance once Kaz had shared his misinformation. She'd just taken what she'd heard and shown no consideration for Callan's side of all this.

Was it so easy for her to cut ties and walk away?

For the first time, he questioned if the partial bond that had started between them before she left was still in place or had her change of heart severed it?

"I take it your silence means you agree, Callan," Zilya proclaimed.

Kenja came striding into the common area just as Zilya made that announcement.

Callan's jaw couldn't clamp any tighter. "If ignorance is bliss, the Governing House must be in a constant state of euphoria with leaders like you."

Zilya's faced warped with rage.

Speaking in a clear and calm voice, Kenja interjected, "Fear not, Governing House, because the Uberons protect this village tonight."

It took a moment for Zilya to regain her composure even as her attack dog Etoi made threatening noises that Callan shut down with one look of warning. He'd lost all desire to deal with either of these two who set themselves above everyone else.

Gaining height by pulling her chin up, Zilya gave Callan a snide look. "See? *Some* MystiK warriors understand how the hierarchy functions."

What a fool. Callan had caught the flicker of threat in Kenja's voice that had obviously flown right over Zilya's head. Becka watched the entire scene with a curious slant of her eyebrows, but kept her opinions to herself.

One blessing.

But allowing Zilya and Etoi to get away with shirking their duties was not fair to the rest of the village. He told Zilya, "We are fortunate to join forces with Kenja and her Uberons, but they are not expected to bear the entire burden for protecting this village. Find your rest, but be prepared to take your place on the security schedule when I call for you or you'll find yourself sleeping *outside* this village."

The dual gasp of Zilya and Etoi confirmed that he'd finally gotten through to the petulant pair.

When Zilya spun to leave, Kenja added, "And you should prepare as well to face reprisal from the report I shall make upon our return."

Zilya turned back. Her eyes would have burned a hole in Kenja if Zilya had possessed that gift. She pointed a finger at Kenja. "You dare to threaten me?"

Kenja shrugged. "Threaten? Telling the truth has never been deemed a threat, unless you see it as such." Then she put steel in her voice. "On the other hand, I find your tone and attitude offensive, but I will allow the insolence to pass this time. Cross me again and I will not be as understanding, and you do not possess Rayen's powers. Any battle between you and I would be over swiftly."

Becka was tapping her foot and making impatient noises that were barely audible, but Callan heard them. *Grant me the patience to survive the women in my life.*

Zilya surprised him by silently turning and walking away.

Until now, he wasn't sure she'd possessed enough survival instinct to recognize a more powerful adversary. Kenja was just as deadly as she projected.

Having witnessed the whole exchange, Becka shook her head. "Zilya should be removed from office. I'm a G'ortian, which puts me above her if she wants to be technical. It's fortunate for her that I'm not interested in governing, but neither do I want to be ruled by someone who annoys me. I think we need a committee created to discuss how to run this village."

Callan wanted to pound his head into the nearest tree.

Kenja sent him a sympathetic glance that he appreciated. She was the sole female not giving him grief at the moment.

"Let's get you settled," he said, towing Becka by her arm again. He shined light from his hands to guide the way or he'd end up carrying her. Not happening. "Have any of your G'ortian powers manifested yet, Becka?"

"Some, but nothing consistent yet."

"What about shining light energy from your hands?"

"Oh, no, that's discouraged by the head of our House. It's far too ... pedestrian. There are plenty of servants capable of accommodating us."

Callan mentally added needy to the list of Becka's unattractive qualities. He was drawn to strong women.

The image of Rayen attacking a croggle single-handedly filled his mind. That was the woman for him.

When he reached the cleared spot in the woods that was much closer to the common area than he'd prefer a sleeping unit, Callan could see why Kaz had chosen this for Becka. She was within shouting distance to call out for service since she viewed everyone around here as her servants.

He released her arm and she kept walking then stumbled, flailing for her balance.

"Callan, where are you?"

Was she serious?

He shined the light at his body. "Right here."

She extended her hand. "Please. I don't want to fall since this is my only outfit until more can be produced."

He didn't even want to ask her what she expected for production of clothes.

A remnant of energy hovered over the spot where Kaz had started her kamara and Callan intended for him to finish it.

Standing only six feet away, she still held her hand out.

He caught her by the wrist just to shut her up and moved her over to where she could stand on a perfectly smooth section of ground.

It was identical to the spot she'd just vacated.

She grabbed his shoulder with a desperation that should be reserved for clinging to the edge of a cliff, then she maneuvered herself up against his chest.

It took all his control to keep from flinging her away.

Callan called out to Kaz telepathically. *Where are you?*

Near enough to watch Becka paw you.

Then come and get her off me.

I'm just making sure you haven't changed your mind.

Not. In. This. Lifetime.

Becka dug her sharp little nails into his shoulder, clutching tighter. "Thank you for making my kamara, Callan. Our parents would want this for us."

There is never going to be an us.

Callan couldn't put off explaining that there was no future for them together. He opened his mouth to tell Becka when a stick snapped behind him. Thank goodness, Kaz was going to peel Becka off Callan's body. Relief rushed through him until he turned and realized it was not Kaz walking up.

Just beyond the glow from his hands, Callan could make out every detail of anger rising in Rayen's face. She swung her gaze from Becka to him. "Please. Don't let me interrupt you love birds."

Becka replied in a sugary tone, "Thank you. We do require privacy."

Callan started, "Rayen, it's not—"

Her voice sliced through his words faster than if she'd used the edge of a broken glass. "Save it."

Then she was gone.

Callan roared, "*Kaz!*"

Chapter 24

I am so stupid.

Maybe that's why my family sent me into a time traveling tornado. They didn't want to risk me reproducing.

Who could blame them?

Fallen branches crackled beneath the slam of my pounding footsteps. I had no idea where I was going, just away from Callan.

I didn't want to go back to the village to face someone like Zilya who would see emotions I couldn't hide right now. I hated this yearning for Callan. It made me miserable. Worrying about him dying tomorrow was hard enough, but watching him and Becka so close together was almost as bad.

I should be the better person and support his future with Becka. A part of me wanted to because it showed I was honorable, but my heart cared nothing for honor. It screamed and stomped around in my chest, refusing to give up Callan to anyone regardless of how absurd it was to want him.

Kaz had explained how Callan was committed to Becka.

No matter how hard I tried, I couldn't make myself think about the future when it was so far from my grasp.

"*We do need our privacy*," I mimicked in Becka's irritating voice. "*Thank you for making my kamara, Callan. Our parents would want this for us*."

The word princess came to mind.

Had my memory just tossed me another nugget or had I known of a princess while growing up? I didn't know, but that description fit Becka.

She'd stood there with her shining blonde hair falling to her waist and her ivory skin. Those hands had never been abused.

I lifted my hands, but thankfully it was too dark to see them. But rubbing my fingers together, I could feel the rough skin and callouses that hadn't happened in the last few days. Whoever I'd once been, wherever I grew up, I'd spent time with weapons and tending the earth.

My hair hung limp around my shoulders. Certainly not the vision of perfection that had clung to Callan. What was wrong with me? That was Callan's world, and it didn't include me, never would. *Get over him and let this go.*

Swallowing was difficult and my eyes burned, but I refused to let a tear fall.

Not for someone who didn't want me.

Out of the dark, a branch hit me in the face and I attacked it, beating the thing away from me until the limb was shredded.

Someone grabbed me from behind, wrapping his arms around to trap mine against my body, and lifted me away from the branch I'd defeated.

Callan.

I knew the feel of his arms and the musk that floated from his warm skin. He hugged me to him, laughing.

He was laughing at me?

"You must have a death wish," I muttered. "Put me down before I grant it."

"We won't have a tree left if I turn you loose."

My heart was pounding fast from anger.

And Now I was lying to myself?

The emotions I suffered were not just anger. My heart was holding a party because Callan was here and holding me. I stopped fighting to see if he'd put me down.

No, and he showed no sign of tiring.

He nudged his face into my hair, inhaling. "You smell good."

I could swear my heart grinned at that.

Stupid organ had no sense whatsoever. It would follow Callan around just to hear his voice, but I had more pride than that. I'd gone looking for him to hear him, but found Becka hanging all over his beautiful body.

Now was not the time to think about Callan's muscular chest and arms. He'd chosen someone other than me and I didn't want to hear anything else from him. "Are you through sniffing me?"

"No." His arms tightened. Not uncomfortably, but to send a message that I was good and caught.

Of all the reactions to choose from, contentment over being so close to him was clearly the wrong one.

"Put me down, Callan. Did you build a kamara that quickly?"

"No."

"So Becka is waiting on you to get back." An ugly feeling clawed through me at the thought of those two together tonight.

"No."I growled. "Is that all you can say?"

He chuckled and started walking. "Why are you angry with me?"

"Because you're still holding me when I said to put me down."

"You were angry with me back when you found me with Becka. Why?"

My muddled mind floundered for an answer.

Why was I upset with him? Because he was going to create a kamara for Becka. That sounded ridiculous in my head. She needed somewhere to sleep. He'd made me one when I'd had no sleeping quarters, but then he'd stayed inside it with me that night.

And that was the reason I was angry.

I did not want him sleeping in a kamara with anyone else and I did not want to admit that, because it sounded ... jealous.

I had no right to be jealous. Callan wasn't mine.

"Rayen?"

"Yes."

"Are you going to tell me why you're angry?"

"I don't think so."

"Why not?"

"Because talking about it will change nothing."

He stopped walking and lowered me to the ground then turned me in the circle of his arms. He held me lightly and let a soft glow emit from his hands. "You don't know that."

"Yes, I do."

"Talk to me."

"No. I don't like this feeling."

A tender thought softened his gaze. "You don't like how you feel about me?"

"No, I mean yes, I don't like it."

"Explain what you don't like."

I snapped, "You won't let this go will you? Fine. I don't like seeing you with Becka. Now I feel even more stupid for admitting it out loud."

He smiled at me.

Maybe if I called up my power and sent him flying into a tree it would knock some sense into him. "Laughing at me is dangerous."

"I'm smiling. Not laughing."

I pushed a handful of hair off my face in a frustrated move. "I don't see the difference."

Lowering his face to mine, he said, "Laughing at you would mean that I find something you did funny. Smiling at you means ... you make me happy."

"Nice that one of us is happy," I grumbled.

His hands came up my shoulders and cupped my face. "I want to make you happy, too."

"That's not possible." Could I sound any more morose?

"You haven't given me a chance."

I took in a deep breath and let it out slowly, trying to find the right words. "You can't fix how I feel. It's my own problem. Go back to Becka and let me work this out by myself."

"I can't do that."

"Why not?"

"Because that's not what I want."

There were a lot of things I wanted, starting with him, but I wasn't getting what I wanted so why should he? "Then it's nice to know I won't be suffering alone."

"Why are you suffering?"

His thumbs swept over my cheeks, soothing me and breaking my heart. I wanted to have this forever, but that was not to be. My patience was long gone and I was tired of playing twenty questions. I asked, "What *do* you want Callan?"

"You. And you want me."

Arrogant warrior. "Don't be so sure."

"I wasn't until now." He pinned me with that relentless gaze of his. "Admit the truth, Rayen. You care for me."

Admitting that would only make walking away from him that much more difficult tomorrow. Why was he doing this to me? Callan had never struck me as insensitive, but making me admit my feelings when we'd never see each other again after tomorrow was inconsiderate. He'd have someone and I'd be alone again.

I circled back to the real issue at hand. "What about Becka?"

He dropped his forehead to mind. "Kaz was wrong to share so much."

"But it was right for you to keep the truth about Becka from me?"

"No. That's what I wanted to tell you when we got back here today. Kaz knew nothing more than speculation that had been going on between my and Becka's Houses. The truth is that no formal agreement has happened. Before I was captured, I told my father I would do whatever was required of me to take Jornn's place, but I could not commit to a woman I had no feelings for and I have none for Becka. If I had, I would have to find a way to break the start of bonding with you."

My crazy heart started beating out of control and I couldn't chastise the fickle thing because I was just as excited. The bonding had started when we were fighting for our lives and Callan had broken through the veil in my mind as a last ditch effort to save me from a bloodthirsty plant.

We'd had a connection since then, but we hadn't actually fully bonded, based on what he'd explained.

I didn't realize until that very moment how much I wanted to bond with him, but to do so would be beyond wrong on my part. How could I bind him to me, which would prevent him from having a life when he returned home? He should have a full life with a family of his own some day even if I had no future waiting for me.

But he was right.

I did care about him. So much it hurt. Was caring for someone supposed to be this painful? My stomach churned and seeing Becka's hands on him had stoked a rage I was surprised to find within myself.

But I still didn't understand something. "If you feel that way, why were you building Becka a kamara?"

Lifting his head, he said, "That bothered you, didn't it?"

His smug tone got under my skin. "No. I'm only curious."

"Liar."

"Just forget I asked."

"But I like that you asked." He was grinning again.

"You find the most irritating things funny. Are you laughing or have I made you happy again. I just want to know before I call up my power and blast that smile off your face."

He gave up a booming laugh that rumbled deep in his chest.

I'd had enough of being made fun of and pushed to back out of his grasp.

He let go of my face, but grabbed an arm, pulling me back to him in a fast move that ended with his arms locked behind my back. "You are prickly as a cactus sometimes. I'm smiling because you're adorable when you're jealous."

"I am not jealous," I lied. Just because he was right didn't mean I had to admit it and feed his ego.

He kissed my hair then my forehead. "It's okay, because I was jealous, too."

That was news. "When?"

"On the ride back from the TecKnati camp. I spent part of the time trying to contact Kaz telepathically. When he wouldn't communicate, I spent the rest of the time considering how many bones I could break without killing him."

"Callan!" I was appalled that he would consider harming his best friend. "Kaz did nothing wrong."

"He was touching you," Callan argued in a dark voice that held no humor. "No one touches you ... but me."

His heated voice claimed me as surely as what he'd declared. I had no defense against the way my heart jumped around at his words, even when I knew there was no hope for anything more than being here with him.

Maybe it was weariness from the past two days that allowed him to knock down the barriers to my heart, but I knew it was more. I would never care for another the way I did for Callan and I was selfish enough to want what little time we had left.

The warmth from his body slowly drained the fight from me. I yawned and dropped my face against his chest to cover it. He smelled warm and male.

"You're exhausted, sweetheart, and I haven't slept since you left to return to the past the last time. Let's get some rest," he suggested in a voice that was gruff with gentleness.

"Where will we sleep?"

"In my kamara."

"But Kaz said—"

"I don't care what anyone says. Time is short in this place. I spent two long days without you, thinking about how I've done everything I had to do and gave it my best." His lips grazed my hair. "But with what little time I have left, I'm doing what I want to do and that's be with you."

Time.

All the worry and fear over him dying exploded in my chest. I pushed us apart enough to face him. "Kaz let me believe your birthday was today and that you had survived the wraiths, but you're turning eighteen tomorrow. What are we going to do? We have to get you out of here."

Callan hid his emotions better than anyone here, but in that one moment I saw how much being here and knowing what was coming soon had beaten him down. He was seventeen. He'd fought and bled for this village, and still had to bury children. He'd watched his friend Mathias be dragged away by wraiths with no way to help him and Callan knew that was his fate at this point.

When he spoke, his words were gentle like the wind. "I don't want to spend tonight thinking about tomorrow. I want to forget about everything else and just be with you."

I reached up and cupped his face, kissing him with all the feeling in my heart. When I stepped back, he stood perfectly still, clearly waiting on my decision.

Was there any doubt? I whispered, "Take me to your kamara."

Chapter 25

Gabby collapsed on the herb-scented bed of feathers in Jaxxson's hut and sprawled. She'd once been forced to run track with a bunch of physical overachievers.

It had taken her three days to recuperate.

That had been nothing compared to how beat up she felt now. "Do you think the ward will hold?"

Jaxxson stood at the entrance of his hut with his back to her as he sealed the passage. The opening disappeared, filled in with more indigo-blue feathers to match the rest of the walls, then Jaxxson turned to her.

Fatigue swiped dark shadows under his eyes. "I'm not sure, but Callan believes we're secure, so I will accept that."

Pushing up on her elbows, Gabby swallowed a yawn. "How are the children?"

On the way back to his hut from powering the ward earlier, Jaxxson had split off from her to check on two children who had shown signs of their magic reacting to the Sphere. "They had mild rashes. I was able to clear that up and ease them to sleep. What about V'ru and Tony? Any progress on the prophecy?"

"Some. They're working late. If anyone can figure out how to make that computer work, it's Tony."

"I don't understand how they determined that we need the computer," Jaxxson commented as he walked over to where he kept a gourd of water on a bench Gabby had used earlier for a chair. "I know the words of the prophecy and nothing was said of a computer."

She chose her words carefully, trying her best not to outright lie to Jaxxson. "The way I understand it, a TecKnati got sent back two thousand years and he built an analog computer that sank a ship near a Greek island. The prophecy started back then. It's some parallel to that ancient computer."

"I've read some on that, but who made the connection to *us* needing a computer now?"

Gabby shook her head thoughtfully. "I would ask more questions, but everyone is working so hard to solve the prophecy and find a way out that I don't want to make it any more difficult than it is for them."

"Me either," Jaxxson assured her as he brought the gourd to her so she could drink first.

While she took a drink that soothed her parched throat, Jaxxson knelt down on the bed.

He turned with a groan and sat hard. "Someone must have beaten me when I was asleep to make me this sore."

Gabby took the opening he gave her to shift the subject away from the prophecy. "I hear you. I feel rode hard and put up wet."

Jaxxson smiled at her. "You say the most unusual things. You are both beautiful and entertaining."

And he made her feel like an amazing woman just for bringing a smile to his face.

Why hadn't they been born in the same era?

She wouldn't dwell on that and turned the subject back to what had drained them physically so much tonight. "Once I understood how to push our power into the ward and got the hang of it, I started *feeling* the energy in the ward."

"You're getting much stronger and gaining more control. I'm so proud of you."

She smiled her appreciation, but she hadn't been fishing for a compliment. "What I mean is, I could tell the ward was struggling to stay intact. We need more power than we're generating. Do you think Rayen could help?"

Jaxxson's face paled. "She might be able to power the entire ward, but she also might blow all of us up. She has no control of her power."

He had a point even if he had made Rayen sound like the antichrist.

Gabby hadn't told Jaxxson that it appeared Rayen was

important to fulfilling the prophecy. The minute she did, he would ask questions Gabby doubted she could dance around as easily as she had a moment ago. Keeping her encounters with Mathias from Jaxxson was chewing her up inside, but Mathias had been adamant that she would put the MystiKs at risk if they knew what had happened to him. Mathias worried that Jaxxson and the others would try to reach out to him and open a door for the wraiths to attack them before they turned eighteen.

Jaxxson drank his fill of the gourd and lay back, pulling her down to his side. A week ago, she would have panicked at merely touching anyone, especially a guy, because she feared hearing thoughts. And she had no experience with boys, but Jaxxson was in a league of his own.

He made her feel safe and comfortable, and loved.

Not that he'd said the L word. That was *her* mind playing the love game, but she'd never had the opportunity for a relationship with a guy, and after years of not even being hugged she craved this closeness.

Jaxxson waved his hand and the glowing rocks dimmed, leaving the room almost completely dark. His voice swept through her with a calming quality that came from his healing powers. "You will eventually leave and not come back."

But those words yanked her right out of Calm City. "I don't want to think about that."

"I do."

"Why?"

"I've been thinking about ... us."

In the silence that followed, she considered what he was saying. At some point, the MystiKs had to go home. Gabby did, too. She had no idea what awaited her, Tony or Rayen in the past, but the longer they remained in the Sphere, the more dire the consequences when they returned. The idea of Tony going to jail turned her stomach and the thought of losing Rayen if they took her away permanently left Gabby with just as sick a feeling.

But the real killer would be waking up the day that she'd never see Jaxxson again.

That was reality, whether she wanted to avoid it or not.

"You are thinking about us, too," Jaxxson whispered.

"Yes." There was no point in trying to lie. He would know. "It's just that I know it's going to be hard to live without ever seeing you again so I don't want to think about it right now."

He hugged her to him and kissed her hair. "There is a way to stay connected."

Gabby turned, pushing herself up to look him in the face. "We can be together?"

His grim expression was answer enough, but he lifted a hand to her cheek, brushing his fingers across her skin. "You are not of age for what I have in mind—"

He had an idea? "Don't even start with me that I'm too young for something at sixteen. In your world, they expect a lot more of someone my age than they do in mine, but I'm an old soul in a young body. It's not the age, but the miles and I've had my share because of my gifts. I've lived alone for so long even among others my age that I'm tired of being alone. What are you suggesting?"

"I will tell you, but this is not something that can be changed once it has been done."

"I'm listening." She leaned down with her arm crossed over his chest and propped herself to be inches from his face. Jaxxson wasn't built like Callan and Kaz who had cut muscles, but more like a toned runner. An Adonis athlete.

Both of his hands moved to her hair where he began to methodically undo each of her eight ponytails as he spoke. "There is a way to stay connected throughout time. It is called bonding, but it is only for a couple who believes they were meant to be together forever. We are halfway to bonding."

What? Wait a minute.

Hadn't Jaxxson executed the equivalent of jailbreaking her mind to help when her power was out of control during her last visit? He'd hesitated, saying if he pierced her mental veil it would start a bonding.

Was she really considering this?

Hadn't Mathias said something about the bonding *must* happen?

Now that she thought on it, Tony and V'ru had mentioned that even if they figured out how to fulfill the rest of the prophecy the last line would stop them.

A bond of two will set us free.

Was that why Jaxxson was bringing this up?

She stayed away from the prophecy discussion, wanting to hear what he had in mind. “Are you saying you have divorce issues in the future, too?”

His lips tugged up in a half grin. “There will always be those who treat a relationship as temporary or disposable, but some believe their soul is meant to unite with only one forever.”

Her heartbeat tumbled along at a fast rhythm that was picking up speed as she realized what he was talking about. “Are you saying you want to finish forming the bond with me?”

Jaxxson’s gaze moved over her as his hands kept unwinding the ponytail bands. “I have a hard time admitting the truth, but yes.”

Call me idealistic, but I love hearing that. “Why is it hard to admit?”

His gaze slid back to mine. “Because it would mean that you would never bond with another, only when you found my soul.”

The light bulb flashed in her head and it had nothing to do with solving the prophecy problem. “Wait, are you saying I could find you in the past?”

“Yes, but—”

“*Oh my God, oh my God...* “ She shoved up, ready to dance around the hut to celebrate this news. “Yes, a thousand times yes. Of course, I’ll do this. I want no one but you!”

Jaxxson wasn’t jumping around celebrating with her. What was wrong? He swallowed and studied on his thoughts for a moment before replying. “You won’t find *me* in the past.”

“What do you mean?”

“If we are bonded, your soul will search for mine and you will find it if my soul is still there.”

“So your soul travels through time?”

He did smile at that. “Not exactly. My soul—and yours—remains in the human body until that body expires then the soul moves to a new body. I researched this with V’ru while you were gone. The way I understand it, once souls are connected they will continue to reunite with each other as soon as both reach maturity. One will always wait for the other one to return. The maturity part is a gray area, but the best I can tell it means whatever adulthood is in a given period of time."

She eased back down to his chest, considering what he'd explained. "So if we bond, I would find you in my time as soon as I hit adulthood?"

"Give or take a year or two, plus the fact that it will not be me physically as you see me right now, but yes, your soul would recognize mine."

She massaged that thought, looking at the possible downside as well as the benefit. Would she be open to caring for someone who was not Jaxxson? "What actually happens during a bonding?"

"We open our minds and cross the veil in each other's mind, which allows our powers to blend."

"Is it painful?"

"It is ... intense. Not painful, but life altering. You will experience a level of understanding for everything around you that feels like the world is amplified at first. Once you become comfortable with the connection then everything will recede, still sharply in focus, but not as overwhelming."

She latched on to the part about their powers blending and couldn't ignore the question hanging in the back of her mind. Was this about solving the prophecy riddle? She just could not believe that Jaxxson would ask her to do this solely for the prophecy. Every ounce of her being wanted him in a way that she doubted she'd ever feel again, but she still had to know. Instead of asking about the prophecy, she chose a parallel that would answer her question.

"If we bond, will you and I be able to offer more power for shoring up the ward, Jaxxson?"

"We could, if I allowed anyone to know, but I won't because I refuse to have you used like a charging source." Jaxxson's calm voice boomed with protectiveness. "Your power is greater than mine. Combined, it would expand and grow, but it takes time to become accustomed to the change. You've seen what happened as your Hy'bridt powers developed. No, this village will have to survive without putting you under that kind of stress."

This really was only about the two of them.

For the next few minutes, she chewed on her lip, thinking how it would be better to take a part of Jaxxson rather than lose all of him.

Jaxxson groaned. "Please do not do that."

"What?"

"Biting your lip."

"Why?" She had a feeling she knew why but the vixen inside her had to tease him. It was Jaxxson's fault after all that she'd come out of her shell of cold indifference to live like a real person.

"Because I want to kiss you and once I start I'll forget about this discussion."

Her hair now fell around her shoulders in a way that hadn't felt normal in a long time. She'd planned to live her life alone rather than face any more heartache over the gift that had been the catalyst for her mother's death. Gabby considered her options now that she knew how to block the thoughts of others and had developed powers attributed to being a Hy'bridt ancestor.

Even if she could now be with another person and protect her mind, she would still be living in the shadows, hiding her gifts. She asked, "If our souls meet in the past, would yours be open to my powers?"

"If we bond, your soul *will* find mine and, yes, mine will have powers as well so it will feel protective over you and your power. However, since that will happen so many years in the past, my soul would very likely need you to help understand those powers."

Somebody in the past needed her, but could she definitely care for someone who was not physically Jaxxson? "What if I meet this person and I don't ... connect to him?"

Jaxxson's smile was full of warmth. "That is the beauty of bonding. You will care for him, but you will not be forced to stay even though it will be difficult to walk away."

"Why?"

"Because he will fall madly in love with you the minute he

sees you and be ready to lay the world at your feet."

She laughed, a light sound that filled the hut. "Like that would ever happen."

"It already has."

Her heart clutched at the sincerity in his words.

Jaxxson lifted up and kissed her. His firm lips moved over hers in a familiar dance that had her forgetting everything around her. The next thing she knew, she was on her back and he was still kissing her. His fingers wove into her hair and touched her so lightly it was if they had moved to another dimension.

When he stopped, he lifted his head, drinking her in with his eyes.

She drank her own fill of him at the same time. "If we do this, will you want to, uh, ..."

He cocked a look at her, but didn't force her to say it. "To truly share my bed and have sex?"

Her face felt so hot she had to be tomato red. "Yes."

"No. That is a physical bonding that should never happen until you have reached the point when you are prepared for that step. In your time, it would be a vow to marry. In my time, it is a vow to marry and a union of Houses."

She probably shouldn't feel such relief, but she wasn't ready to take that step, even knowing she would never get the chance with Jaxxson. "Is it strange that the idea of bonding feels more important to me right now?"

He shook his head. "It is more important than a physical act. To unite two souls is eternal. If we had time to spend together, I would wait to discuss bonding, but I can't live thinking about you alone in the past." His chest moved up and down with a deep breath. "I would be dishonorable if I didn't admit that I have a selfish motive. I want you in my future as much as I want you to have someone in your world. I love you, Gabby, and my soul will never want another."

Her vision swam with tears. No one had ever wanted her, not like this. She trusted Jaxxson to believe that she could care for someone else in a few years, that she'd recognize his soul when she met him.

And now she could do something for him and this village as

well.

If they bonded, that would insure a real chance at fulfilling the prophecy and sending Jaxxson home.

Chapter 26

Byzantine Institue, Albuquerque, NM

Phen-T112 watched his lizard run back and forth across the hall, clearly confused. This was the floor where Rayen, Tony and Gabby were last seen before they disappeared.

Giving a command Phen had programmed into the sentient beast, it began morphing from a lizard to the image of a hunting dog that Phen had seen in a book.

These people still had books with paper pages.

Talk about primitive.

When the dog finished forming, he started sniffing just like the one Phen had read about called a Bloodhound. Now, would he have a nose for finding Rayen and her two friends?

The Browns might give Phen grief over a dog, but he could always order it to morph back into a lizard when they weren't looking. They thought they were so clever running this school under the noses of the government in this world. How difficult could it be to develop a school and be accepted as a superior operation when the people running it had been sent back 175 years in time?

Not Mrs. Brown, of course. Or her son, Nicholas, that Mr. Brown had to have adopted since he hadn't been in the past long enough to have a seventeen-year-old child.

SEOH didn't place women in any vital positions. He had less use for women than he did for MystiKs.

Or scouts.

Phen had never enjoyed being a TecKnati scout, but he'd been moving up the ranks until that stupid Rayen showed up in the Sphere. SEOH held Phen responsible for the intruders.

Twenty-three years as a TecKnati, fifteen of which had been spent either training or working as a scout, and he got sent back to a time when paper and physical computers were still in use.

No more.

TecKnati had served the civilization back home by providing solar energy to heat and cool homes, laser curtains to prevent rabid C'raydonians from entering the cities, and a space program that offered a defense system never seen before.

That was all fine, but Phen had been treated like a number for too long. SEOH thought he'd never see Phen again, but he was wrong. Phen would find that time travel computer and wait for Rayen to return then make her show him how to get out of this place.

He wanted to go home. Something this place would never be.

The sound of voices echoing through the hall that this one connected to snapped Phen out of his musings. He hurried forward, searching for a place to hide, whispering to the dog, which followed at his side and stopped at a door. Phen opened it and rushed inside the dark room, closing the door softly.

"I don't like waiting. SEOH leaves us exposed by sitting on all these MystiK eggs we've harvested in the women's center. We've been here four years. It's time to move to the next location and get started."

Phen recognized Dr. Maxwell's rough voice that sounded as if the man gargled with broken glass.

"Based on the message Phen brought from SEOH, we may not have to continue any operation much longer."

And that would be Mr. Brown, the central cog in all this. He'd tried to get Phen to take classes. Phen had given him a thousand-yard stare he saved for idiots.

Take antiquated classes? He'd probably have to use a pencil and paper, too.

Did they still have pencils in this era?

Phen should find some of the USB memory sticks and take them with him to sell when he returned home. There was always someone who wanted to collect that old crap.

SEOH's minions really thought Phen was going to just accept being ripped from everything he knew and thrown back in time?

"Speaking of Phen," Dr. Maxwell said as the voices came closer to the room where Phen hid. "What are we going to do about him?"

"Let him be. The minute SEOH sends the K-Virus back in time, we'll release it into the atmosphere. The virus will begin attacking anyone not inoculated. SEOH specified only inoculating ancestors of the top twenty percent of TecKnati DNA based on intellect and the eight families protecting future engineers. Do you really think Phen came from that level of breeding stock?"

Dr. Maxwell chuckled and Phen considered turning his sentient beast into something with claws and serrated teeth to unleash on the obnoxious doctor.

So SEOH was even going to wipe out his own people?

"I hope his plan works," Dr. Maxwell said.

"We'll know in another day when the virus shows up. Once we see the first cases of it being reported on the news, it will be time to move into the next phase of this operation. We'll use—" Mr. Brown's voice trailed off as they turned down another hall.

Phen swung around and leaned back against the door. He had to find that computer now and he'd take it to a spot where he could hold Rayen prisoner as soon as she came back through the portal.

She would either help him or watch her friends die.

When his eyes adjusted to the semi-lit room, he stared at a ladder with a pair of commercial cans of tomatoes sitting on the floor then he looked up at the top of the shelf.

Chapter 27

Callan lit the way through the woods with his palms and wished he hadn't had to move his kamara closer to the village, but he couldn't very well ignore his own security orders.

Still, this location was far from anyone else and he'd built a personal ward fifty feet out around the kamara that blocked entrance and sounds from both sides.

Kaz could reach Callan telepathically if any threat arose.

Rayen said, "I'm not sure I even know which direction the village is from here."

He held her hand, keeping a light shining from his other hand as he drew her along. "The good news is that you aren't going anywhere without me and I can find it."

"You sound pretty sure about this. I might change my mind."

He smiled over the teasing in her voice. When was the last time he'd laughed or smiled before Rayen came along? He couldn't remember and he doubted he'd laugh or smile as much again once this ended.

Don't think that way tonight.

When they reached his kamara, he stopped before entering and pulled Rayen around in front of him and kissed her. She wrapped her arms around him without hesitation. This was the woman he envisioned being with forever. Someone who was his equal in every way, and maybe even more powerful than he was. That didn't matter. If anyone or anything threatened her, he would bring the full force of his power to destroy that threat.

Her lips on his brought his world into focus and gave him a reason to hope beyond tomorrow and this miserable Sphere. Callan ran his hands into her hair, letting the wild strands flow over his skin. She had her hands in his hair, too, holding his head as if she feared he'd vanish if she let go.

Nothing could drag her from him right now.

She angled her head and he took advantage, kissing her more deeply, tangling her tongue with his.

He would trade all his tomorrows for this.

When they broke for air, she stared up at him, studying his face for answers he was sure he didn't have. "What?"

"I'm just trying to memorize everything for when ..." She looked away, her jaw moving with unspoken words then she came back to him. "For when I have to depend on memories alone. I have none and I'm filling up every available spot in my mind with you."

If he was honest with himself, he'd admit he was doing the same thing, but he didn't want to admit that. He didn't want to give up the one thing worth fighting for, if only someone would point out who or what he had to fight.

She tried to stifle another yawn.

He kissed her nose. "Let's go inside where it's warm."

"Mm. Sounds good. Chilly out here, but I'm so tired I could probably sleep on the cold ground."

Once he had her inside, she glanced around at the gray zero-gravity chair that emulated the one from his home and the floating, cloud-like bed, silently taking it all in.

Then she froze, turning as she studied the images of her embedded in the walls of his kamara. That was another reason he wanted no one else inside here.

This was the only place he found solace.

He went to sleep and woke up thinking of her and those images now covered the circular walls.

She finished pivoting around until she was back to facing him. "How did you do this?"

"I could show you more easily than explain it, but generally a kamara is created from the most tranquil part of your mind and enhanced with everything that fills you with peace."

"So you *pulled* these images out of your mind and stuck them on the walls?"

"No. I've never had pictures of anything or anyone show up on the walls of my kamaras in the past, not even of my family.

But after sending you and the other two back to Tony and Gabby's time at moonset of your first visit to the Sphere, I woke up the next morning to find that image of your face in here." He pointed at the picture of her lying back while he'd treated her wounds after a croggle attack. Her guard had been down and they hadn't been adversaries in that brief moment.

Clearing his throat, he added, "When you came back and we spent the night in the kamara I built you, I stopped by here for a weapon on the way to rescue Tony and the two boys from the TecKnati. All the other images you see showed up then."

She reached out to touch a vision of herself sleeping that floated past her hand. "Is it because we spent that night together?"

He couldn't waste a moment being apart so he moved behind her and wrapped his arms around her waist, dropping a kiss on her neck. "No, I think it's because we started the bonding even on our first meeting."

Her hands covered his that were folded over her stomach. "Oh. I forgot about that."

While locked away in the TecKnati camp, he'd given two long days of thought to the bond and what it would mean if he left it in limbo the way they were right now. Kaz claimed what was started when Callan pierced the veil in Rayen's mind could not be left that way and Kaz had shared his ideas on how to sever it completely.

Rayen dropped her head back on his shoulder and thick eyelashes brushed her soft cheeks.

Callan pulled her back with him and sat beside her on the bed. Her eyes flew open and she looked up at him. He bent down, kissing her with as much control as he could manage.

Did he want more? Well, yes, but he'd never dishonor her that way.

That wasn't to say he would be satisfied with leaving things the way they were right now, with them half-bonded. Hoisting her up, he tossed her to the side so she landed and bounced on the bed, laughing with a deep, throaty sound that he felt to his bones.

He stretched out next to her and propped his elbow to support his head. Here was the picture to replace all others.

Her black hair spilled around her face like a dark fire. Blue-green eyes twinkled along with the sweet curve of her lips. Her skin was the color of perfectly steeped tea. When he brushed a lock of hair off her shoulder, he grimaced.

Her fingers touched his lips. “Why are you frowning?”

“Your skin is so beautiful. I never realized how unattractive the mixed colors of mine are next to you.”

“I love the way you look, Callan.”

She caught his hand that was still toying with her hair and pulled it to her lips, kissing his hand then his wrist. When her aqua gaze reached out to his again, she said, “Something is bothering you that you’re hesitating to tell me.”

Had she delved inside and lifted his thoughts? No, she wouldn’t do that. He asked, “Why do you say that?”

“I don’t know. I just ... sense it, I guess.”

“It’s the bond trying to form.” He said the words as soon as he thought them.

Her gaze moved everywhere but to his face.

As much as he wanted to push to know what she was thinking, he had to let her work through her emotions on her own and see if she’d come to the same conclusion he had.

Finally, she kissed his hand then tucked it against her chest and addressed him. “We have to do something about this bond that was started.”

“Agreed.”

“Is it something we can do tonight?”

“Yes.”

Her eyes shone, glossy with tears. He never wanted to hurt her and watching her struggle with this was more than he could take. “We can finish the bond now.”

“What?” Her eyes rounded. “Finish it? That would mean we’re bonded forever.”

He drew back at her reaction. “Yes, it would.”

“No, we can’t ... you can’t ... what are you thinking?”

That wasn’t the reaction he’d expected. “I was thinking that you wanted to be with me as much as I want to be with you.”

“I do.”

“Doesn’t sound like it.”

“But you’re talking about bonding our souls forever. I’m

already dead by the time you return home."

"First of all, I probably won't make it back."

She shoved up in his face. "Don't say that! You *are* going home."

This was not going anything like he expected. "Then if I do, there's even more reason to be bonded."

"What if my soul ends up in a TecKnati body in your time? You can't be with a TecKnati." She started nodding. "See? You haven't even considered that, plus if you're bonded to me you'll never bond with someone you have to ... marry."

"I don't care. I don't want to lose you. I know if we bond we'll be together somewhere during our many lives. If I find your soul in a TecKnati, I'll deal with it."

"You hate the TeKs. They killed your brother. They sent you here. SEOH is trying to destroy the MystiKs. I don't have a life to go back to so you'd be losing any chance at happiness by doing this."

For the first time since his brother died, the vengeance Callan lusted after had been moved aside in his heart and

something more important filled the largest spot. He caught Rayen's face between his hands and told her, "I'll lose any chance at happiness if I never find you again. I've chosen you as my soul mate. I want you to choose me. Just answer this. Do you to want to bond our souls?"

She squeezed her eyes shut, holding the tears back, then opened them. "Of course, I do, but I don't have any way back to my home. If we do this and my soul is trapped in the wrong world it may leave yours in limbo."

Drawing her close until their heads touched, he said, "I don't care."

She reached up to fold her fingers around his neck. "That's just it, I do care, too much to allow you to be bound to someone who will prevent you from having a life. I care too much to do that to you. I will miss you forever once we're apart, but I can't bond with you. I couldn't face myself for doing this when I have no idea what it would do to you for eternity."

Could it be any worse than the pain crushing his heart at losing her forever?

Chapter 28

The wind blew through my hair as I raced across the desert beneath a full moon on my trusty Yo-zon. I'd given him a name my grandfather had told me meant swift, because this brindle-colored horse had been fast even as a yearling.

We rode as one through the dark.

Always at night.

That was the only time a C'raydonian was safe from attack. The sentient beasts were not as adept in the dark for some reason. My parents had warned me to always travel with an escort, but I needed to ride and burn off the fear that had clawed at me for three nights straight.

I couldn't face sleep again.

Each night I saw a young man, tall and fit, a warrior as fierce as my father who led our tribe. This warrior called to me in my dreams. He sounded as though he missed me.

How could that be?

I'd never seen anyone like him.

Soft blue-and-brown-colored shapes covered his wide chest and arms, all layered with muscle cut by hours of training. His body was a living sculpture of a fierce fighter. The tanned skins he wore for pants hugged muscled thighs and stopped at his boots. Wild locks of hair blew in the wind, brushing his shoulders and changing from dark brown to golden to a cinnamon color.

He stood in front of a small, waist-high table and told me, "When I do this and I'm gone, my soul will search for you. If I had the choice to lose only my *life in trade for just one more minute with you, I would do it." His throat moved with a hard swallow. "If others did not depend upon me, I would stay here with you."*

"What are you talking about? Where are you going?" And why did his words tear me apart?

Lifting his hand he reached out to me.

I reached out to touch his hand and the world exploded.

I lunged up, gasping for air, no idea where I was until Callan jumped off of the cloud bed to stand in front of me, searching the kamara. He whispered, "What's wrong? Where's the threat?"

"Just ... a dream." One that felt as if I'd had it while living at home, but how could that be when Callan had not even been born by the time I died?

I sat on the bed, still breathing hard, and he turned to me with tufts of hair sticking out everywhere from sleeping on it. Running both hands through the golden-brown locks, he shoved it down and wiped a hand over his face before squatting down in front of me. "Are you okay?"

Staring at him, I tried to come up with an answer that was the truth. "Just rattled with so much going on. Think it's daylight yet?"

"In a little less than an hour."

"How do you know this when there are no windows in the kamara?"

"My body is in sync with the rotation of the red moon. I can feel its pull as the moon nears the time to rise."

I reached out and touched his cheek, wishing he was anywhere but this miserable Sphere. Before I could form a thought, he cupped my hand and kissed the palm.

Then that look entered his eyes. The same one that I'd seen the last time he tried to make me leave. I warned him, "Don't start on me to go back."

"Thylan will attack and if we can't hold this ward against him, he'll come for you. I don't want to run the risk that I can't protect you."

"I'm powerful enough to deal with Thylan."

"*When* your powers show up," Callan pointed out, reminding me of my hit-and-miss defense system. "If we were bonded, I could direct your power."

Ah, his new tactic. "No. I will not condemn you to a

lifetime without the chance to bond with someone else. Don't think it's easy for me to say that. There's a crazy woman inside me who wants to kill any female who touches you, but the warrior in me was raised to make honorable decisions. I can't tell you how I know that since I have regained so few memories I can count them on two fingers, but I can't take that choice away from you."

"You're taking away the choice I'm trying to make."

I kissed his cheek. "Nice try. Not doing it."

Callan sighed and was leaning forward to kiss me when he stilled and his gaze lost focus. He jumped to his feet. "TecKnati have broken through the ward."

Chapter 29

I rushed along behind Callan who lit the way for me with his hands, but I could see other lights coming from the right and the left. "How do you know where to go?"

Callan leaped over a log and I followed him as he explained, "Kenja contacted Kaz and he called out to me."

"How many TecKnati have broken through the barrier?"

"We're about to find out." Callan slid to a stop and held an arm out to block me from passing him.

"What are you doing?"

He leaned over and whispered, "I knew the ward would be breached once the traitor got word out, so I intentionally left several spots vulnerable. Then Kaz and I created a trap inside our ward in those areas and I told Kenja to keep her people clear of them."

"Kenja was in on it?"

"Yes. She wasn't in the Sphere when the traitor released the TecKnati we captured the first day we had you, Tony and Gabby in our prison hut."

I muttered, "I remember that."

Callan kissed me. "That was before we realized you weren't the enemy. Anyhow, Kenja isn't the traitor."

"That leaves Kaz out, too."

"Right."

"So who is it?"

"If we've captured a TecKnati or two, we'll find out."

Kenja came running up to us, but she was quiet as a whisper covering the same ground I'd just crashed through. If I spent much time around her I was going to get a complex about her warrior skills even though I'd used a dose of my power to blast her across the common area one time.

Callan lifted his chin at Kenja. “How many?”

“None on the far side. Kaz and my warriors are watching the second weak spot we created to make sure this is not a distraction so that they can send an army through that area.”

“Good. Ready?”

Insult narrowed Kenja’s gaze. “I will not honor that with an answer.”

Callan muttered something that sounded like a curse and led the way.

As soon as we neared the trap, I could feel energy swirling in a tight weave of ward and spell that had the pull of a magnet. When I focused on the ward trap area, the light Callan shined on it blurred around the edges, allowing me to determine the perimeter of the trap.

Two bodies were stuck against an invisible wall much like oversized insects pinned against a huge sticky surface.

Their arms were stretched out. They struggled, then one of them cursed and they both looked up at Callan.

Or Kenja.

Either sight should put the fear in a TecKnati captured inside this village.

Callan said to Kenja, “I’ll release them one at a time, you contain them and I’ll transport.”

“Fine by me.”

Walking through an open area between the trap and the ward perimeter wall, Callan stepped behind the first TeK and placed a hand on his shoulder.

The guy screamed and fell to the ground then curled up as if he expected to be kicked.

“What did you do?” I called to Callan.

“Nothing. I only touched him and he cries like a baby.”

Callan sounded bewildered.

Kenja passed through the ward and ordered the guy, “Sit up, coward.”

The TeK remained curled in a ball.

“Very well.” She held her hands over him and spun one hand as if wrapping something in the air.

A fine blue film circled the TeK on the ground until he was

completely covered.

I asked, "Can he breathe? If not, he won't be of much use to question."

Kenja nodded. "Air flows through the entire wrap."

They repeated the process with the second TeK, but without all the drama. This scout stood as Kenja wrapped him from knees to head and announced, "You will walk."

When he didn't move, Kenja pointed at him and he started jumping around shouting, "*Stop it! Stop it!*"

She snapped her fingers and he wobbled to the side. "Are you ready to walk now?"

He nodded.

Callan used kinetics to lift the whimpering TeK from the ground and float him to a prison hut I hadn't noticed, but there were still parts of this place I had yet to see.

The hut they tossed the prisoners into was four long strides across, much larger than the one Tony, Gabby and I had been locked in that first time, and it wasn't made of the same vibrating green material. This one looked woven of vines so thick you couldn't see through the seams.

Kenja did her finger trick and the wrap disappeared from the heads of both captives. The wimpy TeK had no choice except to remain balled up and hadn't shown any interest in unrolling himself anyway.

Callan ignored him and speared the standing TeK with an icy glare. "Who opened the ward for you?"

"I don't know."

Kenja didn't hesitate or warn the scout before she pointed her finger at him.

The TecKnati started begging, "No, please don't, I swear I don't know. Please, please... " Tears rolled down his face and he twisted one way then the other trying to stop whatever was upsetting him.

"What's he feeling?" I asked.

Kenja calmly said, "It is much like having a thousand black ants attack your most sensitive and private areas."

The scout cried out, "I swear I'd tell you. I don't know. Please make it stop," he pleaded.

Callan gave Kenja a look and she shrugged then snapped

her fingers.

The guy fell to the ground, shaking and jerking. His voice was much higher and raspy.

Callan squatted next to him. “Are you willing to tell me what you know now?”

“Yes, anything, please don’t do that.”

“How did you know the ward would be open in that spot?”

“Thylan told us it was marked on the outside.”

“Marked how?”

“With a glowing section of grass.”

“Is it still there?”

“We were told it would vanish as soon as a Tecknati touched it.”

Callan pinched the bridge of his nose between his thumb and forefinger.

I could feel his frustration. He’d set a trap to uncover the traitor. If this guy knew, he’d have screamed the name by now. He might have a level of tolerance for pain, but not the kind Kenja inflicted.

Kenja asked, “Why were you sent here?”

“To find the computer and take it to Thylan.”

Standing, Callan stepped out of the hut. Once Kenja and I were out, he sealed it shut and set a ward of power that buzzed with the three of us this close to it.

He clearly didn’t want to risk the traitor letting these two go.

I directed my question at both Callan and Kenja. “How many MystiKs can make the grass glow?”

Kenja glanced at Callan who answered me. “All of them. It’s a simple exercise learned as a child and when anyone other than a MystiK touches it the glow disappears.”

“What are we going to do now?” Kenja asked and I was glad she had decided to stay.

Callan moved us far enough away from the prison hut to talk without being overheard. “We can’t set traps all along this ward. It’s too much area to protect and we don’t have enough people to cover what we do have. It’s not going to take long for Thylan to realize his scouts failed to get the computer. Once he does, he may be crazy enough to attack. He must be getting desperate to send two of his people inside this village.”

I suggested, "What if we reduce the ward protection area so that there's a smaller perimeter to protect?"

"We can't," Kenja said. "Remember the ground cover that emitted a hallucinogenic mist?"

"Oh, yes." I'd encountered that on the last trip. I'd tried to kill Callan because I thought he was a TecKnati and that the village had been destroyed.

"It's mutating and poisoning the plants we've been sustaining on. That in turn will affect the animals. This village is barely surviving on what we can forage inside this ward."

"Then we have to strengthen the ward."

Callan said, "We've tried. Gabby and Jaxxson exhausted all they had to get it to the point it is right now and I only allowed that because I knew everyone was inside. We can't risk losing our strongest healers, but the ward is slowly failing."

"What about my power?" I asked, thinking that was the obvious next move.

Neither Kenja nor Callan said a word.

Chapter 30

While I stewed over being told I couldn't help with the ward, Callan had called in every available power source. He didn't see the point in trying to trick the TecKnati again since we needed to capture Thylan to find out the identity of the traitor.

I believed I could power up the ward, and not kill anyone, but from looks on the faces surrounding me no else held that opinion. It was worth another shot at trying to convince them. "This is a ward," I began, "and I'm a power source. How difficult can it be?"

Kenja explained, "Your power is not MystiK so it may not merge with the current ward or you could force too much power into it and blow up the village."

"She might blow up the ward, but not the village," Kaz offered and I wasn't sure if that was in my defense or not.

"It's too much risk to her," Callan said with the power of his authority that would normally end all debate and prevent anyone else from arguing.

Anyone but me. I told him, "I think I'll know if it's too much for me."

Callan, Kenja and Kaz were grouped on one side of me. Gabby and Jaxxson stood on the other side. Zilya sort of stood with Callan, but in truth she hung back, staring a hole in Callan's back.

Unwilling to bend, Callan shook his head. "We try it again without you."

Zilya argued, "We're draining our power when we'll need it later."

I was in shock. Zilya spoke up to support something I

wanted to do? That surprise lasted only long enough to note the sneer she sent my way. No, she just wanted to conserve her power for herself and would willingly sacrifice me.

We stood twenty feet inside the ward and I could tell there were weak spots when we'd passed through an opening the last time. The energy usually buzzed across my skin, but now it felt more like the brush of friction.

Before I could mount a new argument, Gabby said to Jaxxson, "We have to tell them."

Jaxxson nodded.

I'd noticed something odd about the two of them when they walked up, but couldn't put my finger on it. Gabby always had a glow about her when she was with Jaxxson. For some reason, it was more pronounced at the moment.

Callan had caught Gabby's comment. "What do you have to tell us?"

Jaxxson put a proprietary arm around Gabby then announced, "Gabby and I have bonded. We are far more powerful now as a team."

Zilya gasped.

Kenja's eyebrows dropped low over her confused gaze. Kaz was neutral and Callan sliced a look at me that said *we could have done that*.

Gabby's tentative gaze skittered around until it landed on me. I smiled, but worried what that would mean for her since there was no way for her and Jaxxson to end up together.

Kaz said, "Then let's get busy and try it with Gabby and Jaxxson."

Callan turned toward the ward and everyone followed him, including me. He shook his head at me so I backed up to watch, feeling useless for all the power I possessed.

They spread out six feet apart and raised their hands.

Jaxxson began the chant, then Gabby picked up his rhythm. Blue-green light radiated from the two of them and even Zilya's eyes widened with awe.

Callan jumped in as the chant repeated, followed by Kaz's bold voice and Zilya's murmuring.

I could actually see the spread of power and the spots that were getting stronger, especially where the streak of power originated with Jaxxson and Gabby.

But after five minutes, Kaz and Callan had sweat pouring down their backs, Zilya was trembling and Gabby looked pale. Kenja and Jaxxson were gritting their teeth. Jaxxson took one look at Gabby and told Callan, "We have to stop."

Kenja shouted, "No. The ward is getting stronger."

Jaxxson turned to her. "We're pulling off in thirty seconds.""We can't finish in thirty seconds," Kaz argued in a strained voice.

The heck with this. I walked over and touched Callan's shoulders. He tensed and said, "What are you doing?"

I answered him by tapping on his mind. When he opened to me, I said, *We can do this with my power. I just need to find it without being upset and having my power run out of control.*

He surprised me by sweeping into my mind. *Follow me.*

I let go mentally of everything except focusing on him as he dove inside and found the red glow of my energy. As soon as I saw it, I drew the energy up and pushed it into Callan. His shoulders rolled with the surge of additional energy and he took the power as fast as I could feed it.

Colors swirled and blurred, spinning into a vision as beautiful as it was chaotic. I kept drawing from my core and it felt as if I had a bottomless supply of energy.

Then the flow slowed until I couldn't push it any more.

What was wrong?

A noise pierced my mental sanctity. Voices shouting.

Oh, no. Had I destroyed the ward?

I opened my eyes and stared at the back of Callan's head. He said, "Are you going to release me?"

My fingers were digging into his shoulders. I snatched them back. "Did I hurt you?"

Callan turned, rubbing his shoulder, but grinning. "No."

"You did it, Rayen," Gabby exclaimed and hugged me.

I looked up and the wall radiated energy to the point of glowing. "I didn't blow it up."

Kaz laughed. "No, you would have blown up Callan first as the conduit."

My skin chilled. I hadn't considered that.

Callan gave Kaz a censoring look. "I was never in danger."

Jaxxson said, "I'm being called to the healing hut." He thanked me for my help and took Gabby's hand.

Zilya swiped at perspiration that slinked along her neck. "You could have done that to begin with and saved the rest of us from wasting our time."

"Protecting your people is wasting time?" Kenja asked.

Speaking through a clenched jaw, Zilya said, "Don't twist my words, Kenja. I'm only saying that she's of no real use to this village. We should have had her power the ward on her own. She clearly has enough energy."

Callan's face turned darker with every word Zilya spewed. "You should be thanking her."

Etoi came storming up. "I will take Zilya's place for anything else today. She is too important to use in labor such as this."

Why? Yes, Etoi was Zilya's shadow, but Etoi didn't have Zilya's power for things like the ward or she'd have been out here helping. Was Etoi trying to keep Zilya from using her power to shore up MystiK defense?

Could Etoi be the traitor?

"Thank you," Zilya told Etoi. "I'm going to find a place to cool off and rest. We need pik-pik thread woven. You and I'll do that today."

Zilya basically dismissed herself from anything else and walked off.

Kenja murmured, "She is lucky she was not born Uberon."

Callan scrubbed a hand over his face. "I don't care as long as she stays out of my way. We've got to figure out Thylan's next move."

Neelah came from the direction of the prisoner hut. Callan and Kenja tensed, probably both thinking the first thought that came to me.

Had she gone to see the prisoners? Was *she* the traitor? Tony had warned me about her from our first visit to the Sphere. She was angry and bitter, not that he blamed her, since she was trapped here, but such a person could easily betray others to save her own skin. I just recalled everything Tony had told me and needed to share it with Callan, but not out in the open.

Callan asked, "What is it, Neelah?"

"One of the prisoners is begging to be released from the binding."

Kenja said, "Why should we care?"

"He claims he will share something he knows if we will free him."

Callan and Kenja took off like an arrow shot from a tightly strung bow. I followed with Kaz right behind me. On the way, I tapped on Callan's mind. He was quick to ask, *What?*

I didn't want to say this out loud, because I don't want to falsely accuse anyone, but Tony told me after our first trip here that Neelah had visited him when he was locked in the prison hut. She'd made the comment that she didn't care if he was TecKnati and, in fact, hoped he was because she was looking for a way out of here. She said she'd do anything to go home.

Thanks for telling me.

But that doesn't mean she's guilty, Callan.

I know. I won't accuse anyone without solid evidence.

When we reached the hut, Callan opened it and we all entered.

Before Kenja and Callan started in on this guy, I had a question for the scout. "How is the traitor in this village communicating with Thylan?"

"Messages are left outside the village in the same spot every time. I can show you the spot, but I've never seen the traitor."

I nodded and stepped back.

Kenja looked down her nose at the prisoner who was still standing and warned him, "We do not have to negotiate with you."

"I know. Please don't do that biting, itching thing again. I'm offering this in good faith."

"TecKnatis do not understand good faith," she tossed right back at him. "You have broken our treaty and killed our children."

The knot at his throat pumped up and down with a hard swallow. "That's SEOH, not all of us. I didn't sign on to do this. I've tried to hide the whole time here, because I don't agree with what SEOH is doing, but to go against him is to die. I know you don't believe this, but not all TecKnati are bad. We have families just like you and many of us want to live in peace."

Callan crossed his arms. "Your leader is trying to commit genocide against our race."

"I realize that, but no one back home knows it. There's a board of twelve members he has to answer to on everything he does. My father works in communications and I heard him tell my mother that he thought there was something odd about the Komaen Sphere project, but SEOH delivers Sphere reports on a regular basis to the board members who oversee all TecKnati developments."

"Are you trying to tell me that SEOH is keeping this secret from *all* of the TecKnati?"

The scout nodded.

Callan studied the scout. "Why are you willing to tell us this now?"

"I thought all the scouts would have been sent home by now because the BIRG Con is tonight. But Thylan hasn't even come to see what happened to *us*." The scout indicated himself and the guy on the ground who was sniffling and crying. "He told us once he completes both parts of his plan we'd go home. But I think he's lying about that, too. I'll tell you anything you want to know, but please let me go. I've never hurt anyone." His attention was squarely on Callan when he said, "I wasn't allowed to get close to you when you were locked up or I'd have helped you escape. I didn't have enough rank to be inside the main building. I've been sleeping outside the entire time."

I believed him, but I wasn't sure if Callan or Kenja did. Kaz had a wary expression on his face that made me think he battled internally for a fair decision.

Callan and Kenja exchanged a long look then Kenja nodded and Callan told the scout, "Tell us everything you know and we'll release you once we can confirm what you share."

The hunched body on the floor begged, "Do it, Allen."

Allen, the one standing, looked as if his life had been spared. He didn't need the prodding. "Thylan was supposed to take possession of the computer she brought." He angled his head in my direction. "And send it to headquarters. SEOH intends to reverse engineer it then destroy the computer before the BIRG Con. Thylan was only supposed to test the laser at twenty percent level. When it barely worked on the two boys you came to rescue, Thylan turned it all the way up on you."

Callan grunted, but continued standing with his arms crossed.

"Thylan sent a report back about how much power it had required and that he didn't have the computer yet. SEOH sent more scouts and an order that no one could go home until Thylan captured Rayen and delivered the computer to SEOH. Thylan has always been weird, but he's acting scary strange."

I didn't want to ask what Allen thought was weird compared to what I'd witnessed.

Callan shifted his stance, his hands clutching his arms tightly. "What's Thylan's plan?"

"He's having the laser field dismantled then rewiring it into a machine he's going to use like a weapon to destroy the ward around this village."

I looked to Callan. "Can he do that?"

Before Callan could answer, Allen interjected, "The laser field was designed in layers so that if one level of power didn't work they could keep increasing to the next level at another layer. There are three levels. When he maxed out the power, it was only the final layer. Combining all of them would be ..." Allen hung his head, thinking. When he lifted it, horror blanketed his gaze. "I don't know, but my guess is apocalyptic power. He has no idea if it will break the ward, blow up this village or maybe even blow up the entire Sphere. He's nuts."

Now I understood this Allen's motivation. He wanted to be anywhere but in this village when Thylan unleashed his weapon. Something he said niggled at the back of my mind. "Why do you think Thylan is lying to you about taking you home?"

"Because of the first step in his plan that he's executing today. Some of the TecKnati scouts arrived in the transenders with MystiKs, which means they have to travel back in the same transender or the molecules will rearrange in their body and explode upon arrival. Thylan's destroying all the transender sites before moonset except the one he arrived in."

Chapter 31

Tony carried the laptop and wished he could show it to Bill Gates. He grinned at the half-pint genius beside him who'd shown Tony things he couldn't use back home. Not for another nine years. He'd given V'ru his word and wouldn't break it.

But hot day-am! Tony couldn't wait to see this baby light up if Rayen could do her imitation of a power supply.

When he reached the common area, kids were running around eating some weird yellow and pink fruit that could be the offspring of a watermelon and a pineapple.

Two of the kids were levitating and tossing a circle of pink power the size of a tennis ball between them.

V'ru's face drooped with longing.

Tony assessed the situation and made a decision. He paused, turning his head back and forth.

"What are you looking for, Tony?" V'ru asked looking around. He'd taken to mimicking any move Tony made.

"Rayen and Gabby. I need to talk to them about not sharing anything they see with this computer when we go home. Do you mind hanging out here for a little bit while I find them and talk?"

"You mean out here?" V'ru asked with a bubble of excitement in his voice.

"Sure. You don't mind do ya?"

"Think they'll let me stay?" V'ru was watching the kids his age running around and playing with their powers.

"Mind? Are you kidding? They'll be glad to have you. Go on and I'll be back soon."

"Okay," V'ru answered, not sounding too sure of himself, but he took a step toward the group.

Tony headed toward the healing hut. If anyone knew where Rayen was, it would be Gabby. He rounded one of the shelters where the kids slept then turned around and leaned forward to watch V'ru to make sure that no one made fun of him.

Or hurt him.

Tony had spent many days watching over his kid brother Vinny and sometimes stepped in to keep someone from bullying him. He'd teach Vinny how to defend himself once they were back together again. As soon as Tony got the MIT scholarship, doubled up on his classes and blew through school to get his degree, he'd take any job that would pay enough for him to rescue Vinny from foster care.

The only problem with that plan was Nick setting Tony up for a theft at the Byzantine Institute. Tony hadn't stolen anything, but could he convince anyone he was innocent?

He'd worry about that when he made it home again.

V'ru had walked up to a group of five kids playing some weird game that resembled shooting marbles, but it was a holographic game played on a horizontal level with balls that looked more like tiny stars. When they hit each other, it resulted in a little pop of light and tiny fireworks.

The kids stopped playing as soon as they noticed V'ru.

One boy crossed his arms. Bad sign.

V'ru shoved his hand up in his hair, a nervous twitch.

A little girl stepped up and smiled at V'ru then said something. V'ru tentatively opened his hand, palm up.

The little girl handed him a glowing star that twirled and sparkled on his palm.

The boy with the crossed arms made a put-upon noise, then nodded at the girl and V'ru stepped into the circle.

Tony grinned. V'ru was careful not to rub elbows with the little girl. Not because V'ru considered her below him. The kid didn't have a malicious bone in his body. No, he was being a normal eleven-year-old boy encountering the female species for the first time up close and personal.

V'ru was acting as if she had something contagious like ... cooties. Just thinking of that old term made Tony smile.

The kid was going to be okay.

Tony swung around to continue on his mission and

practically ran into Gabby. He put a hand out, "Whoa, sweet cakes. Last thing we need is for me to drop this work of art."

Gabby stared at the laptop, dismissed it and raised worried eyes to Tony. "We have bigger problems than the prophecy."

"Then why did I stay up all night with V'ru trying to make this thing work?" Tony snapped.

"Don't yell at me. I'm not the one causing the problems."

True, but admitting she was right would do nothing to soothe his irritation. "Sure. Whatever."

Gabby stabbed a hand on one hip. "I'm starting to feel more sympathy for Hannah."

He wasn't sure if he should be angry on his or Hannah's behalf. "Tell me what has your panties is a wad, then I need help finding Rayen."

Bam. Say the right thing and Gabby forgot about being mad at him. She clasped her hands together. Praying or worrying?

Or both.

"Rayen is gone with Callan, Kenja and Kaz."

He tucked the laptop under his arm and cracked his knuckles. "We have maybe four hours until the moon sets. Do they want to solve this prophecy or not?"

"That's not the problem!" she said, grabbing her head. "Listen to me."

He was going to throttle Gabby if she didn't start making sense. "Start sayin' somethin' intelligent and I will."

She glared at him and whispered, "The TecKnati are destroying all the transender sites."

"*What the—*"

"Keep your voice down so the children don't hear." She cut her eyes to the side then came back at him. "Jaxxson just got a telepathic message from Callan, telling us to keep everyone inside the ward. He said it's the safest place and there's nothing he, Kenja, Kaz or Rayen can do to keep us any safer. They're trying to reach the sites first and stop the TecKnati."

Tony clamped a hand over his face, feeling nauseous. If they wrecked all the transender sites, none of these kids would make it home. V'ru would be here forever. Pulling his hand down, he said, "Someone needs to burn SEOH big time."

"That won't be one of us, but if we can figure out the

prophecy SEOH will get his due."

That was putting a lot of faith in words written two thousand years ago, but Tony wisely avoided pointing that out. "Now you want the prophecy solved again, huh?"

"I always did. I just didn't want to talk about it until I told you about the transender sites." Compassion mothered Gabby's next words. "If they destroy ours, I won't be able to go home and you won't make it back to Vinny."

His gut clenched with panic at that thought until he processed it all the way through. "The TeKs don't know about our site."

"Are you sure?"

"No, I'm not, but work through the logic. They've never met us at our transender site for an arrival or a departure. If they had known, I'm thinkin' they would have had scouts watching that site for us to arrive today and ambushed us to steal the laptop. We didn't come in through their transenders so I don't think they know about ours."

"Oh." She stared off into the distance a moment then smiled with relief. "Okay, then let's work on getting the prophecy sorted out and that computer operating so we have a way to send these MystiKs home."

"Wait a minute, sweet cakes. Where'd you come up with that bit about using the computer to send them home?"

Talk about the classic deer in the headlights look and the headlights belonged to a tractor-trailer bearing down on her with the way Gabby's face froze. "Hey, Gab, chill. What's the matter?"

She was back to wringing her hands. Something was up with their mouthy Gabby. "Don't ask me how I know. I can't tell you and even if I could, you wouldn't believe me."

He raised a hand to calm her. "You don't have to tell me, but as far as not believing you? I've time-traveled through a portal in a laptop five times, outrun a croggle, fought a killer plant and watched you float around."

"Right. Okay, I need to sit down with you and V'ru to work on the prophecy while they're gone. Callan promised Jaxxson they would all be back before moonset, but he didn't know how soon before moonset."

"Let V'ru have another fifteen minutes for a break and meet us at his kamara."

"Okay. Thanks for easing my mind about our transender." She went rushing off.

Tony couldn't share her elation. It just dawned on him that the traitor might know about their transender site. If that was the case, he hoped Rayen got to it first.

Chapter 32

SEOH had his assistant block anyone from coming into his office. He tapped the controls on his desk and accessed the video feed from where he kept the three sentient beasts.

He hated to give any of them up, but he could spare one as long as no one in his world knew that he possessed the outlawed killing machines. Thylan had discovered SEOH's stable of sentient beasts, just like Thylan had found out about the laser grid program.

SEOH grinned at the obvious genetics. Thylan might just be the one son as devious and deadly as SEOH.

Thylan had sent a request for help.

The least SEOH could do was support the person who had no conscience when it came to executing a plan.

Tapping keys, SEOH entered the code that would deliver one of his sentient beasts to the transender waiting to take it to the Sphere. Thylan had sworn he could deliver that computer before moonset on the Sphere if he had the beast.

Chapter 33

I ran through the ward opening behind Callan then waited outside the perimeter until Kaz and Kenja passed through before clasping hands with Callan and sealing the opening.

Once that was done, Callan and I turned to face the other two. I asked, "How many transender sites are there?"

Kenja answered. "Four."

"But one transender site is closer to the TecKnati camp and a long distance away from this new village location," Kaz clarified. "I could take that one and you three could go to the others."

Callan didn't waste a second to consider that. "We stay in pairs so that we all have backup. You and Kenja start at the site closest to the TeK camp and the next one on the way when you head back. Rayen and I'll go to the other two. The one where she arrived is a fifth location. We're going there first."

"No, we're not." I was standing firm on this. "The TecKnati don't know about our transender site or we'd have seen them there at some point."

"They might," Callan argued, just as adamant to have his way. "We don't know for sure if they do or don't know."

I wanted these MystiK children to return home, but I had to take Tony and Gabby into consideration, too. "In relation to the other four sites, how far from the TecKnati camp is the one where my group landed?"

Kenja supplied the answer. "Farthest."

Callan wasn't happy with her reply. "That doesn't change anything."

I put my foot down. "Yes it does. We do this strategically, starting with the sites closest to the TeK camp, because Thylan is lazy. He'll do whatever is easiest first. Kaz and Kenja are going to the first two so you and I will start at the third one down from the TeK camp and work our way back."

Callan wasn't through debating it. "What if Thylan gets word from the traitor that we're on to him?"

Ah, victory. I reminded him, "You aren't turning the prisoners loose until we return and no one can get through that ward without me because I'm not MystiK."

Kenja grinned. "She has you there."

Callan finally gave in.

Kenja wouldn't let any of us depart until she wrapped us each in a spell that protected us from the hallucinogenic ground mist still cropping up in places. I was the one most susceptible, so I think Kaz and Callan went along with it just to keep me from feeling like the weak link.

I snapped my fingers. "Wait! We'll take the tortalones."

Kaz sighed. "The mama left with her herd.""What happened to you being the turtle whisperer?"

"I can't make a tortalone stay when she doesn't want to and evidently she left. She was being so affectionate that I'm pretty sure it's mating season."

Just when we could use them, too. Shrugging, I said, "Meet you back here."

Kaz and Kenja took off fast.

Callan and I ran to the first of our two locations and found a transender crushed, lying on its side and still smoking. The big pink fake flower that hid the switch for a hologram control panel had been smashed. Wires and metal parts were scattered around.

How many MystiKs would that deny the chance to go home?

With no time to waste, we made it to the next one and found it in much the same condition except what was left of the transender unit crackled and sparked with a sick sound. Tendrils of smoke curled from sections that had exploded and landed all across the clearing. The flower for the holographic panel had been torched and melted into a puddle of gray and black.

Watching Callan hold back the agony he had to be feeling

over this was killing me. I wanted to put my hands on SEOH and make him suffer pain equal to that he had inflicted on all MystiKs.

If the wraiths came for Callan and I couldn't save him ... I didn't know what I'd do, but I *would* find Thylan since he was the access to SEOH.

On the way to my transender location, I decided to talk about the prophecy more as a distraction than anything. "V'ru and Tony are making headway on the prophecy."

"It's good to keep them occupied." Callan's words fell flat as soon as they left his mouth.

"That sounds like you don't believe in the prophecy."

"Let's just say the days of my believing in everything MystiK have passed."

I didn't know if the prophecy would save them or not, but it was worth the effort to find out. "You have to believe in something, Callan."

"Why?" He cut his eyes at me for a moment before watching the uneven path through what had turned from purple-tinged woods to bright-red jungle spotted with orange, blue and brown plants. "After tonight, we won't ever see each other again even in the afterlife."

This was about bonding?

How could I make him understand that I wasn't sure it would work with us? "Gabby and Jaxxson are both MystiK. What if the bonding doesn't work with me?"

"Then you'll be free to find someone else," he snapped back in an angry tone.

"Is that what you think? I'm not bonding with you because I want someone else?"

He didn't answer.

I started laughing.

He scowled at me and cursed to himself, ignoring my chuckles for a few steps. He finally asked, "What's so funny?"

"You." I let him pull me around a ground fog that looked just like one I'd seen strip the skin from a small animal while it was still alive.

As soon as we got by the deadly fog, Callan released me and nursed his foul mood.

I caught a breath and admitted to him, "How can you think that, Callan? Let's be honest. I won't have a life without you. I'm trying as hard as I can to give you the chance at having someone and believe me that's not easy to accept."

"I understand." He ran along for another stretch then said, "Now that you mention it, I do have someone in mind that I'd consider for bonding."

He was going to tell me about her? I ignored him.

Lifting branches out of our way when the growth thickened, he continued sharing too much. "She's a warrior and fast."

Of course, she'd be from the Warrior House. I could see that, but it didn't ease the ache in my chest.

He continued. "She's fast. *Very* fast, in fact. Great skills with a spear and incredible power." His voice dropped until it sounded as though he was thinking out loud, figuring it for himself. "Pretty, too. No, that's not fair."

She wasn't pretty? Good.

"She's gorgeous. I'll have my hands full just keeping the other warriors away from her, but she'll be worth the battle."

He was killing my mood. I had enough to worry about without hearing the details of the girl who would end up with him.

Was she as skilled a warrior as me?

Sounded like it.

Was she prettier than me?

Callan must think so.

"Rayen?"

"What?" I wasn't short with him, but that probably hadn't come out as pleasantly as it could have.

Another few steps and he said, "Rayen?"

"*What?*" This time I'd snarled it, but it was unfair of him to do this to me.

He was stifling a laugh, but smiling at me.

I sent him a death glare and he burst out laughing until he had to stop to catch his breath.

Served him right to choke on that thought.

Callan grabbed me, swinging around, smiling in my face the whole time.

I put my hands around his throat. "Clearly the mist has

gotten to you and you've lost your mind. I may have to beat some sense into you." It was getting harder to maintain my anger in the face of his delight.

"I love that you're just as jealous as I am."

"The only difference is that I don't have someone to carry on about in front of you."

"Silly woman. I was describing you. I told you. You're all I want."

My hands had forgotten about strangling him and cupped his head to me so I could kiss him. I loved the feel of his lips, the way he took over the kiss, powering into it with his usual Alpha approach. Everything had to be done his way and anything he cared for belonged to him.

The Warrior House, the MystiK village here, and me.

He would always have me even if I couldn't be with him.

Kaz had a point about what I was doing with Callan interfering with his future. I could hold back from bonding with him, but I couldn't resist him here.

I realized we were moving. He held me with my legs wrapped around his waist, kissing me as we walked.

I pulled my lips from his. "Put me down so we can run."

"We don't have to. Your transender site is just ahead."

Twisting around to look, I noticed the jungle had begun to regenerate in areas from the destruction we'd found on the last trip. "Do you think the TecKnati are here?"

"I would have heard them by now, but they may be lying in wait."

He let me slide down, then we snuck toward the transender site where leaves and trees that had been burned the last time now leafed out in aqua blue, a vibrant orange and pink colors.

We found a spot to crouch behind wide palm fronds and watched the transender site for several minutes, then Callan stood up.

I popped up with him. "Is it clear?"

"Kaz just called and said they passed a party of five TecKnati heading toward the TeK camp. He and Kenja have their second site to check."

"I hope it's still intact."

"Doubtful if the TeKs are heading back to camp, but that

gives me hope that this site is still secret."

But for how long? I wondered, then I suggested, "Let's find the flower with the switch for the control panel."

Chapter 34

Byzantine Institue, Albuquerque, NM

Phen had searched three rooms to find the perfect spot for the computer with the time-travel portal once he had it in hand. He needed somewhere that no one would disturb him while he waited on Rayen and her group to return. The perfect location for containing all three of them as soon as they showed up.

Did Rayen's powers function here in the past?

He should have tested her somehow before she left again. It didn't matter. He'd bind her hands, her feet, anything that she could point at him. MystiKs pointed at something to throw their power, right?

How was he supposed to know?

Scouts were trained in isolated areas and taught to ask no questions. He wouldn't have known about what his father heard at work if Phen hadn't snuck around at home.

No one risked talking. SEOH scared everyone with his ability to get information. One wrong word and Phen would have landed in prison.

Wait. How would that be any worse than being sent back in time to historical hell?

"Phen."

He turned sharply at the sound of a familiar voice. "What are you doing here, Kurt?"

"Same thing as you. SEOH sent me here." Kurt had a year of age and about twenty pounds on Phen. His brown hair had been clipped into the new flatter style, rather than the crowned look most TecKnati scouts wore, and his eyes were too small for his wide face.

"When'd you get in?"

Kurt looked up, thinking. "Four, maybe five hours ago. I can't get used to this time change."

Had that been a joke?

Phen kept questioning him. "Why'd SEOH send you here? You screw up something?"

"No. I think it's because I was on the Sphere. I haven't heard of anyone going home from there." Kurt scratched his chin where it sprouted a few hairs. "SEOH used me to send a message to Brown about a schedule change."

If SEOH was so smart, why couldn't he figure out how to send a message back without needing a body to deliver it? Phen didn't really care. When he got home, and there was no question that he'd make Rayen take him to his world, he was finding somewhere to live far away from SEOH and his insanity.

Kurt had mentioned a schedule change. Phen asked, "What's going on back home? Why the change in schedule?"

"Thylan is in the Sphere now. He volunteered, no less, to test a new laser grid system that SEOH has kept secret."

That was news. SEOH's middle son was rumored to be a special level of degenerate. One you didn't want to get caught facing on a dead end street after dark. Phen held his thoughts, letting the silence force Kurt to keep talking.

"Thylan used the grid to capture Callan of the Warrior House. Slick job doing that. Then he offered to trade Callan for the Genera-Y computer. That girl intruder brought a computer to Thylan, but Thylan doesn't believe it's the Genera-Y unit."

Phen suppressed a grin. Thylan had been denied the computer because the Genera-Y that SEOH wanted was here at the Byzantine Institute. Rayen and her two cohorts were using it to travel to the Sphere. "What's SEOH going to do with the computer when he gets it?"

"He just wants to destroy it."

"What about the prophecy crap?" Phen asked.

"SEOH seems to think that after the BIRG Con tonight, no yesterday, no." Kurt scratched his head. "I have no idea how to figure the time difference."

Phen did. He'd been keeping track since he needed to get

back before SEOH sent the K-Virus here. He cleared up Kurt's confusion. "The BIRG Con starts at sunset back home and that's in less than an hour here."

"Got it. Anyhow, SEOH believes once the ceremony starts the MystiKs will no longer be a problem. He's got something up his sleeve."

Just the way Kurt said that alerted Phen that Kurt had not shared everything. "What message did you bring back to Brown?"

Kurt hesitated, his gaze straying from Phen.

"Listen, Kurt. You and I are screwed in this deal. SEOH sent you back with no plan for you to go home. They know that neither of us are a threat here in the past." At least, not in SEOH's mind.

That convinced Kurt, who started talking so fast there was no doubt he'd wanted to share what he knew with someone. "SEOH's message was strange, but Brown seemed to understand. I told him the next TecKnati to come back will arrive tomorrow and that person will carry a final message. He'll be sent as soon as SEOH is done with the Sphere."

Phen felt the blood drain from his face. SEOH was injecting someone with the K-Virus and sending it to this world in twenty-four hours. That had to be what Brown was talking about this morning. "What about Rayen?"

"What do you mean?" Kurt cocked his head in question.

"The intruder girl. What happened after she gave Thylan the computer? Did she go back to the MystiK village with Callan?"

Kurt snorted. "Do you really think Thylan would let any female go? I heard she traded herself for that MystiK warrior. She's not ever leaving the TecKnati camp, not as long as Thylan is there."

Phen's palms were getting damp. "What about her powers?"

"Thylan buried a laser grid around the perimeter. It corrupts their power. She's caught."

Phen could hardly listen as his last hope of finding a way home and stopping release of the K-Virus vanished. He had only a slim chance of survival and that depended upon timing.

How was he going to watch the TecKnati portal spot outside the school compound *and* guard the room for Rayen's return at the same time? Kurt would have to help, but without knowing why, because Kurt might be one of the mindless TecKnatis who thought he was supposed to report everything to Brown and Maxwell.

Hard to tell which TecKnatis were actually susceptible to the brainwashing.

Phen had always been careful to never let on that he was no robot. Keeping calm so Kurt wouldn't figure out anything was up, Phen told him, "We should keep an eye on that portal landing spot to see who else SEOH sends back. Why don't you do that and let me know as soon as he or she lands?"

"Can't get in. Brown sealed the location and has it under guard. We'll see him soon enough. I'm going to find a place to crash. I'm starting to come down from the charge that crazy time travel gave me."

Phen nodded and shrugged. "See you later."

Not being able to prevent the person being sent back with the K-Virus from infecting this world changed everything.

As soon as Kurt walked away, Phen took the service elevator to the floor where he'd hidden in the storage room while Brown and Maxwell had walked by talking earlier. On the way there, Phen pulled his lizard out, stroking its scaly head. Once the elevator spit him out, he went to the storage room and closed the door softly. He flipped on the light and turned to where a ladder was still set up next to tall metal shelves.

A heavy-duty shelving construction that could hold a lot of weight at the top, where it stopped about two feet short of the ceiling. His gaze tracked to the two commercial-size gallon cans of tomato sauce.

Someone had thought they were clever.

Phen had been smarter.

He stroked his lizard one more time and let it hop to the floor where the lizard stretched and shifted, hair replacing scales until a large black dog stood there, flicking his tail back and forth.

Phen patted the dog's side. "Took me a while to figure out why you were so excited about that ladder. Nice job. You stay here."

Phen climbed up to the top of the shelves.

When he stepped on the very top and pushed up, he was eye level with the computer he'd found earlier. The same three circles—silver, bronze and gold—continued to swirl on the monitor. Someone here had called it a laptop.

Who'd want to have that heavy thing sitting in their lap? He missed holograms. He missed everything about his life.

Pulling the laptop to him, he carried it down the steps and placed it on the floor.

His sentient beast padded around happily. His eyes glowed at times. Phen had wanted to keep him and now he could.

He curled his hands into fists that needed a target. SEOH's face came to mind with a crosshair in the center of his forehead. "If I can't go home, then no one else is either."

He lifted his foot and stomped the laptop with everything he had.

Chapter 35

"That flower looks fake," I pointed and ran to the pink bloom large enough to stick my hand down into. It was a perfect replica of the deadly one that had once ambushed Tony. To SEOH's credit, he'd chosen a great camouflage. Once the MystiKs knew the pink flower was connected to a deadly host plant, they wouldn't touch anything resembling that flower. If they didn't know, they'd go around testing all pink flowers for transender switches and die.

Some had.

Nausea threatened at the memory of tiny faces looking out from the tree where the host plant grew at the base.

Callan was right beside me when I reached inside the bloom and felt around until my fingers touched a knob. Tony had twisted it when he called up the panel for the transender so I did the same thing.

A holographic panel appeared, the screen lit up and a feminine voice said, "*One hour, forty-seven minutes left to request transender return from Sphere*."

That was how long we had until moonset, because trasenders couldn't be called up once the moon disappeared.

It wasn't fair that the other sites had been destroyed, but my shoulders dropped in relief. At least I wouldn't let Tony and Gabby down. They were here because of me. My power had pulled all of us into the computer the first time.

Callan murmured, "Thank goodness."

I turned to him, trying to think of anything that would comfort him over the loss of their transenders.

The feminine voice emitting from the panel said, "*Error. Error.*"

I stared at the panel that flashed a red "Warning" over and over.

Wind whirled and spun in the open field.

The transender wavered into view, then blinked out and came back. I held my breath as the spinning continued then the transender turned solid, shook as if a giant hand used it as a toy, then burst into a ball of green and purple flames. Lightning bolts shot up toward the sky.

"*Error. Error. Transender terminating!*"

"*No!*" I shoved my hand on the panel that glowed bright as a hot ember, then shattered into a thousand pieces that floated in the air for two heartbeats.

Then vanished.

Smoke billowed from the pink flower and it sizzled the way water did when it struck a scorching rock. Within seconds, it was all over and the entire flower structure had melted into a smoking pile that smelled of burned chemicals.

I stared at that pile then forced my gaze to the spot where the transender had disintegrated. "It's gone."

Callan's arms came around me, comforting me the only way possible right now.

My words tumbled over each other in a mumbled mess. "I can't get Gabby and Tony home."

"I know. I'm so sorry. This was our fight, not yours, Tony's or Gabby's. I should have found a way to stop you from coming back."

I turned on Callan whose eyes bled with guilt. "Everyone is *not* your responsibility. It's *not* your fault that the MystiKs are here, and it's *not* your fault that I'm here or that I brought Tony and Gabby back. We chose to return. *I* chose to be here right now."

Callan didn't answer, just stared past me to the debris field I couldn't look at again.

I reached for him and hugged my arms around him. "I wouldn't care about this if it was just me. I will never regret coming back for you. I just have to find a way to tell them."

He let out a pent-up breath, crushing me to him. "We'll do it together. Maybe Tony will be able to get the computer working and we can find another way to send all of you home."

The past wasn't my home.

More than that, I didn't have it in me to tell Callan that based on how Gabby explained it to me, if the computer Tony and V'ru worked on was the one required for the prophecy it wouldn't send us home.

It might send the MystiKs home or it might not work at all.

I wasn't even sure that the computer would play an actual role in fulfilling the prophecy that was supposed to put the world back into balance.

Whatever that meant.

Chapter 36

"Concentrate, Gabby." Tony should have calculations spilling out of his ears by now after nonstop work on this laptop.

"I am concentrating." She held the palm of her hand parallel to the keyboard and an inch above it.

Jaxxson stood to the side of where he'd set them up in his healing hut at a table with tree stumps for chairs. Jaxxson wanted to be able to monitor what happened with Gabby as she tried to power up the computer and also be available for anyone in need of healing at the same time.

But right now his hovering was getting on Tony's nerves. Tony turned to him. "Yo, buddy. You got some herbs to mix or something?"

"If I had any that would improve your temperament, I'd gladly start mixing."

"Very funny. Tell ya what. You spend all night trying to turn an inanimate object into something sentient instead of sleeping and we'll see how cheerful you are."

Gabby pulled her hand back and gave Tony her stink eye. "If you want my help, do not insult Jaxxson."

"I didn't insult him, sweet cakes."

"Don't call her that."

Tony started to pop off at Jaxxson about playing caveman when V'ru made a throat-clearing noise, grabbing everyone's attention. "Arguing at this point is unproductive."

How did a pipsqueak like him manage to sound so full of authority at times? "You're right, V'ru Man." Tony took a calming breath and told Jaxxson, "No insult meant."

Jaxxson gave a half smile. "None taken. Now what is it you

expect Gabby to do with her power?"

"Heck if I know." Tony washed a hand over his face and rubbed eyes that felt as though grit lined the inside of his eyelids. "When Rayen puts her hand on a computer, things just happen."

Stepping behind Gabby, Jaxxson leaned down and reached around each side of her to put his hands on the sides of the laptop. "Try it now, Gabby."

She passed her hand over the keys again. Lines furrowed her brow with her deep concentration.

Tony kept the sarcastic comment that came to mind locked behind his teeth, but what *were* those two woo-woos doing now?

Light flickered on the screen.

Are you kidding me? Tony sat up and leaned closer to observe.

Sweat pebbled above Gabby's upper lip and muscles stood out on her neck from strain. Jaxxson's hands gripped the sides of the laptop, white-knuckle tight. The monitor tried to come on twice then the keys glowed for an instant before turning dark again.

Tony rubbed his hands. "Keep going."

Jaxxson pulled his hands back from the laptop. "That took all the power Gabby and I could generate combined as one force."

V'ru asked, "Combined as one?"

Jaxxson was slow to answer the kid. "Yes."

The shock hammering V'ru's face confused Tony. "What's the matter, V'ru Man?"

V'ru's gaze ping-ponged between Jaxxson and Tony. The kid's little Adam's apple bobbed up and down.

Jaxxson must have taken pity on him and explained, "Gabby and I are bonded."

Tony had questions, but not for V'ru's ears. "How about you pull up the prophecy list, V'ru, and let's get moving on it?"

The change of subject turned the kid's discomfort into immediate relief. He jumped up. "Where do you want it?"

"Over on the far side." Tony waved him back. "Make it big like a chalkboard."

At the distant look on V'ru's face, Tony saved the kid from digging through millenia of archived information stored in that little head of his and said, "A chalkboard is just a big display. So make the prophecy list in a font size large enough to see it from over here."

Nodding, V'ru walked several strides across the length of the hut.

While he did that, Tony whispered to Gabby, "Did you and Jaxxson, uh, do the horizontal tango?"

She wheeled on him, eyes furious. "No. Bonding is much more important than mere sex."

Tony tried to wrap his mind around *that* and just gave up. "How can that be?"

"We blended our powers and made an eternal commitment. For the rest of time, our souls will always find each other."

O-kay. Just a bunch of their weird mumbo-jumbo. He could go with that. She wasn't leaving here pregnant. "Got it."

"Is this large enough?" V'ru asked from across the room.

Tony gave him a nod of approval. "Looks good. You want to stand there and add or change things as we talk?"

V'ru gave a vigorous nod that threw clumps of black hair in his eyes. The kid needed a haircut. V'ru pointed a finger at the line that read *A bond of two will set us free*. Next to it, Gabby and Jaxxson's name appeared in a bracket.

That explained the bonding part of the equation.

Gabby must have wanted to stay off that subject. She asked, "What does 'three powers' mean? Why is it in a bracket by *Three must unite?"*

V'ru explained, "I added that. I think it means that it will take three specific powers combined to make all of this work."

"Why can't it mean that Rayen, Tony and I united?"

Gabby threw V'ru a curve with that. The kid studied the display, trying to find an answer. He lived for information and answers.

Tony hadn't given that line much thought earlier, but if V'ru's explanation was correct, then Tony was concerned. Jaxxson and Gabby had only been able to draw a flicker from the laptop. If this prophecy was all about MystiKs, then Rayen's power was of no use.

V'ru wasn't often stumped, but he turned to Gabby and did the shoulder lift. "Maybe it *is* you, Tony and Rayen," he allowed, thinking. He added, "but I think *When three become one* and *Three must unite* are tied together because they both reference an action that would require power. *When the three become one, the End has begun. Three must unite, for the scales to right.* It almost sounds the same, especially if 'End' means the end of chaos and fighting."

Gabby's forehead was scrunched as she studied the list. "You think the line *An enemy leaves as friend* is Tony, right?"

"Yes. It's logical since the TecKnati are our enemy and Tony carries TecKnati markers in his blood." V'ru seemed to catch himself and hurry to add, "But Tony is our friend."

Tony smiled at the kid to ease V'ru's worry. "You bet, buddy."

Gabby continued with her hypothesizing. "If that's the case and Rayen seeking answers is part of this, plus my bonding with Jaxxson plays a role, then that would mean our presence is part of the equation, right?"

V'ru's eyebrows drew together, which meant he was processing and trying to calculate Gabby's answer before she shared it. But when V'ru replied, he only managed to say, "I suppose so."

Gabby sat back, arms crossed and looking smug. "Then just to play devil's advocate, here's another possibility. *When the three become one* could mean when Tony, Rayen and I joined as one to travel here through the computer portal. If that's the case, our arrival here set the clock ticking on *The End has begun.*"

That sounded ominous, but Psycho Babe did have a point.

After studying on it a moment, V'ru lifted a finger he waved over his shoulder without looking at the holographic display. The words "three powers" were replaced with "Rayen, Tony and Gabby."

Just when Tony thought Gabby was on to something with deciphering the code, she admitted, "I don't get that whole scales thing."

Jaxxson mused, "*For the scales to right* would mean to balance something. Correct?"

V'ru said, "Yes," but he didn't rush in with any more ideas after Gabby had surprised him.

Gabby asked, "But what *specifically* is being balanced?"

The silence grew and expanded until Tony expected to hear crickets. He said, "Let's start at the beginning. Why did Damian write this thing?"

Eyes lighting with excitement, V'ru warmed to something he could lecture on. "Damianus wrote it before he met Antonis, the TecKnati sent back two thousand years."

Tony said, "Right. The guy who built an analog computer then sank the ship with it."

"Correct," V'ru said. "But Damianus knew a great deal about Antonis when he came to tell Antonis he was in trouble and had to leave. It's thought that Damianus had a vision of what was to come to pass. It was never stated in specific words, but from all that our historians have gathered, Damianus believed Antonis really wanted peace between the MystiKs and the TecKnatis. That led to the conclusion Antonis was the catalyst for writing the prophecy."

Gabby didn't look the least bit confused. Tony had heard the story behind this earlier or he'd have been lost. Why wasn't Gabby?

Jaxxson propped an elbow on his other arm folded across his chest. He supported his chin on bent fingers and glanced over at Gabby every so often. Maybe he was doing some Jedi mind trick with Gabby, keeping her up to speed.

Tony pushed his attention back to the prophecy list and took a stab. "Based on Damianus and Antonis, *For the scales to right* could mean to bring peace to your world, but it's also a reference to justice. Maybe it means to punish those who created the chaos, too, like SEOH."

"Good point," Jaxxson noted. "I agree with Callan's name next to *Day of birth as Red Moon rises*. I have always believed that Callan may have been the designated one to lead the Houses all along."

Gabby stared hard then said, "You have BIRG Con next to *Night of end when last Moon sets.* I'd call that our deadline."

V'ru quickly agreed. "Yes. I added the BIRG Con, because everything in the records I reviewed leads me to that conclusion."

Or was it just wishful thinking of a child who missed his family and home?

Tony had the urge to go hug that kid. V'ru might talk as if he was a tenured professor at a top academy, but underneath all that incredible knowledge was a little boy who needed to believe in something.

He needed to believe he was going home.

Tony had wanted to rip into Rayen earlier today for giving this kid false hopes—because nothing in that prophecy list said anything about the MystiKs going home—but maybe she was right.

Maybe a little bit of hope went a long way.

Tony angled his head left then right, making a show of studying the list. "That could be what Rayen was talking about this morning, V'ru. Maybe if we figure this out, you'll all go home tonight."

Gabby turned a concerned look at Tony. Was she taking issue with the whole going home tonight part? "What, Gab?"

"You're just throwing things out there."

"So? We're brainstorming here. Everything is allowed." He gave it a beat then said, "Unless you have firm data we haven't received."

"No. Keep brainstorming."

Jaxxson snapped his fingers and said, "*A gateway will open.* That might support the theory about the way home, too."

Tony grinned at Jaxxson's jumping onboard the Hope Train.

V'ru must have agreed, because he added Jaxxson's suggestion then asked, "Now, what does *A path will close* mean?"

Jaxxson's gaze slashed down at Gabby who looked up at him and blanched.

A path will close.

Crap. That had to be the transender sites.

Of course, that was assuming this prophecy was all about the MystiKs here on the Sphere. But if V'ru Man was anything, he was literal, and accurate. He and Jaxxson both thought this was about Callan's birthday and the BIRG Con. Even Zilya and a few others Tony had overheard talking about the prophecy referenced the BIRG Con.

Plus, if Tony looked at this objectively, everything *had* seemed to change for the MystiKs here when he, Gabby and Rayen came together to time-travel as one through the portal. Did that constitute the beginning of the end?

Lot of possibilities.

Gabby and Jaxxson were still staring at each other. Were they doing that mind-to-mind talking thing again?

Tony was starting to feel like the lowest animal on the food chain around these MystiKs, and he could get into Mensa any day of the week. He just didn't need to sit around with a bunch of eggheads trying to prove who was the baddest when it came to crunching code and data.

He'd slam dunk them.

While Jaxxson and Gabby did their mental time out, Tony took in the list to see what they were missing.

The future is in the past [Prophecy]
One will seek and all will forfeit [Rayen]

When three become one [Rayen, Gabby and Tony]
The End has begun [end of chaos, return of peace]

The gateway will open [a way out of the Sphere]
A path will close

A friend enters as enemy [traitor]
An enemy leaves as friend [Tony]

Day of birth as Red Moon rises [Callan]
Night of end when last Moon sets [deadline]

Three must unite [three powers]
For the scales to right [bring the world back into balance and punish SEOH, maybe send the MystiKs home]

The last will lead when others cede [Callan]
All turn to the outcast

The past speaks to alter the present [Rayen's ghost]
A bond of two will set us free [Gabby and Jaxxson]

Tony mentally added destroyed transender sites as a possible *path will close* since that was the only known way home for these kids. That left *All turn to the outcast*.

Who was that?

Jaxxson announced, "We're done here."

When Tony jerked around at Jaxxson's stern words, it took less than a second to realize something had happened.

V'ru's eyebrows lifted. "We haven't figured it all out yet."

Tony chuckled and said, "Hey, I need a break. V'ru Man, would you mind running back to your kamara and grabbing my backpack for me?"

"No problem." The kid zipped out of the hut.

Tony gave him time to be out of earshot before turning on Gabby and Jaxxson. "Cut the woo woo crap and tell me what has Gabby looking like she's ready to toss her cookies."

When Jaxxson frowned, Gabby said, "He means throw up." She still looked punched in the gut when she turned to Tony. "Jaxxson just heard from the security inside the ward that the TecKnati are setting up some machine outside, but no one can get through the ward to take the kids out if we have to evacuate. Rayen used her power to help reinforce the ward so now we need her to open it."

Tony didn't like the idea of taking these kids outside the protective cocoon of the ward. "What kind of machine?"

Jaxxson answerd, "Before Kenja left, she told me the TecKnati prisoners we captured this morning warned about Thylan building a weapon from his laser grid. And the ward is weakening again."

"Thought Rayen and Callan shot it full of their juice."

"They did, which means it's being intentionally corrupted."

A blast rocked the camp, shaking it hard enough to toss Tony and Gabby off their stools.

Tony jumped up. "Jaxxson, you call V'ru and tell him to stay put then come with me. Gabby, you get the other kids locked down in the safest place you can find in the village."

Jaxxson followed Tony out the door. "What are *you* going

to do?"

"You mean because I didn't come with an internal power pack?" Tony didn't wait for an answer. "I'm going to offer them a sentient computer in trade to stop bombing us."

"We don't have a working computer."

"The TecKnati don't know that."

Jaxxson was striding with Tony step for step. "What good will lying do?"

"You're thinking like someone who plays by the rules. I learned survival on the streets of Camden. When in a corner, bluff your way out or at least until backup shows up."

The ward took another hit, sending Tony stumbling and Jaxxson falling down.

Tony gave him a hand up. "All we have to do is bluff until Rayen, Callan, Kaz and Kenja get back. If they can't kick Thylan's butt, then we're out of moves."

Chapter 37

"How close are we to the village?" I asked Callan, because I was completely turned around by the route we'd taken to check transender sites.

"Maybe another four or five minutes at this pace. Kaz and Kenja are a little more than thirty minutes behind us. We'll wait on them to keep from opening the ward more than once. I've got a bad feeling about it holding up."

We were running as fast as we could through the dense jungle. This part had fully recovered from SEOH's attack prior to my last trip. That man had to be stopped, but I had no idea how we could accomplish that now that all the transender sites were gone.

Kaz and Kenja had found the same things we had at the sites they'd checked.

A loud boom sounded in the distance and blue light flashed up in the air. I said, "Was that—"

"The village. Let's go." Callan took the lead, using his kinetics to shove everything out of our way and clear a path.

I ran faster, leaping over everything in the way and trusting him that we wouldn't rush into a threat.

Another blast hit and I felt the shock waves from it.

Thylan was attacking a village filled with children for a stupid computer.

Heat swirled and built inside me, rushing through my body to my arms and legs. I fisted my hands to hold it in, so tightly that my fists glowed red.

But I might not need it. There hadn't been a third blast yet.

As soon as we reached an area where the undergrowth thinned out, Callan slowed and lifted his hand to indicate we needed to be cautious advancing. He whispered, "I just heard from Jaxxson. Tony is trying to negotiate with Thylan to trade for the computer."

"He can't do that!"

"Jaxxson said Tony is bluffing to buy us time, plus he can't get outside of the ward because you have to help open and close it. Tony's been yelling at them and Thylan sent one of his scouts to the ward to carry a message that he's giving Tony one minute to open the ward and hand over the computer or Thylan is going to turn his machine up to full power."

We reached the edge of the tree line as Callan finished giving me that report.

Thylan had built something that was twice as tall as me and on a trailer dragged by a huge beast with scaley gray skin. Four spikes erupted from its head and it stood at least twelve feet tall. The creature snarled and pawed the ground with three-toed feet. When the thing swung toward me, its eyes were unnaturally yellow and black. A nasty stench burned my nostrils.

I knew that smell.

Callan murmured in a shocked voice, "There are no more sentient beasts."

Evidently, there were.

The beast was harnessed to a flat cart that Callan could lie on with his arms stretched out and not touch an outer edge. It was parked with the back end facing the village. Piles of metal components, gears, wires and tubing covered most of the cart body.

Callan whispered, "Those three round barrels as thick as my thigh are set up like cannons.

"What's a cannon?" I knew the word but had no mental picture.

"It's an old device that was used to launch ammunition of some sort at a target. In this case, it looks like he's shooting lasers through them."

Thylan's voice called out, powered by some mechanical device so that it could be heard all the way across three hundred yards to the warded village. "Time's up. You dare to test my patience? That ward is coming down."

Then his voice changed back to normal when he lowered his amplifier and turned to his men. He called to his scouts, "Load up a full charge of all three levels and send it in there."

Someone argued, "It might blow up everything and I mean like the whole Sphere."

"Don't ever disagree with me."

A buzzing sound was followed by someone's scream of pain, then a scout stumbled back from those huddled around the cart and beast. He clutched his chest with both hands, screaming again, then fell to the ground and stopped moving. Blood ran from his mouth and nose.

I looked at my hands and they still glowed. The power had permeated my body until I felt one with it.

Thylan yelled, "Get up there! Blue laser, silver laser then the gold one. Release the blasts in that exact order."

A scout close to my age climbed up on the machine with jerky movements. He pushed two levers and lights started glowing.

I yelled, "Stop!"

Thylan's head stuck up from where he hid on the other side of the cart. He grinned. "Glad you're here. Watch what happens when you lie to me."

Callan lifted his hands and threw a kinetic blast at the machine. The blast hit it and bounced away. He looked at his hands as if they'd failed him.

Thylan hooted. "I enclosed this cart with laser protection. You lose." He pointed a thumb at the village. "And they die."

Blood rumbled so loud in my body it was defeaning. Nothing mattered beyond stopping Thylan.

A stream of blue shot from one of the canons.

Callan took a step toward them, turning his kinetics on the cart again, but it was bouncing off every time and Thylan remained inside the protective area.

Blue washed across the ward.

I heard children screaming.

Lifting my fists and shaking them at Thylan, I yelled, "*Tenadori!*"

The cart lifted ten feet off the ground and started spinning. Blue laser bursts were flying everywhere. TecKnati scouts near the cart were sucked into the vacuum as it picked up speed. Bodies and mechanical parts flew around and around, all of it ten feet off the ground like a huge disk of living bodies and machinery.

A whining noise started, then picked up in volume.

The sentient beast morphed, changing shape over and over from beast to bird to a dog and back to a bird as it was slung around the outer edges of the tornadic storm.

Everything sped up until it was impossible to tell machine from bodies.

I shook my fists again, wanting to close my ears against the screaming.

Then I realized I was screaming.

Callan called to me from a distance. I couldn't find him in the blur surrounding me.

He shouted, "*Rayen! Let me in!*"

I forgot about my spinning storm and answered him with my mind. *Where are you?*

That was all it took for him to slide inside my mind and instruct me in a calm voice. *Slow everything down and allow it all to stop, sweetheart.*

No. It feels good to let out this energy. Thylan wants to kill the children and my friends. I won't let him.

I won't either, Rayen, but your entire body is glowing red. Pull back the energy before it consumes you.

It won't hurt me. The burst of colors filling my eyes were beautiful. Couldn't Callan see them? How could he ask me to give this up? My power was calling to me.

Rayen, you have to stop the spinning now!

Why?

It's heading for the village. Stop. The. Spinning!

I fought to see what he was talking about and blinked away the mash of colors blinding me. That's when I saw what I was doing as if from a distance.

Something was shaking me like a rag doll.

Callan yelled in my head again and again, but the sound was distorted until I finally heard, *Stop it before you kill everyone!*

My mind cleared. I scrambled through the mental chaos and yanked all my power back inside.

The spinning bodies and machinery slowed, dropping to the ground until the cart bounced and landed upright. The sentient-beast-turned-bird wobbled around for a moment then took flight and disappeared.

Scouts lay scattered across the ground, moaning. They held their heads and rubbed their arms.

Callan put his arm around my shoulders, panting and hanging onto me for balance. His entire body was shaking.

What had I done? "I'm sorry."

"It's fine. No one's killed. But you had me scared there for a minute. I've never seen anything like that and your body turned into a fiery red glow, so bright I was sure you would combust."

Callan was looking down at me, his eyes soft with relief, then his gaze slid past my face and turned murderous.

He shoved me away hard, stepping forward as he did.

I stumbled and rolled from the force of his shove. When I scrambled to my feet and turned, Thylan had jumped up behind his machine and pointed it at Callan, shouting, "Die you miserable MystiK!"

Blue light burst from the center canon.

Callan threw up a field of power. The laser slammed it and battered Callan's invisible shield, chewing small holes through it.

The searing beam that poked through holes hit Callan, beating him as if he was being pelleted with rocks. He jerked with every hit. Skin stripped off his arms and legs in areas two fingers wide.

It all happened in three seconds.

Blue rays that bypassed Callan shot toward me in slow motion.

I started forward to meet the attack. Energy roared to the surface and saturated my hands. I raised two fists and jabbed them in Thylan's direction.

Holes blasted up from the ground on each side of him, rocking the machine and cart, but nothing touched Thylan. He was safe inside the protective shield around his machine.

Laser strikes popped my skin, singeing and cutting. If Callan hadn't been blocking the strongest part of the attacked with his kinetics, we'd both be dead already.

He slid back a foot and dug in hard, pushing against the relentless blue blast, trying to hold his tattered kinetic field.

Noises warped in a hollow sound. A voice filled my head, telling me, *Rise up and protect, Ashkii Dighin.*

That was the voice of an ancestor I'd met in a dream. She'd called me that as if it was my given name.

I had no time to talk to ancestors.

The old ghost wavered into view. His words came to me, too. *You must take possession of all your powers now, Ashkii Dighin. Your people need you.*

I didn't know what he was talking about. My people had already died, but the minute the voices disappeared, everything came at me in real time again and twice as fast.

Instinct drove me and I went with it.

Holding up my hands up, I willed a wall of energy to form, something I'd never done before. Moving forward to push that protective energy ahead of Callan, who was taking a beating, required more than willpower. Locking my muscles, I bent forward, shoving as hard as I could.

Pushing the Byzantine Institute building across the desert would be easier.

One foot, then another and the wall moved.

When I reached Callan's side, his body shook with maintaining his kinetic force field. The second canon spewed a silver laser beam that struck next, tearing new strips from Callan's shield and attacking his body.

He fell to his knees. His face had been battered and seared. Skin ripped off his shoulder and chest.

I raged at Thylan and the TecKnati, calling up every bit of power I felt inside me. Energy unlike anything I'd ever felt before exploded through my body.

I couldn't think about overloading and being consumed by the power. Not when Thylan was killing Callan. My body felt twice its size and heavy as I moved forward, but my hands and arms looked the same as always.

My arms shook, straining against the force. My knees threatened to buckle.

Fight, Ashkii Dighin! my grandfather shouted inside my head.

I can't do this.

Yes, you can. You must save your people.

Why did my ancestors think I could save anyone?

The lasers pounded, pushing me back inch by inch.

The female ancestor was back, speaking in my mind, too. *End this now or say farewell to him.*

Him? As in Callan?

Noooo! I screamed in my mind then forced my feet to dig in and my legs to move forward. One step, another step, then another, faster and faster. I bellowed at the top of my lungs, "*Tenadori!*"

Thylan stuck his head to the side of his machine. His face held the first sincere emotion I'd seen on it. Terror. He screamed, "Hit her with everything we've got!"

Gold energy boiled in a plume around the machine for a second then sucked into the weapon and shot out the last canon with a vicious burst.

The thick laser beam struck my energy field, a blind serpent with gleaming gold fangs ready to kill.

My power and this last laser blast clashed.

Brilliant shades of glowing yellow-orange power splashed up and out, spreading across my wall of energy.

Then it slowed. Had I beaten the lasers?

The gold crawled, separating into sizzling rivers of boiling energy, snaking out further and further until it found the perimeter of my force field and curled around the backside toward me from every direction.

What now?

Molten gold struck my skin, burning as it dug in.

I shrieked in pain. Nausea climbed my throat from the smell of scorched skin, and the burns felt bone-deep. My power rushed to the surface and burst around me in a white-hot cloud, sucking me into the core and wrapping me in a protective case.

Callan had been right.

My power had consumed me.

Thylan was going to win.

No! No! No! I shook my fists. Thylan could not win. SEOH could not win. The MystiKs needed Callan.

I opened my eyes and stared through a wall of smoky white.

The lasers continued pulsing toward me. I was on my knees, arms lifted, but I knew if I just lay down it would all be over and the pain would go away. I was tired of being alone and of fighting. Why did it have to be so difficult?

Because the strong will never be given easy tasks, Ashkii Dighin. It is time to show who you are. It is time to protect your people.

How do I do that? I pleaded.

You will find the answers inside yourself. Go now. You no longer need our protection.

I didn't have it in me to argue any more about how I couldn't save a doomed race of people, but in that moment I thought of the ancestors I'd met in a dream and of riding horses with my father. I saw the faces of my parents and felt a stab of longing. Long black hair framed the soft brown skin of my mother's face. Tiny lines creased her blue-green eyes when she smiled at me and hugged my father who stood tall and proud.

My eyes swam with tears.

I wanted to be with them again. Even if going home meant I would die with my C'raydonian race, I wanted one more day with my mother and father.

I wanted a chance for Callan to have his life, too, and one more hour if that was all I'd have with him.

Determination pushed me to my feet. White light spun around me and flowed inside my body, pumping power so hard through me the pounding of blood in my ears muffled everything else.

Was that the protection my ancestor had been talking about?

Hadn't my power been red?

Raising my arms this time, I watched the gold bounce off the white glow around my arms and hands.

The lasers continued shooting, but nothing touched me. Maybe there was nothing left of me and I was dead, but I could feel the strength in my body and had no time to question it.

Thylan and his group of scouts finally realized I was back on my feet and walking toward them. They scrambled to do something, but his three canons were unleashing maximum lasers and it was all bouncing away.

Everything became clear in my mind.

I held my arms straight out and dropped my head back, calling forth my power and directing it to attack.

All the white power surrounding me disappeared.

Glowing red energy burst from my chest and engulfed the world. The power slammed Thylan's machine, pulverizing it. Metal twisted and screeched, ripping parts off that flew across the field. In a heartbeat, my red wave washed over Thylan's army, knocking them to the ground.

Screaming mixed with metal banging against metal, the fallout smelling hot and full of chemicals.

I stood there, weaving until I realized everything had stopped.

The sudden silence terrified me more than the lasers had, then a noise scraped behind me.

I swung around and cried out at the abomination that had once been Callan. What skin was left on his body was covered in blood. Bone showed in places. He struggled to stand.

Running to him, I caught him around the waist and grunted under his weight. Where had all my power gone that I could barely hold him up?

His clothes were in tatters. One eye had closed completely on his swollen face, but the gaping holes in his body were leaking out his precious life. He probably had even more damage on the inside that I couldn't see.

My hands trembled with fear when I carefully touched his chin, turning him to me. My heart cried out at the savage damage. "Heal yourself, Callan."

"I ... I can't. Not yet."

"You can't wait. Please. You're bleeding to death."

He lifted a bloody hand and touched my face. "Love you. Always."

"We'll bond. Do it now. Whatever it takes to use my power to heal you."

"No. You could die ... too."

His knees buckled and we both went down.

Chapter

I dropped down in front of Callan and let his weight fall against me. I shouldn't turn my back on Thylan and his

TecKnati scouts, but if I hadn't killed them yet and they attacked, then I would die with Callan in my arms.

"Callan, can you hear me?" I asked, my voice breaking.

His eyes had closed and his breathing rasped worse by the second. I bumped his mind. *Callan, let me in.*

When he replied, his words came into my mind hoarse and lacking strength. *No. Too painful for you.*

I don't care.

When Callan didn't answer me, I bumped harder. *Let me in or I'll force my way in and that will hurt both of us.*

I feared hurting him more, but if that was what it took to keep him breathing, I would barge through his mental shields. He'd come inside my mind at one time and showed me how to use my power to heal. I could do it again.

But I didn't have his experience. I might do it wrong and kill him, but he wasn't going to survive this way.

His arms hung limp at on each side of mine that were wrapped around his back, holding on to him with everything I had.

"Please, Callan," I begged in a raw voice, terrified he'd draw his last breath any second. "Don't make me hurt you more by forcing my way in."

One of his arms moved slowly, lifting to grasp my waist. No strength in those hands, but he finally entered into my mind and said, *Prepare yourself.*

When he opened the passage fully between us, I rushed by his shields, ready to wrap my power around his.

But it was like diving into the inside of a fire monster. Hot claws and spiked teeth ripped at me. I sucked in a breath, fighting for air and trying not to scream.

He tried to push me out, but I was stronger than he was right now.

Speaking softly in his mind, I clamped my jaw against the moan trying to escape and reassured him. *I'm okay. Show me the worst injuries first and don't waste time arguing. I'm not leaving.*

Unless I passed out from the pain. I was only getting part of what he endured. I didn't see his power anywhere so he couldn't push me around his body to help.

Recalling what I'd learned following him when he'd healed my body, I swept first to his heart and gasped. His heart had been slashed repeatedly by the attack. How was he even alive?

See? Callan whispered telepathically. *You can't fix me.*

I was not giving up. *What if we bond, Callan? Gabby and Jaxxson are stronger now that they bonded.*

If we bond ... A pause followed his words. He was struggling to even speak telepathically. He finished, saying, *You will die if you're inside my mind when I take my last breath.*

You're not dying.

I am, Rayen. I won't take you with me.

If I lost him now, I'd never find him again. But if we were bonded, our souls would hunt for each other.

That was why Callan had been trying to explain to me about bonding. It was all so clear now. Why had I refused?

Because it might not work with me being C'raydonian. It might leave his soul unable to bond with another.

But if it did work and we both died, our souls might find each other again in another life.

More than all that, I was willing to do whatever it took to keep him alive.

I made my decision and had to form the bond now before Callan died. I sucked in a breath at the idea of his lifeless body.

Do this for me, Callan, I begged, still speaking in his mind where it was easier for him. *Bond with me.*

No.

Please. I want our souls joined forever. I don't care if I die today or tomorrow or any other time if I know that our souls will always find each other. Don't leave me alone to never find you again. Do this for us. Do this for me. Tell me what I have to do to finish the bond.

He shuddered with another racking breath.

I pulled my hand around to barely touch his chest at the spot of his heart. *I love you, too, Callan.*

After a quiet moment and the terrifying possibility that I'd lost him, his fingers at my waist squeezed gently.

Or was that all of his strength?

He explained, *I started the bond when I pierced the veil in your mind so we could fight the Frazzle Vine. You have to pierce mine ... then we blend ... powers.*

His voice was fading. I was losing him.

The pain in his body continued to leach into mine, eating at me with jagged teeth. Callan wouldn't be able to tell me much more or show me anything. I had to get through the veil in his mind and blend with his power.

But how?

What had my ancestors told me?

Look inside yourself for the answers, Rayen.

Closing my eyes, thoughts blurred with images. I forced my presence further inside Callan until I could see all of him at once and not just one or two spots. What I found was heartbreaking. I touched where a wound had gone to the bone and clenched my teeth against the pain it caused.

A hiss wheezed out of him.

How was he still here? The damage was everywhere and devastating. His heart fought for each ragged thump.

His pain overwhelmed me, flooding more misery into my mind. I steeled myself against it, ignoring everything so I could search for the veil. Where was it?

The next second stretched until it felt like an hour, and finally translucent colors shimmered into view. They moved softly as a butterfly wing in a gentle wind. That had to be the veil.

I swallowed and pushed on the protective wall.

For as sheer as it looked, the filmy membrane was resilient and denied me entrance.

No one was stopping me, least of all a veil. Backing up, I surged ahead and broke through.

Callan groaned and sagged.

No, no. Tell me I didn't kill him. I clutched him to me, waiting for a sign he was breathing.

His breath hushed against my skin, barely noticeable.

Rushing now, I delved deeper inside him, hunting frantically for the core of his power that should be glowing bright as a beacon. Where was it?

Callan nudged me in another direction, then I couldn't feel him. His hand fell from my waist.

Stay with me, Callan. Please don't leave me, I begged, tears pouring down my face.

He couldn't be dead. I would not allow it.

I fought past the panic paralyzing me and forced myself to believe he still had a chance.

Had he tried to push me toward his power that last time? I dove in that direction, refusing to accept his death until I had the cold evidence of his power extinguished.

It was so dark and quiet inside him.

My heart hurt at every empty turn I made.

Then I saw it. A glimmer of the force that had to be his power. There was barely enough pulsing to keep him breathing.

The tiny ball of bluish light brightened then dimmed. It glowed again then dimmed even more, shrinking.

He said we had to blend our powers.

I had no time to question my actions or to fear doing the wrong thing. Not trying was the only wrong choice.

Calling up my bright red power, I brought it slowly inside Callan, past his mental veil. My power obeyed, moving carefully and in sync with me for once. I would forgive all the times my power failed me if it performed now. When I drew it close to the core of Callan's energy source, I closed my mind to everything except our two powers.

Red swirled around and around in a gentle stream toward the ball of blue light that began to spin slowly.

Bright red spirals continued swirling.

I felt Callan's chest move with one shallow inhale. He whispered, "Rayen." It sounded like his last breath then he went perfectly still.

I wasn't doing something right or fast enough.

It was now or never.

I shoved more power into my energy. The red ribbons of energy wrapped around the blue glow faster and faster until blue light disappeared inside a fiery circle.

No, that couldn't be right. My power would consume his.

Everything I did was wrong.

Heat flashed in an explosion of red flares.

Brilliant blue light burst through the red circles and

detonated into silver-blue shards.

A surge of energy flooded me with an overwhelming sense of happiness, peace and contentment all rolled together. I knew somehow that I'd never experienced anything like this before. I was floating and didn't care where I was, only that I was safe and loved.

Then everything went dark.

I was blinded. Or had Callan died?

"*Callan! Callan!*" I shouted out loud.

"I'm here, sweetheart," he whispered.

Arms I recognized were around my back. I opened my eyes. Two gorgeous brown eyes flecked with blue-green chips looked at me with undisguised love. His face was still cut and bruised, but the swelling had gone down.

I leaned back to look at his chest. Pink skin replaced the open wounds and blood had dried. I touched him to make sure this wasn't some dream. "You're alive?"

"Yes, because of you. Because of our bond."

Lifting my gaze back to his, I saw a flash of worry and hesitation. I shook my head at him. "Don't even wonder if I regret that. I should have agreed last night. Now all I can think about is hoping the bond will really help me find you again somewhere in time."

He reached a hand up to the back of my head and pulled my lips to his, kissing me over and over. I couldn't get enough of him, ever. His mouth loved me and told me how much I meant to him. I gave that back two-fold.

His fingers slipped down to my neck, massaging the muscles that whimpered from what I'd put them through. With a gentle squeeze that I recognized this time as him being careful, he pulled back and said, "We are connected forever and that is all that I could ever want."

"How do you know the bond took, Callan?"

"Look inside me again. You have only to think it and you'll be there now that we're bonded."

I closed my eyes and slipped inside him with an ease that surprised me. What I observed shocked me.

Both of our powers had turned into a dazzling purple glow.

I searched further to see his body rapidly repairing itself.

I withdrew and smiled as I looked at him again. I would never get tired of this view. His eyes held a peace and happiness I hadn't seen before and I would give anything to continue seeing for the rest of my life.

He used a finger to wipe a stream of tears off my face. He kissed the path he left. Pulling his head up, he whispered, "Thank you."

"Did you really think I was going to let you get away from me that easily?" I teased, needing to breathe a moment now that I knew he'd live.

At least until dark. We still had to face the wraiths.

Was reaching eighteen this hard for everyone?

I bent my head back so I could see the moon's position in the sky. "We're getting close to moonset, Callan." Bringing my head forward again, I said, "I'm not giving up on getting you out of this Sphere alive."

Callan got to his feet and pulled me up.

His clothes were still shredded, but now it showed a slightly battered, yet powerful body. One I had every intention of keeping out of the hands of those miserable wraiths tonight.

He glanced past me. "Are any of the TecKnati still alive?"

"I don't know." I didn't want to look at Thylan and his people, but I had to at some point.

With Callan alive, I could face anything else.

The transender sites were gone. Even if Tony had the computer operating, we didn't know what the prophecy meant. No one could leave this Sphere except the TeKs at this point, *if* they had survived my counter attack.

Callan took my hand and we walked across the fifty yards to where bodies were scattered over the open field. He frowned as his gaze scanned the fallout. "What happened to their hair?"

I'd been avoiding looking down until he said that.

All the TecKnati had white hair and eyebrows. Huh. I watched their chests move slowly. "They're breathing."

"More's the pity," Callan muttered.

I nudged him gently, but his body was back to rock hard again and not easily moved. "I don't like the TeKs either, but I didn't want to kill them. Well, maybe Thylan. But the others were raised to believe in their leaders like you were raised to believe in yours. From what you've told me, both TecKnatis and MystiKS need new leadership. If we solve the prophecy, maybe that will be possible."

He squeezed my fingers. "There's Thylan. I want five minutes alone with him."

"No. We need him alive."

"Why?"

"Because I have a plan."

Callan wasn't acting too keen on allowing Thylan to live, so I laid out what I was thinking. "The TecKnati have the only transender location that can transport out of the Sphere. I'm betting that SEOH is capable of setting up all the original transenders again. We're going to hold Thylan hostage. If we don't solve the prophecy, then he's our backup plan."

Now, Callan grinned. "I love that devious mind of yours."

One little compliment from him and my insides turned into a gooey mess. "Can you use your kinetics to move Thylan into the village?"

"Not yet. I need maybe an hour to fully rebuild my body and power, but here comes Kaz and Kenja."

I saw the pair running toward us then I gazed over at the red moon. There wasn't much space left between it and the horizon. "We might not have an hour."

Chapter 38

2179 ACE, in ORD/City One

"Where have you been?" SEOH barked at Rustaad who came striding into SEOH's office.

"Things are not going as simply as you'd thought."

"I never expect simple."

"No, but you expected the MystiKs to behave as they always do and that has not happened."

SEOH slapped his hand down and the holographic monitors on the side of his desk disappeared. "What's wrong?"

"We never found the last four G'ortians. I think three were snuck into the city as part of the staff supporting those two Hy'bridts."

"We were led to believe G'ortians were the equivalent of all but deity level in the Houses. Why would they pretend to be staff?"

"My guess would be that those two young Hy'bridt's and G'ortians got together and came up with a plan on their own that didn't include the leaders of the Houses."

SEOH paused, shocked that a bunch of teens had defied fifty years of MystiK customs and habits. "What are they doing?"

"I'm not sure, but the laser curtains are corrupting for no traceable reason. It has to be due to those MystiKs."

"What? Why would they do that and risk letting C'raydonians in?"

Rustaad's gaze narrowed at that comment, but SEOH was not going to open a discussion on C'raydonians right now. SEOH said, "Power up the laser grid now. Weaken the

Hy'bridts."

"It's too soon," Rustaad argued.

"We're just under an hour from the opening ceremony for the BIRG Con. They'll all be too busy to notice anything and the leaders obviously know nothing if the Hy'bridts and G'ortians are making a rogue attack on our laser curtains. In fact, we'll expose those brats to the House leaders as soon as we meet. The MystiK leaders may hate me, but they will not tolerate anyone daring to undermine their authority and put their lives at risk."

Rustaad rubbed his chin.

That action was the equivalent of someone else having a panic attack. "Is there something you want to tell me about the C'raydonians, SEOH?"

"No." Just as there was nothing SEOH intended to tell Rustaad about the sentient beasts he still possessed. "What are you waiting on?"

"You to reconsider this laser grid entirely. If we power up and it doesn't perform as expected, the MystiKs will turn on us. All of us. I have real concerns about these G'ortians and Hy'bridts joining up."

"That bunch of weirdo kids has you running scared? Where's the Rustaad I hired?"

"I'm standing here trying to keep you from losing everything you've worked to build. I've seen what the MystiKs can do, but not this level of power from them. The combined strength of the G'ortians and Hy'bridts has to be the reason for our sporadic breakdown in the laser curtains. What bothers me is the uniform corruption, as if the MystiKs can actually target that much damage and be specific. Thylan's laser grid test proved we still have more to find out about this grid system. Powering it up for the first real test when the most powerful MystiKs are together in one city will be suicide if we fail."

"Then don't fail. Go activate the grids now or I'll send someone else."

Chapter 39

Callan waited for Kaz to deliver Thylan to the center of the common area. He normally would never allow a TecKnati this close to children, but there was little time and Callan could not risk succumbing to the wraiths and leaving the Sphere without solving one last problem.

Thylan was regaining consciousness when Kaz dropped him on the hard ground. The TecKnati groaned and flopped over on his back.

MystiKs emerged from community structures and some drifted in from the woods protected by the ward. All of them eyed the white-haired TecKnati who was sitting up and trying to pull his hands apart. Kenja had offered to bind him head to toe, but Callan only wanted his eyes covered, plus his wrists and ankles cuffed.

Neelah rushed in, pushing past several children. "You bring that scum inside here? Kill him and toss his carcass outside the ward."

Rayen walked over to stand beside Callan and whispered, "That statement would fit the traitor."

He nodded. "I thought the same thing."

"Any ideas yet?"

Callan said, "Yes, but I'll wait to see if I'm right."

Zilya and Etoi marched up to the central area and both paused, staring down at Thylan. Etoi twisted her face into a frown that wanted to be a threat and ended up just unattractive. "Why does he live? He tried to kill us." Etoi stepped up her anger when she pointed at Rayen, but her words were still for Callan. "She's made you soft. First you let her TecKnati friend stay in the village. Now you bring this pig to taint our air."

Zilya showed no reaction at all, which was unusual. Maybe she was trying to figure out which response would be of greatest advantage to her.

Callan asked Kenja, "Would you remove his blindfold?"

Kenja pointed a finger then made a flipping motion with it and the blindfold ripped off.

"Ow," Thylan complained. "That was stuck to my hair."

Zilya's eyebrows lifted and she angled her head, which gave her a better position to see Thylan's face. She turned to Callan, her gaze snapping from him to Thylan and back. "This is perfect. Let's demand SEOH send us home or we'll kill his son."

Thylan twisted slowly around and stared at her.

She gave him a haughty snub. "Do not look at me, you worthless TecKnati."

Thylan actually chuckled. "That isn't going to play, Zilya."

"You do not know me," she argued a little too strongly.

Callan had heard enough. He addressed Zilya. "But you know who he is and you were the only one who had the autonomy to make decisions that would protect your deceit."

"How dare you!" Zilya said, but not with the kind of certainty it should have had.

Callan continued, "And for a while I thought it was Etoi."

"What?" Etoi screeched.

"But then it dawned on me that she wasn't creative enough to do this on her own, plus I couldn't figure out her motivation for standing by as our children died."

Zilya's voice shook. "You will pay for accusing me of treason, Callan."

Thylan had scooted around to face Zilya, but he tossed his words over his shoulder at Callan. "You want to know her motivation?"

"Shut up, Thylan," Zilya ordered.

"Are you kidding? I'm sitting here tied up in the middle of a bunch of crazy MystiKs, stuck on a Sphere that there's only one way off of, and I'll never get to use it at this point. You were supposed to open the ward for my two scouts and make sure they got the computer."

"Shut. Up!" she screeched, losing her superior composure.

Thylan's anger rose with his words. "I sent men inside right where you left a marker outside the ward. They never came out."

Callan offered, "We're turning those two loose as you speak. I made a deal with them."

Thylan grunted. "Figures. Zilya was doing this because she thinks she's going to end up as part of my father's inner circle with all the money and power she could ever want once the MystiKs are eliminated completely from our planet. She offered to be the MystiK consultant to the TecKnatis to help them catch and prevent MsytiK interference in our space program until that time, didn't you, fool?"

Etoi was staring at Zilya as if she'd changed into a croggle.

Zilya snarled at Etoi, "Don't look at me that way. You helped."

"I didn't know what you were up to. I thought you were going to get us out of here."

Children started shouting, "*Traitor. Traitor*."

Callan's voice cut through the melee. "I've heard enough. Lock up Zilya and Etoi with this TeK.

"You can't do that," Zilya argued. She and Etoi backed away as one, but they froze and their arms jerked down to their sides.

Screaming, Zilya tried to break loose, but Kenja appeared next to Zilya and continued moving her hands in a motion that spun a wrapping around Zilya and Etoi, pinning them back-to-back when she was finished.

Etoi yelled, "You will die when I am free."

Kenja gave a tired shake of her head and gagged both of them.

As Kenja transported all three prisoners in an impressive display of her kinetic strength, Rayen spoke to Callan in a low voice for his ears only. "How could she live with herself after the death of those kids and you-know-who?"

He understood that Rayen meant Mathias. Callan squeezed her fingers. "I don't know and she will have to answer for her actions, maybe even to him some day."

Nodding, Rayen looked around. "Where are Tony, V'ru, Gabby and Jaxxson? We have to find out if they've unraveled the prophecy."

"Rayen, that may not make any difference."

She swung around in front of him with her fierce warrior face. "We *will not* quit trying. Would you call to Jaxxson and find out—"

"I already called to him a few minutes ago. Here he comes now behind you."

Jaxxson and Gabby walked up with Tony and V'ru following. V'ru still wore Tony's hooded jacket that swallowed the kid, but Callan had to admit that Tony had reached V'ru on a level that no one else had, including Callan. V'ru had no brothers or sisters and Tony treated him as a brother.

Callan had never thought he'd feel a kindred spirit with a TecKnati, but Tony had surprised him.

"What are we doing, people?" Tony asked, reminding Callan why Tony still grated on his nerves at times.

Rayen asked, "Did you get the computer working?"

"Yes and no."

"This is not the time to joke around, Tony," Rayen snapped.

"Hey, do I look like I'm jokin'?" Tony handed the computer to Rayen. "That is beyond state of the art for ten years ahead of the best we have to offer back home right now."

V'ru lifted a worried gaze to Tony and prompted, "But?"

"But I'm not using that technology until six months before it will be discovered anyhow in our world." He patted V'ru on the shoulder. "My word is better than gold."

"I know." Still, V'ru now looked reassured.

Gabby piped up, "We have most of the prophecy figured out except the traitor and the outcast."

Callan filled them in on what happened, saying, "So Zilya's the traitor entering as a friend, but leaving as an enemy. Who is the outcast?"

V'ru scratched his nose. "I think it's Rayen, because she's C'raydonian and in our world that would be an outcast." As soon as V'ru said that, he looked over at Rayen, "But we don't think of you that way."

"It's okay, V'ru. I've felt like an outcast and it has nothing to do with all of you. It's just because I don't understand why my family sent me through time, but I don't hold it against them either."

Tony searched the sky. "If this show has to go on by moonset, we got maybe fifteen minutes. Everyone needs to figure out their places and what we're doing."

"You're right," Rayen agreed. "We need somewhere to put the computer."

Jaxxson walked to the center of the common area and everyone backed away. He pointed both hands toward the hut where Callan and Kaz had used a table to strategize ways to defend the village.

A small slab they'd used as a work spot floated to the center of the common area and paused waist-high in front of Jaxxson. He turned to Rayen. "Will this do?"

"I don't see any reason it shouldn't." She placed the computer in the center and the laptop covered most of the surface. "Okay, V'ru, what should we do now?"

V'ru said, "Me?"

"You're the one who knows the most about the prophecy, right?"

"Of course, he's the one," Tony said, giving V'ru a pat on the shoulder. "Do your stuff, V'ru Man."

V'ru's shoulders squared and Callan thought his chest puffed out some. Moving his hands up and out, V'ru produced a holographic display with "Damian Prophecy" at the top. The following lines read:

The future is in the past [Prophecy]
One will seek and all will forfeit [Rayen]

When three become one [Rayen, Gabby and Tony]
The End has begun [end of chaos, return of peace]

The gateway will open [a way out of the Sphere]
A path will close

A friend enters as enemy [Zilya]
An enemy leaves as friend [Tony]

Day of birth as Red Moon rises [Callan]

Night of end when last Moon sets [deadline]

Three must unite [three powers]
For the scales to right [bring about balance and punish SEOH, send the MystiKs home]

The last will lead when others cede [Callan]
All turn to the outcast [Rayen]

The past speaks to alter the present [Rayen's ghost]
A bond of two will set us free [Gabby and Jaxxson]

Callan started to ask V'ru why he thought the prophecy meant the MystiKs would end up going home, but changed his mind. Mathias had said to keep hope alive with these kids.

V'ru pointed out, "We haven't determined what *A path will close* means."

Gabby and Jaxxson exchanged a quiet look. Tony sent Rayen a little headshake that Callan read as saying to not mention the destroyed transender sites.

When Kaz quirked an eyebrow in Callan's direction, Callan said, "It means no more MystiKs will be sent here."

"Ah." V'ru pointed at the display and filled in that bracket. Sounding more sure of himself than he had in a while, V'ru started dictating instructions. "The prophecy requires power to activate the final stage."

"What is that final stage?" Jaxxson asked.

V'ru cut his eyes at Tony who nodded so V'ru said, "Tony and I think the prophecy will reach fulfillment when a time lock opens. Based on what we know about the history of Antonis, Lysandra and Damianus, I believe the computer must be powered up to maximum capacity to activate that last step."

When he got head nods, V'ru said, "Based on the words *three must unite* and *a bond of two will set us free,* and the fact that it points to *one who will lead when all others cede*, I think Callan, Gabby and Jaxxson should power the computer."

Callan ignored the sick feeling that this wouldn't work and stepped up to the computer.

Gabby ran over to Rayen and hugged her. "I hope you

manage to go home."

Rayen whispered something and Gabby said, "I'm at peace because of our bond."

That gained a smile from Rayen in spite of tears that were threatening.

Gabby hugged Tony who stiffened then shrugged and hugged her back. He said, "See you on the other side, Sweet Cheeks."

Hurrying, Gabby joined Jaxxson and Callan.

The last thing Callan wanted these children to witness was wraiths dragging him to his death. He paused and caught his breath at that thought.

He could do this.

Mathias had faced his final hour with honor.

Callan would do no less, but he could admit to himself that he had never expected eighteen to mean the end of his life and regretted losing the chance to experience that life.

Kaz's empathic gift meant he knew exactly what Callan was going through.

When Kaz took a step forward as if he wanted to help, Callan gave him a subtle hand signal to stay back. Nothing Kaz could do would change the fate Callan faced.

With effort, Callan calmed his breathing and prepared for the end. He'd shared the truth about Mathias with Kenja and Kaz. The two of them had been ordered to throw a shield spell over everyone except Callan and Rayen as soon as a wraith showed up.

She wouldn't want to be blinded during that moment any more than Callan would if the tables were turned.

But he had asked Kaz to do whatever it took to prevent Rayen from sacrificing herself.

Rayen said, "Hurry up you three."

Callan forgot about everyone except her. Would the bond hold and their souls eventually find each other?

He took one last look at her and swallowed the lump of regret clogging his throat. Why couldn't they have had more time together? He drank in his last vision of her.

This was worse than facing death.

He took a step toward her.

Rayen had been leaning forward, pulling against an invisible tether her mind held. When he moved, she ran into his arms, kissing him first.

He hugged her tightly. Why did he have to give her up? She was his reason for breathing and looking forward to the future. Closing his eyes against the onslaught of emotions, he pulled inside himself and opened his mind to her. *Rayen?*

She was there, filling him up and bursting with love yet hurting at the same time. Purple energy misted around them in a soft haze. No one could intrude when they were together this way.

Her voice whispered, *I don't want you to go, but I don't want you in this Sphere any longer either.*

He would be strong for her. "*When I do this and I'm gone, my soul will search for you. If I had the choice to lose only* my *life in trade for just one more minute with you, I would do it.*" His throat moved with a hard swallow.

You said those words to me in a dream. I want to believe our bond is solid, but what if it didn't work with me? I might have doomed you to never having a life with anyone else, Callan.

I don't care. You're all I ever want. If this is all we get, then the memory of holding you will comfort me forever, because I will never replace you.

She shook with a sob. *I can't do this, but you have to go before the wraiths come.* Rayen pushed back from him, eyes red and tears glittering in her eyes. She smiled past her sadness. "Go before it's too late."

He kissed her once more and walked back to the computer.

When he glanced over at V'ru, the kid had tears in his eyes. Callan forced a smile for him and said, "What do we do, V'ru?"

Scrubbing a hand over his face, V'ru said, "Each of you place a hand on the keyboard, starting with Gabby, then Jaxxson, then Callan."

Gabby and Jaxxson stacked their hands, then Callan put his on top. The computer whirled and the monitor brightened with one circle that was braided with gold ... bronze then silver.

Chapter 40

Rustaad came busting into SEOH's office, screaming, "We're under attack.""What the—" SEOH had just walked around his desk to go to the BIRG Con. He'd planned to show up late enough to send the message that all others wait on him.

"The MystiKs are ripping apart our laser curtains. They're looking for the source of what's making some of their people sick."

"Then turn the furkken thing up to high!" SEOH shouted. "Why do I have to tell you that?"

Rustaad sounded like a vicious attack dog, snarling, "I did turn it up. The grid is failing. I think the Hy'bridts are interfering."

SEOH's assistant Leesa flashed into his office as a hologram. "The Hermes II Explorer has exploded, SEOH. ANASKO's research center is being rocked by an earthquake." She disappeared.

Rustaad's tan skin lost its vitality, turning an unhealthy pallid shade. "What are we going to do? The leaders are on the way here for you. Now!"

That was no earthquake.

Those MystiKs want a war? He'd give them one.

SEOH pulled himself under control. He told Rustaad in a deadly calm voice, "How fast can you eject the K-Virus into our our host body and send him back with a message to destroy all the MystiK eggs now!"

"I can have him launched through our time-travel portal in three minutes then it depends on how quickly Brown and Maxwell execute your orders."

That would run it to the minute for the official start of the

BIRG Con. Brown knew that SEOH expected his orders executed immediately. SEOH smiled at finally getting a real shot at these miserable MystiK charlatans. He told Rustaad, "Do it."

Then SEOH rushed back to his desk and called up his monitor. Two holographic displays jumped into place.

Rustaad was on his communicator ordering the injection of the unaware TecKnati scout SEOH had chosen to be the incubator for the K-Virus. When Rustaad finished the call, he stepped over to stand at the side of SEOH's desk. "What are you doing?"

"Closing the last transender site on the Sphere."

"What? Your son is there."

"If he'd gotten the computer, he might have had a value to me."

"But why are you shutting down the transender?"

"Preventing a backlash of astronomical proportions." SEOH typed faster.

"We're facing war breaking out any second, SEOH. I'm betting the Hy'bridts have figured out we have those kids imprisoned somewhere. We need to be strategizing on how to face the leaders and diffuse this."

SEOH ground out a scoffing sound. "Am I the only one who believes in the superiority of technology? The only one who realizes that we have more power than they do?"

Rustaad shouted, "If this goes to war, the destruction will be catastrophic. They will tear apart our cities."

"Only if they have all their soldiers and right now we've got a major chunk of their MystiK power sitting in the Sphere. Remove that from the equation and we have the edge." SEOH continued tapping on the screen closest to him.

"What are you doing?"

SEOH waited for the last code to appear on screen then tapped in the other half that would begin the sequence. He did that and hit "Enter," then turned to Rustaad. "I'm ending project Komaen Sphere. In three minutes, the Sphere and all those furkken kids will be history."

Chapter 41

I was holding my breath, waiting on something to happen, but Gabby, Jaxxson and Callan still had their hands stacked on the computer. Nothing happened beyond the one multi-colored circle appearing.

Children moved around the common area, watching with a mix of wonder and fear.

Kenja had returned. “What’s wrong?”

V’ru admitted, “I don’t know.”

The computer *had* responded. That should mean we were close to making it work. Right? I asked Tony, “What do you think?”

“Heck if I know, Xena. V’ru and I built a piece of technology that should launch spaceships, but it’s not going to do squat unless it gets the power source it wants.”

So we had the wrong power mix? I asked V’ru, “Who else could be the three?”

He studied on my question then excitedly answered, “Maybe it’s a Hy’bridt, a MystiK and C’raydonian?”

Callan’s gaze fixed on a distant point.

I followed the direction to find the horizon had swallowed two-thirds of the red moon. At this point, it would disappear in another two minutes, maybe three. “Let’s try it.”

Jaxxson stepped away, opening up a spot in front of the computer that I filled.

Gabby asked, “What about the bond of two bit?”

Oh, boy. What could I say?

Callan didn’t hesitate. “Rayen and I are bonded.”

Gasping sounds and murmurs raced around the common area. I glanced at Kaz who smiled at me, in the nicest way.

"Whatever, people," Tony said. "You know the drill. Put your hands together and let's see if that does it."

He was right. With time so short, we couldn't waste another minute.

Gabby put her hand down, then Callan covered hers, then mine on top of his. The monitor blazed brightly. My heart thumped hard at that. We'd done it.

Then the monitor screen's brightness dimmed and the circle now switched from silver to bronze to gold, rotating through the colors.

Gabby whispered, "V'ru looks close to a panic attack."

Callan shot a quick look at V'ru then over at Tony, his face indicating that he weighed some decision. Then Callan told Tony, "V'ru is very important to all of us, but not just as a G'ortian or because of his extraordinary skills in the Record House. He is valued as a MystiK and someone I think of as a brother."

V'ru's face crumbled into a watery mess, but he stood there like a little soldier.

Speaking from his heart, Callan asked Tony, "Will you keep him safe until I can return to carry him home?"

My heart was breaking for Callan, because either they all went home, if V'ru was right, or the wraiths would succeed in tearing him from this world.

Tony announced, "I give you my word as Anthony Asklepios Scolerio that I will protect him like my own brother, now try that power thing again because the moon is almost gone."

V'ru's eyes rounded and he became animated, bouncing on his toes. "What did you say, Tony? What's your name?"

Tony repeated it. "What's wrong, V'ru Man?"

"I didn't know. I didn't know that was your name."

"What's the problem with my name?"

"The original ancestor of SEOH was documented as having come to power in your time." V'ru lost all of his usual authoritarian sound and rattled on like a kid trying to get a story out faster than his mouth could work.

"That's where the name ANASKO came from," V'ru rattled on. "SEOH's ancestor was an international business mogul who changed the face of technology in the early third millennium. He was eventually known only as SEOH ANASKO, but he started out as CEO Anthony Asklepios Scolerio and he shortened that to form the acronym for his empire."

V'ru's gaze stayed glued on Tony when his voice dropped off into a whisper. "SEOH is your descendant."

All eyes turned to Tony.

As in *all eyes turn to the outcast*? Tony was the outcast.

My skin pebbled with fear at the realization that if the MystiKs killed Tony then SEOH would cease to exist.

Just as SEOH was trying to wipe out the MystiKs.

Callan stepped down away from the computer and crossed the short distance to Tony.

If he raised a hand to harm Tony, I would have to ... I couldn't consider that possibility.

I believed in who Callan was as a person.

Tony waited, calm in the face of being labeled as the origin of MystiK agony. "So you think I'm the TecKnati devil incarnate now, huh?"

Callan shook his head. "No, you are not SEOH. You are our friend, but I ask one thing of you."

Answering with a hint of confusion, Tony asked, "What's that?"

"If you find a way home, and I hope you do, that you will show others how to bridge the differences between our people so that by the time my generation is born maybe we'll have a real chance at peace." Callan offered his hand.

Tony's voice came out thick and earnest. "You have my word on it."

They shook, then Callan returned to the computer.

Only a sliver of red moon remained. It would disappear in another minute.

Callan said to me, "Let's try it again."

"*Wait!*" V'ru shouted.

We all turned to him.

V'ru said, "We need Tony instead of Gabby."

Gabby said, "Hey, I'm good with that, but Tony has no power."

Here came the voice of authority again from V'ru. "I told you once before that he does. Every human is born with powers, but it's recessive in TeKs because by our time they didn't believe in it so they their powers stopped developing."

"Sorry," Gabby said. "You did tell me that."

But no one looked as though they believed V'ru. His eyes danced from person to person until V'ru rushed over to Callan.

Callan bent down to keep V'ru's words secret, but I could hear them.

"I'm not supposed to admit this, because I'm the only G'ortian born to the Records House. That means I'm the only one who can read blood by touching it between my fingers. I figured out when I was four that our House is not the same as the other MystiK Houses, because we carry MystiK *and* ... TecKnati blood. I am a descendant of Antonis and Lysandra."

Poor kid sounded like he'd just admitted to killing a pupple.

Callan pulled V'ru to him and hugged him. "Thank you for telling me. No one will ever know." When Callan stood, he waved Tony forward as V'ru ran back over to stand with Kaz.

Tony faced me with an I'll-try-but-don't-expect-woo-woo-from-me look.

I said, "Hurry up, Tony, we're out of time."

"Keep your shorts on."

That was the irritable Tony I knew and cared for, and owed a debt to for all he'd done. "Thank you, Tony. I'm so glad I met you and Gabby. If we never see each other again, I'll miss you. I hope you live through this, find your brother and get everything you want in life."

Tony's eyes were shiny. "It's been a trip with you and Psycho Babe, Xena. No regrets. Just take care of you."

"I will."

A rogue wind came out of nowhere, swirling.

The last slip of that blood red moon barely showed and would be gone in seconds. My heart dropped to my stomach.

Tony stepped up on my left. Callan returned to my right.

Howling came from a distance.

Gabby yelled, "*Hurry up, Rayen, he said they're coming*!"

That would be Mathias talking to Gabby. What was it going to take to make this work?

Find the answers inside you, Rayen.

Had that been my thought or a voice? I didn't know, but when I lifted a hand toward the computer, my palm was yanked flat against the monitor.

I froze, waiting to be sucked in again.

Didn't happen.

Three circles appeared, identical to the silver, gold and bronze ones on our time travel computer.

"Why didn't you do that the first time, Xena?"

A high screeching joined the howling that was approaching.

"Shut up, Tony, and do what I tell you."

"Whatever, just get on with it."

The wind batted my hair everywhere. I told Callan, "Put your hand on the keyboard."

He did it without hesitation and his eyes remained steady on mine. He said, "I *will* find you."

My heart was trying to climb out of my chest and cling to him. I nodded then told Tony, "Your hand on Callan's"

He did as I asked and muttered, "Can't believe I'm gonna die without getting laid."

I could see the black wraiths coming from far off toward Callan's back. They were flying fast as a laser beam toward their target.

This was it. I looked at Callan. "I *will* find you somehow."

Black wraiths flew in a mad dash for him.

As the first wraith extended black claws toward him, I slapped my left hand down on top of his.

My world exploded, warping with twisted shapes and colors. I was pulled in three directions and whipped about like a tangled, broken kite. Where was everyone? What had I done?

The sound of air rushing past me blocked all other noise.

Faces of ancestors I'd met flew around my head, going in and out of focus. I could hear the wraiths screeching and calling for blood. Gabby and Tony flickered into view then stretched and disappeared. MystiK faces surrounded me, their gazes locked in shock then they were snatched away as if a giant hand had grabbed their feet and yanked.

Callan spun toward me. He reached out.

I lunged for him.

At the last second, he was pulled away, yelling my name the whole time.

I tumbled and flipped until I just gave up and let go of my struggle.

The swirling colors and shapes whipped into a spinning tunnel.

Then it all sucked into a vacuum, and me along with it.

Chapter 42

Voices hummed nearby, disturbing me.

I stayed still, eyes closed, to discern where I was and who owned those voices.

Dry heat warmed my skin. That was familiar. It felt like a desert. I'd been in a desert before. Had awakened to a beast hunting me.

My mind caught up to my body and memories came at me as fast as I could absorb them.

Albuquerque. Byzantine Institute. The Sphere.

Wraiths flying toward Callan.

My heart was wide-awake and pounding against my chest. I opened my eyes to soft light spilling in through a sheer window covering. The room wasn't large or small, but comfortable. Just big enough for the bed I was stretched out on. Two chests with drawers were carved from wood and trimmed with paintings of warriors on horses and a rocky setting stood against the walls.

I sat up and felt lightheaded, but it passed quickly.

The floor was covered in a woven geometric red and white rug. A rocking chair hewn from piñon pine waited in the corner. The blanket covering me had been woven with lightning designs I recognized. They were the same designs as on the clothes of ancestors I met in a dream.

The entire room came into focus as a sharp memory.

I knew this room and furniture.

A tear plopped on my face and my happiness struggled to push past the pain.

I was home, which meant I'd never see Callan again.

Climbing out of my bed, I padded over to find clothes and fished out a dress my mother had made me. The tears wouldn't stop as my heart jumped from happy to miserable and back again, unable to make up its mind.

Once I had the pale blue dress and soft boots on, I walked out into the great room, the source of the low voices humming.

A man and woman stood up, staring at me as if I was a ghost. Next to them, a boy V'ru's age and a girl two years younger than me rose slowly. They both had blue-green eyes. He was Torg and her name was Aleah.

My brother and sister.

My heart clenched at thinking of V'ru. Had he made it home, too?

Breathing hurt.

They all rushed me at once, hugging and crying. I let myself enjoy being wrapped in the love of my family, being home again. I felt whole once more, because little by little my memories were returning.

But I also had new ones from my time away. Now I knew what would happen to my family in the future.

How was I going to tell them what was to come? That we would all be exterminated like dangerous animals.

That conversation would have to wait for another day when my heart felt stronger. Right now it was whimpering over all I'd gained and lost in one moment.

My beautiful mother couldn't stop stroking my hair. "Let's let Rayen catch her breath."

Aleah and Torg hugged me, then left when my father echoed my mother's request.

I panicked. "Don't let them go outside."

My father asked, "Why?"

"Sentient beasts."

"The beasts can't get past our barriers. They are safe as long as they stay inside the perimeter we protect."

Safe for now, but at some point all that security would fall apart. I stood silently, wondering if I'd have to watch my brother and sister die at some point.

How had Callan survived losing a brother?

"Come sit with us, Rayen," my mother said, gently guiding me to a wide sofa covered with woven fabric. She gave me a glass of water as the three of us sat down. "I was afraid you would never wake up."

"How long was I asleep?"

When my mother tried to talk, but couldn't speak past crying, my father said, "You just appeared, sleeping in your bed, ten days ago. Your mother found you, but you slept through everything we tried. Our elders performed a healing ceremony that should have brought you around. You didn't ever stir."

My father sat with his elbows propped on his knees, leaning forward. "I'm sorry about sending you to the shaman that night. We spent months trying to figure a better way, but when the elders came to us and said you, your brother and sister would not survive unless we allowed you to fulfill your destiny we ..." My father looked away, blinking back tears before he turned to me again. "We didn't want to lose any of you. I offered to take your place, but the elders said it would mean sure death for all of us if anyone tried to take your place."

My destiny, huh? If only they knew that I'd failed, because I never figured out what I was supposed to have done. I'd let my family and my people down.

Now I had guilt on top of heartbreak.

Someone had to shoulder the blame. I'd been the only one given an opportunity to save them, but I hadn't come through so the end of our people would be my fault.

If I admitted that, would my father only feel worse for what he'd done? I might as well explain what I did know. "I understand that we have to follow our heart and read signs in life along the way. As for my destiny—"

Torg came running in. "Father, an army is outside our barriers."

My father jumped up. "That can't be. No one has ever found us here. How many?"

"The guards say it's at least five hundred. The leader demands we send out Rayen."

"No!" My mother shouted. "I won't lose her again."

My father hugged my mother.

I stood. "Let me speak to them. If they aren't attacking, they may only want to talk."

"People of the cities cannot be trusted. We've hidden here

for many years to avoid them. They kill C'raydonians on sight."

Had the K-Virus been released in this world yet? "Are our people infected with a virus, Father?"

"Some were infected, but not for a long time now. We tried to treat them, but they went mad and died."

"It's contagious, right?"

"Yes, but those of us who heal protect ourselves from the deadly virus if we know someone is infected."

That meant eventually someone would get inside these defenses and contaminate the entire race. "Let me talk to the leader waiting outside our gates." Maybe this would be my chance to protect our people. If I could convince the TecKnati to allow us to quarantine and prevent a major outbreak of the K-Virus among the C'raydonians, maybe they would leave us be.

Maybe that was the reason my destiny was to go back in time.

This had to be the way to save my people. I could only hope that Callan was able to save his. I had to believe in my heart that if I was here, then he had made it home, too. That would have to be enough.

My father walked over to get his spear. "I will not risk my children again. Not for the entire C'raydonian race or anyone else. We'll figure out how to save our people with you safely guarded."

"Allow me to walk with you. I think this may be part of my destiny. Trust me on this. Please."

My father lifted his spear and exchanged a look with my mother, who nodded even though she cried the whole time.

He held a hand for me and I joined him. Walking outside onto a fifteen-foot wide ledge covered by an overhang of more rock, I looked around to find a circle of mountains enclosing what I remembered as a five-mile-diameter valley lush with plants, trees and a glistening lake.

Barns dotted the area. Horses grazed in a far section.

But we lived in a desert.

More memories bombarded me. Memories that had hidden the whole time I was gone and now came rushing out to say hello. C'raydonians had found this canyon in the Sandia Mountains. Over time, they used magic to encourage the mountains to grow and completely enclose it with the exception of a narrow ward-protected passage that allowed riders to leave and return.

From the outside, that ward section would appear like the rest of the mountain.

How had the TecKnati found us?

I took in the hundreds of homes chiseled out of the face of the rock bowl. People moved around in the valley over a hundred feet below me. They tended to farms and animals. Some sat on ledges outside the entrance to their homes, ledges furnished with hand-made furniture and plants in pots.

Looking down, I sucked in a fast breath. We were ten stories above the ground and I saw no steps.

Before I could go into full-blown panic, my father took my hand then he stepped off the ledge.

Following him had to be out of instinct.

We floated down.

My pulse raced, but I trusted my father. We landed softly on the ground. He chuckled. "For a moment there, I thought you once again feared heights. Training with your powers cured that."

Now I remembered that I had power inside me to control levitating up or to drop down, too. But no one here knew I could destroy a croggle with it.

We walked toward the narrow passage in the mountains. Two men and a woman, all appearing to be around thirty, approached from that direction.

The woman addressed my father, referencing the strangers outside our compound. "The leader has not spoken other than to demand your daughter be brought to the gates."

My father digested that then said, "No one knows of my children. No one should know of our location."

My palms dampened.

Did they think I was infected? How would they know if they shouldn't even know about this valley?

What ancestor of SEOH had found us?

We continued walking through two lines of guards who

filled in behind us.

My father paused to open two wards on the way and I felt the power sizzle over my skin. We were as well protected as we could be from TecKnati, but not from the K-Virus if a C'raydonian brought it inside this area.

But how would that happen?

A traitor.

Was this unexpected meeting how the infection is brought inside the valley?

The MystiKs had suffered a traitor inside their village on the Sphere.

If we had one, that would explain how the K-Virus is eventually brought in to infect the Craydonians. As soon as this was over, I would tell my father that we have to flush out the traitor for any hope of surviving.

First, I had to be on guard to push my father back inside if this turned out to be a trap.

The passage we traversed was twenty feet tall and wide enough for two people on horseback to ride through side by side. With sun shining on both ends, we walked through a dark tunnel.

As we reached the exit into the desert, heat blanketed me. I covered my eyes and squinted against the glaring sun.

When my vision adjusted to the light, I was prepared to argue that we had a right to live here and to warn that the first sign of aggression would be met with a power unlike anything TecKnati could imagine.

I wasn't prepared for the deep voice that said, "Took long enough, but I found you."

Chapter 43

Callan sat atop a chestnut horse fifteen hands tall.

"You're alive," I whispered. Or was this even real?

He climbed down and draped the reins over the neck of his horse, but he rode bareback. Of course.

When he turned to me, I tried to move forward.

My father stopped me. "Do not go near them, Rayen. Have you forgotten? They are MystiKs. We have been hunted by them as well as the TecKnati."

"I know this one."

"It is a trick. We have lost people to tricks."

"Not anymore," Callan called out, taking easy steps forward. "Things have changed. That is why I must speak with Rayen."

Callan continued moving toward me.

I sensed power rising behind me. "Callan, stop. They don't know everything yet and I'm not even sure how you are really here."

"I'm here and so are you, because you were not born fifty years ago as you thought. You were born in my time." He smiled at me, not backing off one bit as he kept heading straight for me.

This was 2179. That thought struck me so hard I took a step back from the blow.

How were the C'raydonians still alive?

I turned to my father with questions on my tongue, but he was lifting his spear, preparing to attack.

Callan was unarmed, but MystiKs didn't need physical weapons.

I had to stop a potential battle, or war.

Calling up my power, I felt it roll through me in a gentle wave.

Careful not to break my father's arm, I burst past him, running to Callan.

My father yelled, "No!"

Callan lunged forward, meeting me halfway and we collided in a mash of arms and lips. His kiss touched me all the way to my soul. It unwound the hurt and misery balled inside me, allowing my happiness to finally dance free. I didn't care if this was all a dream as long as I didn't wake up.

His powerful arms held me close, lifting me and swinging me around as he turned. I felt him outside my mind and opened up to him. When he flowed inside, the world turned a beautiful shade of purple.

That was all the confirmation I needed.

I was laughing, then he joined me with a happy sound that came from deep inside, the kind that overflowed with joy. I'd never really heard that from him before. Not with such abandon.

That was the sound I wanted to hear forever.

When he finally put me down and we pulled apart a few inches, we were surrounded by his riders on one side and an army of C'raydonians on the other side.

Hostility and heat threatened a meltdown.

I turned in Callan's arms to face my father, because Callan would not release me and I couldn't let him go either. "This is Callan of the Warrior House. I have promised myself to him."

"With your blessing we hope," Callan added, but whispered for my ears only, "You are mine regardless of what is decided here."

My father stared at us without a word.

I whispered over my shoulder, "Father will come around."

But the C'raydonian warriors were making sounds that warned this was not going to end well.

My father lifted his spear and stabbed it into the ground.

I hoped that was not a signal of war, but I honestly didn't know. I hadn't gotten *all* my memories back yet. How could this be 2179?

Father crossed his arms, staring at us. "Do you know of her

destiny?"

"Yes." Callan stood tall and strong behind me. "I have seen her battle to save my people, to save her people and to save people in many worlds. She is a gift to all of us, but she is mine and her future is with me."

My smile should have been all the evidence needed to convince my father that I would not be deterred, but I could understand his being confused. I had hated it when I flailed around with no memories.

So I squeezed Callan's arm. "Give me a minute."

He allowed me to step from his embrace, but his hand snagged mine and he stepped up beside me. "I'm not letting go of you again."

My heart danced all around my chest at the determination in his voice.

Callan gave an order over his shoulder and his entire army dismounted, leaving their swords sheathed as we walked to my father.

"You didn't have to bring an army to get to me, Callan."

"I didn't bring it for that reason. I would have found you on my own no matter what. I brought an army to make a statement so that your father would know I will always protect you."

"You and I managed pretty well on our own."

"And I watched you too close to death more than once to go through it again. I also want the C'raydonians to know that I will defend them with every resource under my control."

My throat felt thick with emotion at that declaration.

We'd reached my father. I stopped in front of him and said, "When our shaman sent me away, I want to another time and place. It's a long story and I'll share all of the details, but Callan was there with me. If he hadn't been, I wouldn't be here now."

The look on my father's face was priceless. He took stock of Callan with one long perusal and after several tense seconds he extended his hand. "I will be forever grateful that she was returned to me."

"You're welcome."

My father told me, "We must discuss this with your mother. She is just now speaking to me again."

So my poor father had taken on the decision to send me away on his own. By the grim look when he'd shared that, he'd suffered for it. One thing I did recall was that my mother and father loved each other completely.

For that reason, I had no doubt my mother would understand about Callan once I told her how I felt and how we'd bonded.

Father continued, "I see a lavender glow surrounding the two of you. I admit that I had hoped you would choose a C'raydonian to marry, but if this is who holds your heart—"

"He does," I answered quickly.

"Then I will honor your wishes if your mother agrees," Father finished then turned to Callan. "This may create a conflict for you, though."

"There are none I can't overcome to have Rayen."

"That's good, because to have Rayen you must give up the Warrior House."

~*~

I stepped out of the upstairs library in my parents' home onto a wide ledge decorated with furnishings created by my people, the C'raydonians. The veranda overlooked our valley, but between the high railing and remembering how I'd been trained to deal with heights I wasn't panicked standing here. Torchlights and silk lanterns lit with magic-infused rocks glowed deep umber around the valley, shining a spray of light against the darkening sky.

My father explained everything to me. C'raydonians had always been reclusive, but prior to the virus outbreak they had begun to move away from this valley. Once the virus began spreading, many came back, running from the TecKnati and MystiKs.

C'raydonian healers quarantined those who were ill, but in a different location to prevent the sickness from entering the area where my people now lived. Just as my father had said, those infected died.

The ones who did not catch the virus were allowed to return here and the C'raydonians sealed the valley, hiding it from both MystiKs and TecKnati for fifty years.

Until today.

Callan strolled out behind me and put his arms around my waist.

Dinner had been strange, especially when I recalled that I'd never been in a relationship with a boy before Callan. No wonder I was out of my depths when we'd met.

My parents had drilled it into me that as the firstborn I was expected to take over as the leader of the C'raydonians at some point. Never had the firstborn been a girl in all the C'ray generations, which was another reason the elders were adamant that I had a destiny.

It boiled down to me being the C'ray princess.

Now I knew why the word princess had sounded familiar.

I smiled at finding out why no one was allowed to grow peanuts. Every C'ray leader was born with that allergy. The elders had been perplexed when I was born a female so they tested the peanut theory on me and I'd become violently ill.

That confirmed I would be the next leader of the C'ray.

My father made the terms clear for his support of my and Callan's union. I had a responsibility to the C'raydonians.

But Callan had one to the Warrior House and the MystiKs.

Why did we have to always face difficult decisions?

Callan chuckled. "It's just part of becoming an adult."

"Did you hear that in my mind?"

"No. You mumbled the words. Stop worrying over your father's decree. I never wanted to lead the MystiKs. I plan to convince my House that Kaz will be a solid choice, because as much as Becka is high maintenance, she's also intelligent and fair. She'll be an asset for Kaz."

"Kaz and Becka? Really? Amazing. Okay, so what happened to Zilya, SEOH, Thylan, Etoi—"

"Hold it, sweetheart, and let me explain." He resettled his hold on me and said, "Let me think. First of all, every child still alive in the Sphere when we activated the computer was returned home."

"Because of the computer?"

"The Hy'bridts came together to explain the elements of the prophecy. Evidently, we managed to bring the world back into balance when you, I and Tony powered the computer, which turned it sentient."

"So everyone was sent back to their respective worlds?" I asked, thinking about Tony and Gabby.

"As far as I can tell, yes. The Sphere is gone, too. I heard that SEOH entered the code to destroy it, because the explosion was seen seconds after we appeared at home."

I'd missed that entire event while I slept for ten days. "What about Zilya and Etoi?"

"Zilya has been charged with treason against the MystiKs, which will have serious consequences. She will have to face each family who lost a child, then she'll spend the rest of her life in a MystiK prison. That is not somewhere you ever want to visit. We are expected to use our powers to benefit mankind, not destroy other humans."

I shuddered. That sounded like a fitting, but awful punishment. "And Etoi?"

"Unfortunately she disappeared."

"You mean escaped?"

He shook his head. "No. She was from one of the last families to disappear due to the egg harvesting program SEOH instigated at the schools in the past like the Byzantine Institute you told me about."

"Oh, that's awful." Rayen meant every word, then remembered, "That's what they were going to do to Gabby until we found and released her."

"Then you saved her and all her descendants."

"And SEOH?"

"Thylan appeared at ANASKO headquarters in the midst of MystiK leaders surrounding SEOH and Rustaad, SEOH's right hand man. SEOH was in the process of sending a TeK infected with the K-Virus back to the past to kill MystiK ancestors, but the MystiKs were able to prevent that. Thylan tried to roll on SEOH and Rustaad, but Thylan's testimony meant nothing. In the first few days that I was back, our world was filled with chaos and squabbling. Every House was still represented at the BIRG Con."

"So you and the other MystiKs all appeared in the *same* location?"

"Yes."

"How did that happen? You were captured in different areas, right?"

"The only reason I can figure for us returning to one spot together is that either the united power of the Hy'bridts and G'ortians were pulling us to them or the prophecy controlled it."

I thought back on what I'd learned of Hy'bridts and G'ortians while I was in the Sphere. "Aren't Hy'bridts reclusive? MystiKs who are not considered team players?"

"They were until two Hy'bridts, one nineteen and one twenty, crossed paths while searching for a lost MystiK. They talked and decided they would be more powerful as a team, something the older ones would never have considered. The Hy'bridts had a vision that clued them in that SEOH intended to attack MystiK power with technology of some sort during the BIRG Con. They convinced G'ortians to travel to the BIRG Con with them under cover."

"So this is why SEOH feared the Hy'bridts and G'ortians so much?"

"He sensed that these reclusive ones might be less resistant to change than their MystiK counterparts. They might communicate with one another if they had the chance and, by sharing information, come to conclusions he didn't want reached until it was too late. And in this he was right."

I'd been so wrapped up in what was going on while we were on the Sphere that I hadn't considered what SEOH might be doing back in Callan's world.

Uhm, *my* world.

I asked, "Did the Hy'bridts prevent the laser attack?"

"Yes, and over the past ten days they've met several times with the TecKnati board members who admitted they feared what MystiKs would do so they agreed to sending the future leaders to the Komaen Sphere, but they all thought it was more like a summer camp based on what SEOH had shown them during progress reports."

"Summer camp my butt," I grumbled.

"And a very nice one." Callan leaned over and kissed my cheek. "Anyhow, the Hy'bridts and TecKnati joint council have come to several agreements. One is that they'll have a committee of ten TecKnati and ten MystiKs, including G'ortian leaders, to vet any decisions that affect this world or space travel. The list goes on and on, but basically for the first time since the K-Virus, the MystiKs and TecKnati are going to work together in a peaceful way."

"The world really is coming into balance," I murmured.

"I hope so. Only time will tell."

"You still didn't tell me about SEOH, Thylan and Rustaad."

"I did get off track. This joint committee heard enough evidence from the imprisoned MystiKs and Mathias, who spoke through a Hy'bridt, to convict SEOH of crimes against humanity, murder, theft of TecKnati funds, and maintaining a stable of sentient beasts, which have since been destroyed."

I had to interrupt. "What about the beast sent back in time and Phen?"

"V'ru was right about the time lock. Everyone the TecKnati sent back in time returned to our world when we activated the computer built by Tony and V'ru."

I studied on that. "So it wasn't about having that *exact* computer for the prophecy that Tony, Gabby and I had opened a portal in for traveling with to the Sphere?"

"No. The Hy'bridts said that computer was not any more sentient than the one Tony and V'ru built. The combined energy of you three—a MystiK ancestor, a TecKnati ancestor and a C'raydonian—is what opened the portal."

I thought on the elements of the prophecy. "That's why it took the same combination to open the computer Tony and V'ru built."

"Technically, yes, but it was more than that," Callan explained. "As per the Hy'bridts, the prophecy was set in motion two thousand years ago when the C'raydonian Damianus, the MystiK, Lysandra and the TecKnati, Antonis joined their energy. The Damian Prophecy was fulfilled, and everyone sent back to their original places in time, by combining three *specific* energies, not just *any* C'raydonian, MystiK and TecKnati."

I kept sorting through it out loud. "You were the one who leads when others cede. I was the one who will seek and all will lose," I admitted, in spiter of how it still bothered me.

"Tony was the outcast who entered as an enemy and left as a friend."

"Correct, but our bond was crucial to the outcome, too," Callan pointed out.

I almost prevented all of this by refusing to bond with him. I would have lost Callan forever.

A lot of things might be different right now.

"So it was about the power of humans joining together for a common goal," I murmured.

Callan's arms pulled me closer to him when he whispered, "The power of caring. And of love."

"Yes," I answered just as softly." But I still wanted something confirmed. "That meant the sentient beast that attacked me in the past was definitely returned to our world, too, right?"

"Yes, but the Hy'bridts contained it the minute it showed up. Two men from that Byzantine Institute you told us about were convicted along with SEOH, Rustaad and Thylan."

"Was one of them a Dr. Maxwell?"

"Yes, and the other one was called Brown."

I nodded, waiting on Callan to continue.

"SEOH, Rustaad, Thylan, Maxwell and Brown were sentenced to spend the rest of their days on the planet discovered in ANASKO's space program."

"That doesn't sound like a tough punishment."

"Oh, but it is, sweetheart. All the dangerous plants and creatures in the Sphere came from *that* planet. The TecKnati board left the punishment to the MystiK leaders. SEOH and his group will be dropped off with the same rudimentary tools that we were given on the Sphere. They'll have to figure out how to survive croggles and killer plants—and wraiths—on their own. And they'll have to find non-poisonous food without the help of someone like V'ru."

Now I felt better. I couldn't feel any sympathy for men who had killed children and tried to wipe out a race of people. That was a fit punishment. "How is V'ru?"

"He's good. Better than good. He slept for four days and scared everyone, but when he woke up he said history had changed and he had needed the down time to process it."

I was still in awe over V'ru.

Callan said, "Tony promised to leave V'ru a package buried like a time capsule. The first thing V'ru demanded was to go to the location Tony had told him. Everyone in the Records House quakes in their boots now with the new and improved V'ru."

That tickled me even though I missed Tony and Gabby just hearing this. I asked, "What did V'ru find?"

"The sealed container had a library of printed comics plus a letter that V'ru cried over, but they were happy tears. He shared some of it with me. Tony went to something called MIT, but it took him longer than he'd hoped to accomplish his goals because of the Byzantine Institute vanishing overnight. He did get his brother back who he brought into his company, which was where a woman named Hannah came to work. Tony married her. He had known her at the Byzantine Institute, but she hadn't recognized him when they met again."

"Hannah didn't remember anyone from the school?"

"No. Tony found Gabby once he had the money to do what he wanted. He said he and Gabby seemed to be the only ones in their time who could recall anything about the Byzantine Institute. It was as if the world had paused long enough for everything to swing back into balance. He and Gabby agreed to protect the secret."

"What about Gabby?" I hurt thinking about how she and Jaxxson would not be together."Gabby created a world organization that focused on gifted children, regardless of the type of gift. She was a highly respected clairvoyant of her time and met a man that Tony said reminded him so much of Jaxxson that it was weird."

I laughed as a breeze stirred and made a few strands of my hair dance across my cheeks. "Tony thought everything he didn't understand was weird." I breathed a deep sigh.

"What's wrong?"

"They're all gone."

"Yes and no." Callan rubbed a hand up and down my arm, his touch soothing me as much as his words. "Jaxxson is in our time period and hasn't found his soulmate yet, but the Hy'bridt from the Healing House described a vision of Jaxxson in the future with a young Hy'bridt who possessed a sharp wit and the couple was surrounded by six kids. Oh, and Tony funded a special humanitarian program he called Woo-Woo, Inc. and Gabby was on the board. SEOH was still SEOH when we returned, but there are positive signs that Tony and Gabby have both influenced the future."

It was hard to imagine all that had happened. I tried not to dwell on the children lost, but I couldn't stop thinking about one in particular. "You said Mathias testified."

"Yes, a Hy'bridt called him to the committee meetings and transmitted his memory of the wraiths, plus she brought me in and drew from my memory of what happened to Mathias, then used her magic to show it to the committee. That was what convinced the TecKnati to defer to the MystiKs for SEOH's punishment."

"Is Mathias at peace?"

"Yes, he told our Hy'bridt that he had Gabby to thank and that he would watch over her descendants for the rest of time. The TecKnati are erecting a memorial to the dead MystiKs in every city, but they're casting Mathias' profile on a new currency to be an icon for reminding us of the selfless leadership we should all strive for."

"You don't need that reminder, Callan. You've always been selfless when it comes to others."

"Maybe at one time, but the minute I had a dream of where you were and knew how to finally find you in my own time, I would not allow anyone to deter me. I told the Warrior House and other MystiKs that anything else they needed would have to wait until I returned."

"What about uniting all your Houses?"

"Kaz and Becka will work with the Hy'bridts to that end."

The sound of voices singing drifted from far below.

Callan turned me to face him and I dropped my head against his solid chest. I would have him forever, but I wanted to be with him right now. "I don't want to wait, Callan."

I heard my father clear his throat on the ledge below us.

Callan's warm breath teased against my cheek when he whispered, "Two years does seem like an eternity, but your father's right about waiting until you turn twenty and that we should get to know each other without being under duress. Plus you have two years of training ahead of you to become the next leader of the C'raydonians. We don't have to rush to start our life together."

"What about you? You said all you ever wanted to do was lead your warriors."

"Kenja will take over that position and the Warrior House will be more powerful than ever in history. I have no problem moving to live here in the valley. I will train with your father's warriors and learn their ways so that when the day comes for us to stand guard over them we will be a strong team."

Callan looked down at me with the kind of love I knew only happened once in a lifetime. I didn't think my heart could expand any more until he kissed my forehead and whispered, "Your people will be free to leave this valley whenever they choose and our children will roam this entire country just as their forefathers once did."

A tear ran down my cheek.

I'd turn eighteen in a month and celebrate it with Callan and my family. Eighteen no longer meant the possible end of his life, and here he was with me when I'd thought I'd *never* see him again. I could wait two years. It would be torture, but nowhere near as bad as the idea of watching him face the wraiths.

He would be here to share each precious day with me.

Standing there, I stared up at my destiny and saw my future in his eyes as a red moon moved gently across the skies above us. I whispered, "You're right. There's nothing we can't overcome now that we have time."

The End

A word from the authors:

Creating this trilogy has been a huge undertaking and a blast at the same time. We have had the great opportunity of meeting many teen and adult readers who have shared their excitement over this trilogy. Thank you for the many messages and emails. Your enthusiasm means the world to us. If you have a moment, we'd really appreciate a review anywhere that you would like to leave one.

Thank you for reading the Red Moon Trilogy,
USA Today bestseller Micah Caida

Red Moon Trilogy
TIME TRAP
TIME RETURN
TIME LOCK

To be alerted of any Red Moon Trilogy news or about an appearance, sign up for our newsletter at MicahCaida.com.

Acknowledgments

Micah Caida is the union of two creative writers – *USA Today bestseller* Mary Buckham and *New York Times* bestseller Dianna Love. We thank both of our husbands for the constant support (and cooking!). We'd like to thank our early read from Cassondra Murray who has a sharp eye and also does the last copy edit for us. Joyce Ann McLaughlin was also a very early reader who never fails to sprinkle her much appreciated enthusiasm along with detailed notes on the story. Additionally, we have our next round of beta readers to thank for being the first ones to see the "almost finished" book before final copy edits – Alex Bernier (teen), Angela Catucci (college), Alexandra Fedor (teen), Hannah G (pre-teen), Emily Gifford (teen), Brooke McClure (teen) and Lynn Fedor (mom). Thanks also to Judy Carney who does the first round copy edits and to Andrew LoVuolo for sharing his knowledge of the comic book world. Andrew also designed our beautiful website that web architect Scott Martin worked his magic in building and coding. Kim Killion has once again outdone herself with designing us a beautiful cover and Jennifer Jakes provided professional formatting (thank you both for doing your parts so quickly each time!).

We love to hear from readers – micah@micahcaida.com
Website – http://www.MicahCaida.com/
Facebook – Micah Caida
Twitter – @MicahCaida
Goodreads – Micah Caida

About the Author

USA Today bestseller Micah Caida is the melding of two voices, two personalities and two minds of *USA Today bestseller* Mary Buckham and *New York Times* bestseller Dianna Love, which often produces the strangest ideas. From this collaboration, Micah enjoys exploring how different characters react and deal with similar situations. Life is often filled with the unexpected – both good and bad. While creating the Red Moon series, Micah hit upon a very unusual "what if" that exploded into an epic story filled with teenagers who face impossible odds, but are the only ones who can save the world from itself. For more on Micah and the Red Moon Trilogy, visit MicahCaida.com

CPSIA information can be obtained
at www.ICGtesting.com
Printed in the USA
BVOW06s1135031017
496545BV00016BA/62/P

9 781940 65180